THE FIRST MOUNTAIN MAN:
PREACHER'S
FIRE

THE FIRST MOUNTAIN MAN:
PREACHER'S FIRE

William W. Johnstone
with J. A. Johnstone

PINNACLE BOOKS
Kensington Publishing Corp.
www.kensingtonbooks.com

PINNACLE BOOKS are published by

Kensington Publishing Corp.
119 West 40th Street
New York, NY 10018

PUBLISHER'S NOTE
Following the death of William W. Johnstone, the Johnstone family is working with a carefully selected writer to organize and complete Mr. Johnstone's outlines and many unfinished manuscripts to create additional novels in all of his series like The Last Gunfighter, Mountain Man, and Eagles, among others. This novel was inspired by Mr. Johnstone's superb storytelling.

All Kensington titles, imprints, and distributed lines are available at special quantity discounts for bulk purchases for sales promotions, premiums, fund-raising, educational, or institutional use. Special book excerpts or customized printings can also be created to fit specific needs. For details, write or phone the office of the Kensington special sales manager: Kensington Publishing Corp., 119 West 40th Street, New York, NY 10018, attn: Special Sales Department; phone: 1-800-221-2647.

ISBN-13: 978-0-7860-2127-7
ISBN-10: 0-7860-2127-6

First printing: January 2010

10 9 8 7 6 5 4 3 2 1

Printed in the United States of America

Chapter 1

The killers lying in the tall grass heard the singing while the two men were still on the other side of the hill. Their voices were loud and raucous, and although the members of the Pawnee war party didn't really understand the words, it was clear from the tone that the song was a bawdy one.

It was a shame the white men had chosen such for their death song.

Because most certainly, they were about to die.

The six Indians waited patiently. They had spotted the riders and the two pack horses heading toward them and had concealed their own horses in the trees. Watching from the top of the hill, they had seen the white men coming straight toward them and had decided to lay their ambush here. Two of the warriors had rifles they had taken from dead white men in the past. The other four were armed with bows and arrows. The riflemen would attack first, standing up and firing at the whites. Then the bowmen would finish them off, if they survived the shooting.

Then the Pawnees would take the scalps of the white men.

It would be a good afternoon's work.

The song came to an end. One of the whites, an old man by the cracked sound of his voice, said loudly, "Whoo-ee, Preacher, that's a good 'un! Let's sing another. How about the one about the one-legged gal and the deacon? You know that one? It goes like this."

The old man topped the hill as he started bellowing out the new song. The two Pawnee riflemen leaped to their feet as soon as they saw the wide-brimmed felt hat and the long white hair and the white beard. They had raised their rifles to their shoulders before they realized that the saddle of the horse next to the old man was empty.

Off to the left, the dull boom of a flintlock sounded, and one of the Pawnee died as a heavy ball smashed into the side of his head, collapsing his skull and pulping his brain. He hadn't even had time to turn toward the unexpected threat.

His companion did, though, and he saw a tall white man with a dark beard stalking toward him on the side of the hill. The white man tossed aside the empty rifle, and his hands swooped down to pull two flintlock pistols from behind his belt. The Pawnee let out a cry of angry surprise and tried to swing his rifle around, but the movement had barely started before smoke spurted from the muzzle of both pistols. Three out of the four balls from the double-shotted loads slammed into the Pawnee's chest, driving deep into his body and knocking him backward off his feet.

All the shots had roared out in a matter of heartbeats, shocking the other four Pawnee into immobility for a second. But that spell broke, and they leaped to their feet, yipping and howling in outrage at the deaths of their companions.

Their reaction came too late.

Death was already among them.

A couple of long-legged bounds took Preacher into the middle of the war party. Dog was right behind him, leaping through the tall grass. Preacher swung the empty pistol in his right hand and caved in a warrior's skull as Dog took down another one and ripped his throat out with a slash of sharp teeth and powerful jaws.

Preacher pivoted and kicked another man in the groin, doubling him over. Dropping the pistols, Preacher grabbed the Indian's head, and brought his knee up into the man's face. Blood spurted from the Pawnee's crushed nose as Preacher shoved him into one of the warriors who remained on his feet. Their legs tangled, and both Indians fell toward Preacher.

He yanked the long, heavy-bladed hunting knife from the sheath at his waist and brought it up into the body of the uninjured Pawnee. The blade went in cleanly, penetrating deep into the warrior's chest. Preacher ripped it free and stepped back in time to see the lone remaining Pawnee about to loose an arrow at him.

From the top of the hill, Uncle Dan Sullivan's rifle boomed. Blood, brains, and bone combined into a pink-ish spray as the ball blew away a good chunk of the warrior's head. The arrow flew from the bow, but it went into the dirt halfway between Preacher and the Indian.

As the echoes of the shot rolled away across the

grassy hills, Preacher looked up at Uncle Dan and called, "Could've been a mite quicker on the trigger. He almost had me."

The stocky old-timer grinned and stroked his long white beard as he rested the rifle across the saddle in front of him. "Wanted to make good and sure of my shot," he said. "These old eyes o' mine ain't as good as they used to be."

Preacher grunted. He happened to know that Uncle Dan's eyes were almost as keen as those of an eagle.

A groan made Preacher look around. The Indian whose nose he had busted was still alive. The man lay on the ground, writhing from the pain in his nose and his balls. Still holding the knife, Preacher went over to him and dropped to a knee beside him.

With his left hand, Preacher took hold of the Pawnee's long black hair and jerked his head up. He laid the razor-sharp edge of the blade against the man's throat, pressing hard enough so that a drop of blood welled out and trickled down the taut skin.

"You thought to ambush us," he said in the Pawnee tongue, having recognized the warrior's tribe by the markings painted on the man's face and the bead-work on his buckskins. "That was a mistake. Are there any more of you around here, or were you and your brothers raiding alone?"

"I speak your filthy . . . white man tongue," the man gasped, his voice choked by the blood that had run from his ruined nose into his mouth.

"Is that so?" Preacher said in English. "All right, then. You can answer my question. How many more of you are there in these parts?"

"Go ahead and . . . kill me! I will tell you . . . nothing! Cut my throat, white man!"

Preacher thought about it for a second, then shook his head and said, "Nope, I reckon not." He took the knife away from the nicked place on the Indian's throat. "Dog!"

The big, wolflike cur edged closer, his lips curling away from his teeth as he snarled at the Pawnee.

"I ain't gonna cut your throat," Preacher went on. "I'm just gonna let Dog here gnaw on you for a while."

He saw the fear in the Indian's eyes as Dog approached.

"He's got a mean streak in him," Preacher went on. "Likes to play with his food for a while before he eats it. He's liable to start at your toes and just sorta . . . *nibble* his way up."

The Pawnee swallowed hard. His eyes were wide, and he seemed to have forgotten about his busted nose and the kick in the crotch.

"What band are you from?" Preacher asked. "Who's your war chief?"

"St-Standing Elk," the Pawnee said.

Preacher nodded toward the other members of the war party, who lay scattered around the hillside, dead. "Is he one of these fellas?"

The Pawnee shook his head. "No. We were scouts . . . from a larger party."

"Where's Standin' Elk and the rest of your bunch?"

The Pawnee started to look stubborn again. Preacher made a small motion, and a snarling, slavering Dog bent his head toward the Indian's legs.

"One sleep toward the sunrise!" the Pawnee cried. "It is the truth!"

Preacher waved Dog back. The big cur retreated with obvious reluctance.

"How many?"

"As many as the fingers of four hands."

Twenty more warriors, then. A formidable bunch. He and Uncle Dan would avoid them if possible, Preacher thought.

"All right," Preacher said as he straightened to his feet. "I reckon we'll tie you up and leave you here. The rest of your bunch will come along and find you sooner or later."

The Pawnee sneered up at him. "Go ahead and kill me. I have shamed myself by talking to you."

Preacher's eyes narrowed. "There are a few hombres in this world who're bad enough I might be tempted to kill 'em in cold blood. You ain't one of 'em, old son."

"Then let me . . . die in battle." The Indian's fingers groped for the handle of the knife at his waist.

"You ain't fit to fight right now. I reckon I kicked your balls halfway up to your throat."

Preacher started to turn away. Behind him, the Pawnee struggled to climb to his feet. Uncle Dan said warningly, "Preacher . . ."

With a sigh, Preacher turned around again. The warrior had made it upright and managed to pull his knife from its sheath. He raised the weapon and lunged awkwardly toward Preacher.

Preacher waited, hoping that the stubborn varmint would collapse or pass out or something, but when the blade started to thrust toward his chest, he had to act. He knocked the Pawnee's knife aside and stepped in to bring up his own blade and bury it in the warrior's chest. The man sighed and dropped his knife as he sagged toward Preacher.

"What's your name?" Preacher asked.

"Bent . . . Stick," the Pawnee forced out.

"Well, if anybody ever asks me, I will tell them that the warrior called Bent Stick died in battle, with honor."

Gratitude flickered in the Indian's eyes, then died out along with everything else. Preacher lowered the corpse to the ground.

Uncle Dan had ridden on down the hill and now sat nearby on his horse, still holding the reins of Preacher's horse and the two pack animals. The old-timer nodded toward the body and asked, "How'd you know he'd talk if you threatened him with Dog?"

"I saw him eyein' the old boy," Preacher replied. "Some folks are more scared of one particular thing than they are of anything else. Might be dogs or snakes or, hell, I don't know, bugs. I took a chance that with this fella, it was dogs."

"Looks like you was right. We gonna try to avoid that war chief Standin' Elk and his bunch?"

"Damn right," Preacher said. He pulled up a handful of grass and used it to wipe the blood from his knife before he slid the blade back into its sheath. "We've got places to go and things to do, and I don't want anything slowin' us down."

He walked over to retrieve his pistols from the place he had dropped them. He reloaded them first, then picked up his rifle and loaded it. He always felt a little naked when his guns were empty.

"If you hadn't seen them birds fly up and guessed there might be somethin' waitin' for us on this side of the hill, them redskins would've had the drop on us," Uncle Dan said as Preacher swung up into the saddle on the rangy gray stallion known only as Horse. "That was pretty smart of you, havin' me go on singin' whilst you slipped around the side of the hill and snuck up on 'em."

"But if there was no ambush, I'd've wound up lookin' a mite foolish, wouldn't I?"

"Better to be foolish and alive, I always say."

Preacher couldn't argue with that.

"How far you reckon we are from St. Louis?" Uncle Dan went on.

"Be there in another week, just about, I'd say."

"That arm of yours gonna be good and healed up by then?"

Preacher lifted his left arm. It was splinted and wrapped up from elbow to wrist, but at this point, that was more of a precaution than anything else.

"It's pretty much healed now," he said. Several weeks had passed since the bone had been broken about halfway down his forearm. "I can use it without any trouble. It just aches a little ever' now and then."

"Well, you best be careful with it. You want to be at full strength when we get there. Killin' that bastard Beaumont ain't gonna be easy."

"No," Preacher said, thinking of all the evil that had been done because of the man called Shad Beaumont, "but it sure is gonna be satisfyin'."

Chapter 2

Preacher had left his family's farm at a young age, driven by an undeniable wanderlust. Many of the years since then had been spent in the Rocky Mountains, although his fiddle-footed nature had taken him as far south as Texas and as far north as Canada. He had also made a number of trips back east to St. Louis, and that was his destination now.

He wasn't going there to sell furs that he had trapped in the mountains, though, as he had done in the past.

This time, he was going to kill a man.

Twice now, Shad Beaumont had dispatched agents to the mountains in an attempt to take over the fur trade. Beaumont was the boss of the criminal underworld in St. Louis, but that wasn't enough for him. He wanted to branch out, to spread his unholy influence over the mountains, and when Preacher had helped foil his first effort in that direction, Beaumont hadn't hesitated to send hired killers after him.

Preacher was still alive, and those would-be assassins were dead, but they weren't the only ones who had died. Innocent folks had been killed, and Preacher was filled with righteous wrath over those deaths. Some of the people who had died hadn't exactly been what anybody would call innocent, but they hadn't deserved to die, and Preacher wanted to avenge what had happened to them, too.

It all added up to Preacher going to St. Louis and confronting the arch-criminal on his own stomping grounds. Venturing into the lair of a vicious animal was always dangerous, but it was also the fastest, simplest way to deal with the threat.

So Preacher and Uncle Dan Sullivan had ridden out of the mountains, following the North Platte River to the Missouri and then following the Missouri on its curving course through the heart of the country toward St. Louis. Uncle Dan had his own grudge against Beaumont, since his nephew Pete Sanderson had died as a result of Beaumont's latest scheme. Over and above that, Preacher and Uncle Dan had become friends, and the old-timer hadn't wanted Preacher to set out alone with a broken arm. It was true that by now Preacher's arm was almost healed, but he had to admit, it had come in handy having Uncle Dan around to help with setting up camp and tending the horses and all the other chores that had to be taken care of when a fella was riding just about halfway across the continent.

Today, of course, Uncle Dan had proved to be even handier than usual by blowing that Pawnee's head off before he could ventilate Preacher's hide with an arrow.

The two men rode roughly parallel with the river, through the rolling hills about a mile south of it. The Pawnee and the Cheyenne liked to lurk in these parts, waiting for unwary travelers to come along, and they were worse along the river. Of course, you could run into hostiles just about anywhere out here, as Preacher and Uncle Dan had seen with their own eyes today.

They didn't encounter any more trouble before nightfall, but they made a cold camp anyway and had a skimpy supper of jerky and hardtack. The two men took turns standing guard during the night.

Other than the sounds of small animals, the prairie was quiet and peaceful, and there had to be about a million stars up there in the deep black heavens, Preacher thought as he lay in his blankets and gazed upward briefly before dozing off. The stars were like jewels, shining with a brilliant intensity, and Preacher felt as if he could just reach up and pluck them out of the sky. He would be a rich man if he could do that.

But he wouldn't be a free man anymore, not with the sort of freedom that he had craved all his life, and he wouldn't trade that for all the diamonds and emeralds and rubies in the world.

The next day, they pushed on south and east toward St. Louis. Around mid-morning, Preacher reined in suddenly and leveled an arm to point at the ground ahead of them.

"Look at those tracks," he told Uncle Dan.

The old-timer had brought his mount to a stop, too. Now he edged the horse forward and leaned over in the saddle to study the faint markings on the ground.

"Unshod ponies," he said after a moment. "Looks like about twenty of 'em, too. That'd be Standin' Elk and his glory boys, just like ol' Bent Stick said."

Preacher's eyes narrowed. "Headin' north toward the river, I'd say. Maybe figure on ambushin' a flatboat or

some pilgrims who come along on horseback, headin'
for the mountains."

Uncle Dan spat on the ground. "None of our business.
Anybody venturin' into this here country had damned
well better know there's Injuns about. It's ever' man's
duty to keep his own eyes open and his powder dry."

"You're right," Preacher said. "Looks like Standin'
Elk and his war party passed through here early this
mornin'. I'm glad we missed 'em."

"You and me both, Preacher."

Preacher lifted the reins and heeled Horse into
motion. With Dog bounding out ahead, as usual, and
the pack animals trailing them, the two men rode
across the trail left behind by the Pawnee war party.

They didn't see any other signs of human beings
until later in the day. The solitude was magnificent, with
just the two men and their horses—insignificant specks,
really—moving leisurely across the vast, open prairie.
Eagles cruised through the arching bowl of blue sky.
Antelope raced by, bounding over the landscape with
infinite grace and beauty. Herds of buffalo as seemingly
endless as a brown sea drifted slowly this way and that,
following the grass and their instincts. Preacher always
felt more at home in the mountains than anywhere else,
but the prairie held its own appeal, too.

Came a time, though, late that afternoon, when
Uncle Dan pointed to the northeast, toward the river,
and said, "Look at that dust up yonder."

Preacher nodded. "Saw it ten minutes ago."

"Well, why in blazes didn't you say somethin' about
it then?"

"Wanted to see how long it'd take you to notice it,"
Preacher replied with a grin.

"Uh-huh. And if you *hadn't* spotted it first, you wouldn't admit it, would you? Let a feeble old man beat you to it."

"You're about as feeble as a grizzly bear. You *are* old, though."

"You will be, too, one o' these days, if you live long enough. Which means you better stop mouthin' off to your elders. Now, what're we gonna do about that dust?"

"Why do we have to do anything about it?" Preacher asked as he shrugged his shoulders. "Probably just some buffs driftin' along the river."

"You know better'n that," Uncle Dan said. "Buffler move too slow to raise a cloud o' dust except when they're stampedin', and if that was the case, there'd be even more of it in the air. No, I seen dust like that before. It comes from ox hooves and wagon wheels."

"A wagon train, in other words."

"Damn right."

Preacher sighed. The same thought had occurred to him, but he had pushed it out of his head. He didn't want anything else interfering with the mission that was taking him back east to St. Louis.

Now that Uncle Dan had put the problem into words, though, Preacher knew he couldn't very well ignore it.

"And you know what them pilgrims may be headed right into," Uncle Dan went on. "They keep movin' upriver, they're liable to run smack-dab into Standin' Elk and that Pawnee war party."

"They're bound to know they might encounter hostiles. You said it your own self this mornin', Uncle Dan. Anybody who's gonna come out here on the frontier needs to keep his eyes open and his powder dry."

The old-timer ran his fingers through his beard

and scratched at his jaw. "Yeah, I did say that, didn't I? But I was thinkin' more o' fur trappers and river men. Fellas who can take care o' themselves. There's liable to be women n' kids with that wagon train."

Preacher figured it was a safe bet there *would* be women and children with the wagon train. He had seen it happening all too often in recent years. With the population growing back east, folks were starting to get crowded out. They wanted to come west to find new land and new opportunities. He supposed he couldn't blame them all that much. He had done pretty much the same thing himself, after all.

But he hadn't dragged a wife and a passel of young'uns with him when he lit out for the tall and uncut. In fact, he'd been nothing but a youngster himself, with no one else to be responsible for. He couldn't imagine a man packing up his family and bringing them out here.

These days, a lot of men did just that, though. Preacher didn't figure the trend would stop any time soon, either. Once it had started, trying to stop it was like standing in front of an avalanche and hollering, "Whoa!"

"You think we ought to go warn 'em," he said now to Uncle Dan. "Tell 'em to be on the lookout for Standin' Elk."

"Seems like the neighborly thing to do."

"I don't recollect askin' a bunch of immigrants to be my neighbors," Preacher pointed out. "Fact of the matter is, I wish they'd all stayed back east where they belong."

"Wishin' that's like tryin' to push water back up a waterfall," Uncle Dan said, which worked just as well as thinking of the tide of immigration as an avalanche, Preacher decided. "We won't have to go all that far out of our way, and it won't take that long. We can just tell 'em about them Pawnee and then go on our way." Uncle Dan paused. "Or they might invite us to stay the night with 'em. Might be nice to eat a woman-cooked meal for a change, or unlimber that fiddle o' mine and play a few tunes with some other fellas."

Preacher had to admit that didn't sound so bad. At most, detouring to warn the wagon train about the war party wouldn't cost him and Uncle Dan more than part of a day. And that wouldn't make a bit of difference in the long run.

"All right," he said. "Let's go see if we can head 'em off."

They turned their horses and rode due north toward the river. That would put them in front of the wagon train. Fifteen minutes later, they came to the broad valley of the Missouri. The Big Muddy had some size to it here. In fact, it wasn't even muddy at the moment. It was a wide, pretty blue stream that flowed between green, grassy banks. Preacher and Uncle Dan rode down to the edge of the river and reined in.

Dog ran at some ducks floating around at the edge of the stream and barked enthusiastically at them. The ducks continued paddling around regally, ignoring the big cur until Dog couldn't stand the temptation anymore and splashed out into the water. Then the ducks squawked and took flight, rising above the water. Preacher had to laugh as Dog emerged from the water, dripping wet, and then shook off sheepishly.

"Yeah, you showed them ducks who's boss, all right," Preacher told him.

"Yonder come the wagons," Uncle Dan said.

Preacher looked along the stream. The wagon train was on the same side of the river he and Uncle Dan were. Several men rode out in front of it on horseback, about fifty yards ahead of the lead wagon. They ought to have at least one scout farther ahead than that, Preacher thought, and wondered if the man had already gone past this spot. Behind the outriders came the wagons themselves, a line of canvas-covered prairie schooners so long that Preacher couldn't see the end of it, each wagon being pulled by a team of either four or six oxen.

"Fella in charge is probably one of those out in front there," Preacher said. "Let's go talk to him."

He and Uncle Dan heeled their horses into motion and rode toward the wagon train. The four riders leading the way brought their mounts to a halt, evidently waiting for Preacher and Uncle Dan to get there. As they came closer, Preacher saw that one man was sitting his saddle slightly ahead of the other three. He was a barrel-chested hombre wearing a flat-crowned hat. A brown beard came halfway down his chest. Preacher pegged him for the boss of the wagon train.

As they came up and brought their horses to a stop again, Preacher lifted his right hand, palm out, in the universal sign that said their intentions were peaceful.

Those fellas with the wagon train must not have known that, though, because the one with the beard snapped, "Now!" and the other three suddenly jerked pistols from their belts and leveled the weapons at Preacher and Uncle Dan.

Chapter 3

Preacher fought down the impulse to lift the rifle he carried in front of him across his saddle and blaze away at the men before they could open fire. He didn't cotton to having guns pointed at him, and his instincts wanted him to do something about it.

But he noticed that the men hadn't cocked the pistols. Their thumbs were looped over the hammers, so they could cock and fire in a matter of a second or two if they needed to, but it seemed that gunplay wasn't imminent.

"Hold on there!" Preacher said. "We're peaceable men."

The big, bearded wagon master, if that's who he was, glared at Preacher and said in a booming voice, "You look more like highwaymen to me, mister! If you have any thoughts of robbing these poor immigrants, you'd better put them out of your head right now."

"Highwaymen?" Uncle Dan repeated. "We're just poor, honest fur trappers, on our way to Sant Looey."

"That's right," Preacher said. It was getting harder

and harder to just sit there with those guns pointed at him. It made his trigger finger itchy. "His name's Dan Sullivan, and I'm called Preacher."

The wagon boss shook his head. "Those names mean nothing to us. We don't know any of the trash that currently inhabits the Rocky Mountains."

"Trash, is it?" Preacher muttered under his breath. He was starting to like this pompous windbag less and less.

But he kept a tight rein on his temper and went on, "The only reason we rode up here is to tell you folks that there may be a Pawnee war party waitin' up ahead for you, somewhere in the next few miles. If Uncle Dan and I spotted the dust from your wagons, you can damned well bet the Pawnees did."

One of the other men lowered his gun slightly and said, "You hear that, Mr. Buckhalter? Savages!"

"I heard," the barrel-chested, bearded man said. "And I told you, Donnelly, that there was a chance of encountering Indians on our way to Oregon. You knew the risk when you joined the wagon train."

"Yeah, but shouldn't we listen to these fellas?" the man called Donnelly asked. "They're bound to know this part of the country. I mean, just look at 'em."

"I know the country, too," Buckhalter snapped. "This isn't the first wagon train I've guided west. And I know that this isn't Pawnee territory. The only Indians in these parts are friendly ones."

Uncle Dan couldn't stand it anymore, and Preacher understood the feeling. "Why, you tarnal idjit!" the old-timer burst out. "Half a dozen o' them so-called friendly Injuns tried to lift our hair yesterday, and they was just scouts from a bigger war party. You keep goin' the way you're goin' and they'll jump you, sure as shootin'!"

Preacher looked along the line of wagons, which had come to a stop while he and Uncle Dan talked to the riders. "How many men do you have along with you?"

Buckhalter gave him a stony stare and didn't answer, but Donnelly said, "Between fifty and sixty, counting the boys who are almost grown. There are thirty-eight wagons in the train."

"Well, then, you've got that war party outnumbered almost three to one. Maybe they'll see that and decide not to attack."

"Do you think we can count on that?"

Preacher leaned over in the saddle and spat on the ground. "Mister, you can't count on *nothin'* where Indians are concerned. Just when you think you've got 'em all figured out, they'll do somethin' else to surprise you. I reckon it's a fifty-fifty chance on whether that war party will jump you. It all depends on how they're feelin' at the time."

Donnelly turned to Buckhalter and said, "I think we should do something about this."

"What would you have us do?" Buckhalter demanded. "Turn back to St. Louis? Give up on all your hopes and dreams?"

"I didn't say that—"

"Nothing worthwhile in this life comes without risk," Buckhalter went on.

Preacher couldn't argue with that sentiment. He knew it was true. But that didn't mean a fella had to be foolish when it came to risks.

"None of you folks asked me for my advice—" he began.

"That's right, we didn't," Buckhalter said.

"—but I'm gonna give it to you anyway," Preacher went on as if he hadn't been interrupted. "Get some scouts on fast horses well out in front of the wagons. When you make camp for the night, pull the wagons in a tight circle and get all the livestock inside. Post plenty of guards and make sure they're hombres who can stay awake and alert. The Pawnee will slip up on a man and cut his throat before he knows what's goin' on if he ain't mighty careful. Make sure everybody who can use a gun has one handy, and keep 'em loaded. They ain't gonna do you any good otherwise, 'cause the Indians won't wait around until you're ready to put up a fight."

"Is that *all?*" Buckhalter asked coldly. "Or would you like to insult our intelligence some more?"

"Mister, what the hell is wrong with you?" Uncle Dan said. "Preacher and me are just tryin' to help you, and you go outta your way to insult us."

Preacher lifted a hand and said, "Forget it, Uncle Dan. Some fellas just don't like havin' their authority challenged. I reckon Buckhalter's the boss here, and what he says, goes."

Buckhalter sniffed and then jerked his head in a nod, as if to reinforce what Preacher had just said.

"That means the blood of all them folks in the wagons will be on *his* head if somethin' goes wrong," Preacher continued. "It ain't none of our business."

He started to turn Horse away, but before he could do so, Donnelly prodded his mount ahead of the others and said, "Wait a minute."

When Preacher looked back at him, Donnelly went on, "I don't know if you're right about the Pawnee or not. Mr. Buckhalter hasn't given us any reason to doubt his experience. But I'd like for you to make camp with us tonight so that everybody can hear what you have to say."

Wearing an angry expression on his bearded face, Buckhalter moved his horse alongside Donnelly's and said, "I'm the chief guide and wagon master of this train, Mr. Donnelly, and I don't appreciate you casting doubt on me by listening to these tramps. We all agreed that *I'm* in charge here."

"I mean no offense," Donnelly said, "and it's true you're the wagon master, Mr. Buckhalter. But those folks elected *me* their captain before we left St. Louis, and I feel a great deal of responsibility for them. I don't think it'll hurt any of us to listen to these men."

"We've heard them already," Buckhalter said. "And I say they're mistaken."

"Hard to be mistaken about six dead warriors," Preacher drawled. "And one of 'em, a fella called Bent Stick, talked before he died. He told us about a chief named Standin' Elk leadin' a war party through these parts. Uncle Dan and I crossed their trail earlier today, back yonder a ways. They number at least twenty men, and they were headin' for the river. Like I said, you've got 'em outnumbered . . . but chances are, most, if not all, of those fellas are seasoned killers. That means they're more dangerous than a bunch of immigrants."

"Ride with us, and make camp with us tonight," Donnelly urged. "You'll have a chance to speak your piece, Mister . . . Preacher, was it?"

"Just Preacher. No mister."

"You can speak your piece," Donnelly said again, "and I promise that we'll all listen."

Buckhalter snorted and shook his head, but he didn't say anything else.

Uncle Dan ran his fingers through his beard. "I was just tellin' Preacher earlier that it'd be mighty nice to eat a woman-cooked meal again. And the strings on my fiddle are just achin' to have a bow scraped across them."

"We have some pretty good fiddle players among us," Donnelly said with a smile. "We have music almost every evening, and I'm sure they wouldn't mind if you joined in."

"All right," Preacher said. He agreed almost as much to annoy Buckhalter as anything else. He felt an instinctive dislike for the hombre.

Donnelly turned to Buckhalter. "It's fairly late in the afternoon. Should we go ahead and start looking for a place to make camp?"

Buckhalter jutted his beard toward Preacher and said, "Why don't you ask him?"

Then he turned his horse and rode toward the wagons.

"Didn't mean to cause trouble betwixt you and your wagon boss," Uncle Dan said. "We just wanted to let you know about them Injuns."

Donnelly shook his head. He was a middle-aged, solemn-faced man with graying hair who looked like he might have been a storekeeper or a lawyer back east.

"He's been touchy the entire trip," Donnelly said. "He'll get over it. I think he's just a very proud man who doesn't like having his judgment questioned."

Preacher said, "It's a good thing for a man to take pride in himself . . . just not so much that he can't listen to what other folks have to say."

The men turned their horses and rode toward the wagons. Donnelly gestured toward his two companions and said, "This is Mike Moran and Pete Stallworth, two more of our scouts and guides."

"How many scouts are out now?" Preacher asked.

"Two. Fred Jennings and Liam MacKenzie. Don't worry, they're good men."

Preacher figured he'd reserve judgment on that. Not that it was his place to be passing judgment on any of these folks, he reminded himself. He didn't like it when people did that to him.

Moran was a tall, burly gent with a face that looked like it had been hacked out of the side of a granite mountain. Stallworth was short and stocky, with thick blond hair sticking out from under a hat pushed back on his head. Preacher said to them, "You fellas work for Buckhalter?"

"He's the wagon master," Stallworth replied with a friendly grin. "It was Mr. Donnelly here who hired us, though, and him and the rest of those pilgrims who're payin' us."

"So there are five guides, countin' Buckhalter?"

"That's right."

"Been to the mountains much?"

"I trapped out there a couple of seasons," Stallworth said. "Know my way around pretty good, I reckon."

Preacher turned to Moran. "How about you?"

The big man just grunted. Evidently, he wasn't overly fond of talking.

Preacher let it go. They were approaching the wagons now, and he saw lots of curious looks directed his way. These folks had to wonder if there was some sort of problem. He saw fear on many of the faces.

Fear of Indians, fear of the wilderness, just fear of the unknown in general . . .

But the desire to make a new start in life had overcome those fears, or else these people wouldn't be here, a long way west of where civilization came to an end.

Donnelly raised his voice and called out, "We'll go ahead and make camp! Pass the word! These gentlemen have some things to tell us!"

Uncle Dan leaned closer to Preacher and asked quietly, "What gentlemen?"

"He means us."

"Oh. Been a long time since anybody called me a gentleman. Ain't sure I fit the description no more . . . if I ever did."

Donnelly rode along the line of wagons, instructing the drivers to pull the vehicles into a circle. Preacher wondered if they had been doing that all along. From the awkwardness with which the drivers handled the maneuver, he would have guessed that they hadn't.

He looked around for Buckhalter but didn't see the man. He was beginning to think that Buckhalter was a fraud, that the man had taken the job as wagon master but didn't really know what he was doing. These pilgrims should have been circling the wagons every night since they left St. Louis.

The same thought must have occurred to Uncle Dan, because the old-timer said, "These folks need help, Preacher. Somethin' ain't right about that fella Buckhalter. That must be why he acted like he had a burr under his saddle right off. He didn't want anybody comin' around tellin' these folks that he's a damn fool."

"I expect you're right . . . but we can't take over and

guide this wagon train all the way to Oregon Territory. We got business of our own waitin' for us downriver."

"Yeah, I know." Uncle Dan sighed. "Still, though, you can't blame a fella for thinkin' about it." He gazed past Preacher. "Especially when he's feastin' his eyes on what I'm lookin' at right now."

Preacher was curious enough at the comment that he had to glance around. When he did, he saw immediately what Uncle Dan meant.

Because the woman coming toward them was pretty enough to make any man think about spending more time with her.

Chapter 4

The woman wore a long skirt and long-sleeved shirt, like most of the women from the wagon train, but unlike them, she wasn't wearing a bonnet at the moment. The late afternoon sunlight shone brilliantly on the reddish-gold curls that fell around her lovely face. The drab attire wasn't enough to completely conceal the womanly curves of her body.

Preacher and Uncle Dan still sat on their horses. The woman came to a stop a few yards away, smiled up at them, and said, "Hello. Welcome to our little community on wheels. Ned tells me that you're going to be staying with us tonight."

Preacher recovered his wits with a little start, hurriedly swung down from the saddle, and motioned for Uncle Dan to do likewise. He plucked the wide-brimmed brown felt hat from his head and gave the woman a polite nod.

"Yes, ma'am, I reckon that's right, although I don't rightly know who this fella Ned is."

"My husband, Ned Donnelly," she said.

"Oh." Preacher tried not to appear too crestfallen at the discovery that this fine beauty was married. "Yes, ma'am, we're acquainted. Seems like a right nice fella."

"He is." The woman extended her hand. "I'm Lorraine Donnelly."

Preacher gripped her hand. He could tell from the calluses on her palm that she must be handling the team attached to one of the wagons. Reins left marks like that on a person's hands when you used them all day, day after day. Despite that, her touch had a womanliness to it that affected him, as it would any man who spent most of his time on the frontier, far from the presence of any female.

"They call me Preacher. This is Uncle Dan Sanderson."

Lorraine Donnelly smiled again. "Oh, you're uncle and nephew."

"No, ma'am," Uncle Dan said as he shook hands with her, too. "I ain't related to this here tall drink o' water. Folks just call me Uncle Dan 'cause I was trappin' partners with my nephew Pete. He got hisself kilt a while back, though."

Lorraine's smile went away. "Oh, I'm sorry."

"So am I."

Looking slightly uncomfortable now, Lorraine changed the subject by saying, "Ned tells me there may be hostile Indians close by."

Preacher nodded. "Yes, ma'am."

"Do you know what Mr. Buckhalter intends to do about it?"

Preacher and Uncle Dan exchanged a glance, then Preacher said, "I ain't sure Mr. Buckhalter believed us. He seems to think this ain't Pawnee territory."

"But you believe it is."

"We kilt half a dozen of the varmints yesterday," Uncle Dan said.

Lorraine's eyes widened, and although her face had a healthy tan from being outside most of the time, Preacher thought she paled a little. "Killed . . . half a dozen of them?" she repeated.

"They ambushed us," Preacher said shortly. "We'll be tellin' the whole bunch about it directly. I think your husband wants everybody to hear about it."

"Yes, that sounds like Ned. He thinks everyone should have a voice in any decision."

That was an admirable goal, thought Preacher, but sometimes it wasn't practical. Too many people didn't know enough about a particular situation and didn't have enough experience to make a wise decision. And some were just damned fools to begin with. When it came down to life and death, it was usually better to let somebody who knew what he was doing make the decisions for everybody, and save the dithering for later.

Lorraine recovered her smile and said, "You'll have dinner with us tonight. No arguments."

Uncle Dan gave her a gap-toothed grin. "I wasn't plannin' on arguin', ma'am. Was you figurin' on givin' the lady an argument, Preacher?"

"Nope," Preacher said.

"Fine. We'll eat about sundown."

"Yes'm," Uncle Dan said.

Lorraine nodded and turned to go back to the wagons. When she was out of earshot, Uncle Dan said quietly, "That there is a *mighty* handsome woman."

"Yeah . . . and a mighty married woman, too,"

Preacher reminded him. "I reckon you can forget any ideas of courtin' her, Uncle Dan."

"Me? Hell, boy, I thought you might try to find out how she'd feel about doin' a little sparkin'. I'm too old for such foolishness."

"See this gray in my hair? I ain't no spring chicken, neither."

"No, but it's still summer for you. I'm closin' in on winter in my life!"

"Let's just go tend to the horses," Preacher said.

While they did that, the pilgrims finally succeeded in maneuvering their wagons into a reasonably tight circle, which was then tightened up even more as each team was unhitched in turn and the wagons backed closer to each other, leaving only one fairly wide gap where the first team could be hooked up the next morning. Preacher and Uncle Dan brought their saddle horses and pack animals into the circle and picketed them where they would be out of the way.

The guides led their mounts into the circle, too, and Preacher spotted Buckhalter again for the first time in a while as the bearded man unsaddled his horse and rubbed the animal down. Buckhalter might be a prickly son of a bitch, Preacher thought, but at least he was taking good care of his horse. That had to count for something in Preacher's book.

Preacher could tell which wagon belonged to Ned and Lorraine Donnelly, because he saw Donnelly tending to the team and Lorraine taking supplies from the wagon to start preparing the evening meal. She set up a cook pot while two boys about eight and ten years old took wood from the wood box and began building a fire under the pot. The youngsters had the same reddish-gold hair as Lorraine, so it was obvious they were her sons.

Preacher nodded toward the wagon and told Uncle Dan, "I'm gonna go talk to Donnelly."

"You wouldn't be goin' over there to be around Miz Donnelly, now would you?"

"No, I wouldn't," Preacher said. "I got an eye for a pretty gal, same as the next man, but I don't mess with married women, Uncle Dan."

"Never said you did. Nice just bein' close to one, though, ain't it? A pretty gal, I mean."

Preacher didn't answer that. He walked over to the wagon where Donnelly was putting out buckets of grain for his oxen.

"Preacher," the man said with a friendly nod. "I figure I'll gather everybody after supper, and then you can tell them what you told us about the Pawnee."

Preacher hooked his thumbs in his belt and leaned a hip against the wagon. "And what good's that gonna do?" he asked.

Donnelly turned to him with a frown. "What do you mean?"

"I been thinkin' about it. Buckhalter's got his mind made up. He's not gonna believe me and Uncle Dan now. To him, that'd look like backin' down. Anyway, what can you do except push on? Buckhalter's right about one thing. You've come too far to turn around and go back to St. Louis. The rest of the folks would never go along with it."

"So what do you suggest?"

"I already told you, and you're doin' it already. You need to be ready for trouble all the time, day and night. Just because things seem quiet and peaceful, don't never take that for granted."

"But what if Mr. Buckhalter says that everything is all right and there's no reason to worry?"

Preacher started to say that Buckhalter would be a blasted idiot if he thought that. He bit back the harsh words and said instead, "You hired Buckhalter and those other fellas to get you to Oregon. I reckon you either have to have some faith in him . . . or not. Maybe he knows what he's doing and where he's going."

"Maybe?" Donnelly laughed humorlessly. "That doesn't sound very comforting."

"There's nothin' comfortin' about takin' a wagon train clean across this wild country, mister. Sooner you get that notion out of your head, the better."

Donnelly thought about it for a moment, then sighed. "So you're saying that you *don't* think we should have a camp meeting tonight?"

"Wouldn't serve any purpose. Do you believe me about that war party?"

Donnelly looked steadily at him. "Yes, I think I do."

"Then talk to the other men you can trust. Spread the word that you've all got to be more careful and more responsible for your own safety, instead of just leavin' it all to Buckhalter. Keep scouts out durin' the day, and fort up like this at night. Keep your guns clean and loaded and your powder dry. If there's trouble, circle the wagons and fight. Fight like the very devil was tryin' to get his hands on you." Preacher paused. "Because with the hostiles out here, that's just about what it amounts to."

After another moment, Donnelly nodded. "All right.

I see your point. There's no reason to panic all the women and children."

"That's right. Your wife knows about us runnin' into them Pawnee yesterday, so you might want to tell her to keep it to herself. Are those guides, Moran and Stallworth, married?"

"No, they're single men. They don't have wagons in the train."

"Tell them not to be flappin' their jaws around camp, too." Preacher paused. "You said there are two scouts up ahead now?"

"That's right. MacKenzie and Jennings."

"What time do they usually come in?"

Donnelly frowned again. "About this time. They're always back before nightfall, and it's almost sundown."

Preacher rubbed his jaw and didn't say anything. There was a chance those two fellas had run into Stalking Elk and the rest of the war party. If their horses weren't faster than the Pawnee ponies . . .

No use in borrowing trouble, though, he told himself. They could wait a while longer before they started worrying about the scouts.

Sure enough, the two men rode in less than ten minutes later. They looked a little surprised at seeing the wagons drawn up in such a defensive posture. Preacher made it a point to be close by when they dismounted and Buckhalter strode over to talk to them.

"Any signs of trouble up ahead?" the wagon master asked.

One of the men shook his head. From his lantern jaw and rusty hair, Preacher figured him for MacKenzie, the Scotsman. "The way is clear," the man reported.

"No hostiles?"

"No people at all."

Buckhalter shot a sneering glance at Preacher, who paid no attention to it. He didn't put a whole lot of stock in what Jennings and MacKenzie said, either. If the Pawnee were out there and didn't want to be seen, chances are the scouts wouldn't have seen them.

Preacher felt a tug on the sleeve of his buckskin shirt and looked down to see one of the boys who'd been helping Lorraine Donnelly earlier. The youngster said, "My ma told me to tell you that supper's ready, Preacher."

"Much obliged, son. You see the fella who was with me around anywhere? Old-timer with long white hair and a white beard?"

"You mean Uncle Dan?" The boy grinned. "He's already over at the wagon talkin' to Ma."

Preacher chuckled. Uncle Dan might be old, but he wasn't dead. And being around a pretty woman would make him feel a mite younger for a while.

Preacher followed the boy over to the wagon. Lorraine smiled at him and said, "Ned will be back in a few minutes, and then we can eat."

"Where is he?" Preacher asked.

"Going around the wagons talking to some of the other men."

Preacher nodded. Donnelly was proceeding as he had suggested and discreetly spreading the word among the other men. That would improve the chances of these pilgrims making it all the way to Oregon.

The two boys went over to Uncle Dan. One of them asked the old-timer, "Will you show us your fiddle?"

"Why, I'd be plumb happy to. I put it back here on

the tailgate. Figure on scrapin' out a tune or two after we've et."

The three of them wandered off to the back of the wagon. Lorraine turned to Preacher and said, "Would you mind helping me with something for a minute?"

"Nope. What do you need?"

She led him over to the front of the prairie schooner, where she said, "Do you know anything about wagons like this?"

"A little. I ain't never traveled much in one, though. I'm more of a horsebacker."

"This brake lever keeps sticking . . ." She tugged on the lever as if to demonstrate. "And I can't seem to figure out what's wrong with it."

"Has your husband taken a look at it?"

Lorraine laughed softly. "Ned was an attorney before we came west, Preacher. He doesn't know any more about such things than I do."

Preacher stepped closer to the vehicle and reached out to grasp the brake lever. Lorraine was still holding it, too, but he was careful not to touch her hand.

"I'll take a look at it, but I ain't promisin' I can—"

He didn't get to finish, because at that moment, a hand came down hard on his shoulder and jerked him around roughly, and then a fist smashed into his face.

Chapter 5

The impact of the unexpected blow knocked Preacher against the driver's box on the front of the wagon. The back of his head banged painfully against the boards. A loud, angry voice bellowed, "Get the hell away from Miz Donnelly, you no-good polecat!"

The punch was so hard it blurred Preacher's vision for a second. As his eyesight cleared, he saw Mike Moran standing in front of him, both hamlike hands clenched into fists now. The tall, burly guide sounded mad, but his face still looked like it was carved out of stone.

"Mr. Moran, what in the world are you doing?" Lorraine cried. "There was no reason for you to hit Preacher."

"I seen him grab your hand and try to kiss you, ma'am," Moran said. His voice was loud enough to carry to everyone who had heard his first shout and started to gather around the Donnelly wagon to see what the ruckus was all about. "I seen him makin' advances to you, plain as day."

Lorraine gasped. "That's not true."

"I seen it with my own eyes," Moran grated, then without warning he lunged forward, clapped his massive hands on Preacher's shoulders, and flung him away from the wagon. Preacher's feet left the ground for a second before he came crashing back to earth in a rolling impact that sent a twinge of pain jabbing through his left arm.

"Don't! This isn't necessary—"

Preacher looked up and saw Lorraine tugging at Moran's arm as the man stalked forward, obviously intent on continuing the fight. Although it hadn't been much of a fight so far, Preacher thought. Moran had taken him by surprise, something that didn't happen very often, and Preacher couldn't help but wonder if it was because he'd been distracted by being so close to Lorraine Donnelly. Then that pile driver punch had addled him for a minute.

But his brain was clearing now. Anger blew away the fog that had clogged his thinking.

Moran jerked free of Lorraine as Preacher started to get up. "I'm gonna stomp you into the ground, mister," the guide said. "Anybody who'd molest a married woman deserves it."

Even though Preacher was mad, he was thinking clearly enough to realize something. Ever since this started, Moran had been bellowing like a bull about how Preacher had acted improperly toward Lorraine. The guide was trying to turn the rest of the immigrants against him, Preacher thought.

He suddenly wondered if Buckhalter had something to do with this.

He could ponder on that later. Right now, Moran still

loomed over him. Preacher had only made it up on one knee, and Moran had a big foot drawn back, ready to kick him in the face.

Preacher was ready when that booted clodhopper came at him, though. His hands shot up. He grabbed Moran's ankle, stopping the kick before it could cave in his jaw. Then he heaved upward and put the strength of his legs into it as he surged to his feet.

Moran yelped in surprise and alarm as he felt himself going over backward. Unable to stop himself, he crashed down on his back like a falling tree.

Out of the gathering crowd, Pete Stallworth rushed with an enraged expression on his broad face. "You can't do that to a friend of mine!" he yelled as he swung a punch at Preacher's head.

Preacher didn't want to fight Stallworth, or Moran, for that matter. He jerked his head aside so that Stallworth's fist whipped harmlessly past his face and grabbed the man's arm. Using Stallworth's own momentum against him, Preacher swung him around and rammed him into the side of the Donnelly wagon. Stallworth bounced off, and when Preacher let go of him, he stumbled and fell.

Moran was getting back up by now, though. He charged Preacher, arms flailing. A lot of the bystanders were shouting now, some of them yelling encouragement to Moran since they had heard his accusations against Preacher and believed them, others asking questions. Lorraine was still trying to stop the fight, but since Moran ignored her, Preacher had no choice but to do so as well. He wasn't going to just stand there and let Moran whale on him without fighting back.

Problem was, Moran outweighed him and had a

longer reach, plus Preacher had to be careful about reinjuring that left arm. He couldn't risk slamming punches into Moran's face or body with that hand. The impact might damage the healing bone.

Preacher ducked under Moran's wild blows and stepped in close. He hooked a right into the guide's belly. The punch was so hard that Preacher's fist sunk into Moran's gut almost to the wrist. Moran bent forward, the breath gusting out of his mouth. Preacher came up and drove his right elbow under Moran's chin. That jolted Moran's head back. Like using a hammer to drive a nail, Preacher pounded the side of his right hand into Moran's nose. Blood spurted. Moran howled in pain and stumbled backward.

He tripped over Stallworth's legs and went down again. Stallworth still seemed to be stunned from his collision with the wagon. With both of his opponents down for the moment, Preacher reached for one of the pistols at his waist, intending to make sure this fight was over.

That was when Uncle Dan yelled, "Look out, Preacher!"

From the corner of his eye, Preacher spotted Buckhalter pointing a pistol at him. Preacher twisted aside as Buckhalter pulled the trigger. Smoke and flame spouted from the weapon's muzzle. Preacher heard the low-pitched hum of the heavy ball as it went past his ear, then the thud as it struck one of the sideboards of the Donnelly wagon.

"Hold it right there, mister!" Uncle Dan said. "You best not reach for another pistol. I'll blow a hole in your noggin if you do!"

Breathing a little heavily, Preacher saw that Uncle

Dan had drawn his own pistol and now had Buckhalter covered from behind. He was pretty sure that Buckhalter's shot hadn't hurt anybody, but he looked around quickly to make certain. He wanted to see with his own eyes that Lorraine Donnelly was all right.

She appeared to be, although she was pale and seemed shocked by the violence that had broken out with no warning. Preacher asked quietly, "That shot didn't hit you, did it?"

She shook her head and said, "I . . . I'm fine."

"Uh . . . Preacher?" That was Uncle Dan's voice. "We got a mite of a problem here."

Preacher turned his attention back to his friend and traveling companion and saw that several of the men from the wagon train had pistols and rifles leveled at Uncle Dan. That was a reasonable enough reaction, Preacher supposed. He and Uncle Dan were strangers, after all, and the way these folks saw it, the two of them had come into camp and started attacking members of the wagon train.

"Everybody just take it easy," he said. "There don't need to be any more shootin'."

"That's right," Ned Donnelly said as he pushed his way through the crowd. "Everyone, put your guns down! Lower your guns, please!"

With obvious reluctance, the men from the wagon train followed his orders. Preacher said, "I reckon you can put your gun down, too, Uncle Dan."

"But this polecat's liable to have another pistol hid out somewheres on him," the old-timer protested.

Donnelly said, "If he does, he won't use it." He moved so that he was between Preacher and Buckhalter. "I give you my word on that."

Buckhalter's face was flushed with anger above his jutting beard. "I was just trying to save my friends!" he said. He pointed a finger at Preacher. "That man attacked them! If you ask me, Donnelly, *he's* the real savage around here . . . and you invited him into our midst!"

"Take it easy—" Donnelly began.

"Why don't you ask Moran what he saw Preacher doing to your wife?"

With a frown, Donnelly turned sharply toward Preacher. "What's he talking about? I heard a lot of yelling, but I was on the other side of the camp and couldn't understand any of it."

Before Preacher could say anything, Lorraine hurried forward and put a hand on her husband's arm. "It's nothing, Ned," she told him. "This is all just a terrible misunderstanding."

Moran sat up, holding a hand over his broken nose as it continued to leak crimson. "I saw him pawin' your wife, Donnelly!" he declared. "Saw it with my own two eyes!"

The whole thing was clear to Preacher now. Buckhalter had set it up. Moran had been waiting for some excuse to pick a fight, and when Preacher and Lorraine had gone over to the wagon to have a look at that brake lever, either Moran had recognized the opportunity or Buckhalter had and told the guide to start the ruckus. Then Buckhalter would step in at the right moment, shoot Preacher, and claim that he had been reaching for a pistol. That way, Buckhalter could say that he had killed Preacher in order to protect Moran.

Yeah, something was rotten here. Preacher didn't know what it was, but Buckhalter had to be at the center of it, and Moran was mixed up in it, too. Possibly Stallworth as well, although he might have jumped into the fight simply because Moran was his friend.

Donnelly looked past his wife and asked coldly, "Is there any truth to what Moran says, Preacher?"

Lorraine moved so that he couldn't help but look at her. "I just told you there isn't, Ned. Preacher didn't do anything improper. I just asked him to take a look at that brake lever on the wagon while we were waiting for you to get back for supper. That's *all*."

Donnelly frowned. "You're sure?"

"I think I would know, don't you?"

Donnelly looked past her again. "Preacher . . . ?"

"Your wife's tellin' you the truth," Preacher said. "Nothin' happened."

"Well, how was Mike to know that?" Buckhalter blustered. "It's getting dark. He looked over there and thought he saw something going on. Maybe he jumped to the wrong conclusion—"

"No maybes about it," Uncle Dan put in.

"That doesn't change the fact that when he tried to go to Mrs. Donnelly's assistance, Preacher attacked him!"

Lorraine shook her head. "I'm sorry, Mr. Buckhalter, but Mr. Moran struck the first blow."

Buckhalter looked like he was on the verge of a fit of apoplexy. "Mike got carried away by his concern for you—"

"That's enough," Donnelly said. "I can see now that it was all a misunderstanding, like my wife told me. An unfortunate misunderstanding. We're just lucky that no one was badly hurt."

Moran said, "My nose is broke!"

"We have several men with medical training among the company. Your nose will be tended to, Mr. Moran. In the meantime . . ." Donnelly faced the crowd and raised his voice. "Everyone go on back to your wagons. There's nothing more to see here."

The other two scouts, Jennings and MacKenzie, helped Moran and Stallworth to their feet as the immigrants began to scatter. The fight had provided them with some excitement, a break from the routine of the journey, but now it was time for supper, and they were hungry after a long day on the trail. Aided by their friends, Moran and Stallworth stumbled away. Buckhalter followed them, casting hostile glances over his shoulder toward Preacher as he did so.

Donnelly turned toward Preacher and began, "I'm sorry about what happened here—"

"Forget it," Preacher cut in, his voice hard as flint. "I reckon it'd be better if Uncle Dan and me left. We'll get our horses."

Donnelly and Lorraine looked surprised, and Uncle Dan appeared to be downright devastated. "Leave before *supper?* What in tarnation are you *thinkin'*, son?"

"I'm thinkin' everybody in this camp believed those lies Moran was yellin'," Preacher said. "We ain't welcome here."

"That's not true!" Lorraine exclaimed. "It was all just a—"

Preacher held up a hand to stop her. "A misunderstandin', I know. I've heard it said often enough the past few minutes. But that don't change anything. Buckhalter didn't want us here from the first, and he's the wagon master. Be simpler all around if we're gone. Better for everybody."

"I don't know about that," Donnelly said. "What about those Pawnee?"

"I've already told you everything I can tell you to do. You remember what I said, and you'll be all right. Main thing is to always be ready for trouble."

He had allowed himself to forget that for a few moments, he reflected, had let down his guard because he was talking to a pretty woman and about to eat a good hot meal. All it had gotten him was a bust in the snoot and more guns pointed at him.

Lorraine stepped forward. "I really wish you wouldn't go, Preacher."

"Sorry, ma'am." He reached up and tugged on the brim of his hat. "We're much obliged for your hospitality, ain't we, Uncle Dan?"

"What?" the old-timer said. "Oh. Yeah, I reckon. Much obliged." Preacher took his arm and started leading him away from the wagon, and as they went, Uncle Dan added under his breath, "But I'd'a been a heap more obliged if'n I'd got on the outside o' some supper first."

"Hush up," Preacher said, equally quietly. "We ain't goin' very far."

Uncle Dan looked over at him, frowning in puzzlement. "What?"

"Buckhalter's up to somethin'," Preacher said, his voice grim, "and I damned well intend to find out what it is."

Chapter 6

They saddled their horses and got the animals ready to travel. As they were doing so, Ned Donnelly came over and asked, "Is there anything I can say to get you to change your mind about this, Preacher?"

"Nope," the mountain man replied. "Look, Donnelly, it's just one night's difference. Come mornin', you'd have headed west and we'd have headed east anyway. Uncle Dan and I got business in St. Louis, and it can't wait."

Donnelly shrugged. "I suppose that's true. I just hate to part when there are hard feelings involved."

"There ain't no hard feelin's," Preacher said with a shake of his head. "Not where you and your wife are concerned. You seem like fine folks, and I hope you make a good life for yourselves out yonder in Oregon Territory."

Donnelly stuck out his hand. "Thank you. Good luck with your business in St. Louis."

Preacher didn't hesitate. He gripped the man's hand and gave him a brisk nod.

Two minutes later, Preacher and Uncle Ned were riding away from the camp. As they went out through the gap between wagons, Preacher had seen Buckhalter watching them.

The wagon master wore a satisfied smirk on his face, as if he had gotten what he wanted after all. Preacher had the urge to knock that smirk right down Buckhalter's throat, but that would have to wait. It was more important to figure out exactly what was going on here. Preacher's gut told him that some sort of threat loomed over the wagon train, but he was damned if he knew what it was.

Once they were well away from the wagons, Uncle Dan said, "Now, you want to tell me what in the blue blazes is goin' on here, Preacher?"

"That's what I want to know," Preacher said. "Buckhalter dreamed up that scheme, and I want to know why he was so desperate to get rid of us that he'd set a trap to murder me."

"What are you talkin' about?"

"You saw how he was ready to step right in there and blow a hole in my hide. He knew there was gonna be a fight before Moran ever threw the first punch. He would've likely got away with it, too, if you hadn't been so quick to holler that warnin' at me. Even with that, it was a mighty near thing."

"Yeah, I thought you was a goner." Uncle Dan scratched at his beard as they rode along in the thickening darkness. "You're sayin' that Buckhalter told Moran to jump you like that?"

Preacher explained the theory that had formed in his mind, and as he put it into words, he became even more convinced that he was right.

"Buckhalter was scared to have us around," he concluded. "Scared that we'd mess up some plan of his."

"What sort of plan?"

"That's what we got to find out. Whatever it is, it must be happenin' quick, maybe even tonight, for Buckhalter to get so spooked just because we were there."

"So you weren't really mad at those pilgrims? You were just puttin' on so we'd have an excuse to leave and do some pokin' around?"

"I was a mite put out," Preacher admitted. "But yeah, it was mostly just to make Buckhalter think he'd done got rid of us."

Uncle Dan cackled. "He's gonna be mighty surprised when he finds out he's wrong, ain't he?"

"I damn sure hope so," Preacher said. He reined in and went on, "Let's wait here a few minutes, then we'll turn around and head back to the camp so we can keep an eye on it tonight."

As they sat there on their horses, Uncle Dan sighed and said, "I sure wish ol' Buckhalter had waited until after supper to spring that little trap o' his."

"After we find out what's goin' on, maybe Mrs. Donnelly will have some leftovers you can scrounge," Preacher told him with a smile.

"Preacher . . . you wasn't really makin' advances toward Miz Donnelly, were you?"

Preacher's smile went away and was replaced by a frown. "Hell, no. You oughta know me better'n that, Uncle Dan."

"Well, I didn't think you would, but you gotta remember, I ain't really knowed you all that long. And you can know a feller for years and years and then have him surprise you when it comes to women."

"I suppose that's true. But in this case, naw, there was nothin' dicey goin' on—"

Preacher stopped short as a growl came from Dog. He looked down at the big cur, and despite the poor light, he could tell that Dog was standing stiffly and gazing off to the east as another growl came from his throat.

"Quiet, Dog," Preacher said softly.

"What's got him stirred up?" Uncle Dan asked. "Some sort o' animal, maybe?"

"Yeah. Maybe some two-legged ones."

Uncle Dan's breath hissed between his teeth. "Them Pawnee!"

"Chances are, it ain't them," Preacher said. "The last sign we saw, they were west of here."

"Could've circled around."

"Yeah." Preacher waved a hand toward some trees along the riverbank. "Let's get over there in the shadows under those trees. Come on, Dog."

Quickly, the men and animals moved over into the concealment of the trees. Preacher listened intently, and after a moment he heard the drumming of hoofbeats.

"Riders comin'," he whispered to Uncle Dan. "I reckon Dog smelled 'em before we could hear 'em."

"Dogs is good about that," the old-timer agreed. "I hear 'em now, too. Sounds like a pretty big bunch."

Preacher thought the same thing. Enough riders were moving through the darkness that they could be the Pawnee warriors led by Standing Elk, as Uncle Dan had suggested. Something about that struck Preacher as wrong, though. He thought it was much more likely that the Pawnee would lie in ambush somewhere up ahead along the river, rather than circling around to attack the wagon train by night.

The riders came into view, a dark mass moving from left to right in front of Preacher and Uncle Dan. Dog growled again, as if his instincts wanted to send him charging forward. "Stay, Dog," Preacher told him. "Steady."

"Too dark to count 'em," Uncle Dan said. "Got to be thirty or forty of the varmints, though."

"And I'm bettin' they're white, not red," Preacher said. "You know what I think is goin' on here, Uncle Dan?"

"Nope, but I'm bettin' you're about to tell me."

Preacher nodded toward the group of riders. "Those fellas are workin' with Buckhalter. They've probably been followin' the wagon train since it left St. Louis. As soon as everybody's settled down for the night, they're gonna jump the camp, kill those pilgrims, and loot the wagons."

Uncle Dan let out a low whistle of astonishment. "And you think Buckhalter knows about this, you say?"

"I figure he's the one who planned the whole thing. He knew the attack was scheduled for tonight, and that's why he didn't want us around. Didn't want us stirrin' up Donnelly and the others, either. He had 'em thinkin' that everything's peaceful and they ain't in any danger, so they won't be as watchful and can be took by surprise easier."

"Well, we sort of fouled that up by ridin' in with news of that Pawnee war party."

Preacher nodded. "Yeah. But it's probably too late to call off the attack, especially if there's a chance the wagons might be ambushed in the next day or two by Indians. Buckhalter will want to get his hands on the loot before that can happen."

Uncle Dan ran his fingers through his beard and then said, "You know, Preacher, we ain't got a lick o' proof that this idea of yours is right. Those fellas who just rode by might not have a damned thing to do with Buckhalter or that wagon train."

"That's true," Preacher admitted, "but there's one good way to find out."

"Follow 'em?"

"Damn right," Preacher said.

"You know there's thirty or forty o' them, plus Buckhalter and however many o' them other guides are really workin' for him, and only two of us."

"We got somethin' they don't, though . . . the element of surprise."

"Oh, yeah," Uncle Dan muttered as he and Preacher rode out from under the trees and started after the men they suspected of being bandits and outlaws, "*that'll* even up the odds."

It became clear in no time at all that the riders were headed for the wagon train's campsite. Preacher and Uncle Dan followed several hundred yards back, far enough so that the men wouldn't be likely to spot them, although Preacher thought they probably wouldn't suspect that anyone was behind them. From time to time, he and the old-timer stopped to listen, and as soon as they heard that the hoofbeats had stopped, they reined in, too.

"Hope the varmints didn't hear us 'fore we stopped," Uncle Dan muttered.

"Not likely," Preacher said. "We were bein' pretty quiet." He swung down from the saddle, and Uncle Dan did likewise. "Chances are, they'll sneak up on the wagons on foot, so nobody will hear their horses comin'."

"And we'll sneak up on *them*, right?"

"That's the plan," Preacher said. "Come on, Dog. Stay quiet."

The two mountain men and the big cur stole forward, all their senses alert. Preacher didn't want to blunder right into the middle of the mysterious riders. He was convinced they were up to no good and were probably ruthless killers.

Of course, if he was wrong he'd probably wind up looking like a fool. But as he had told Uncle Dan about that Pawnee ambush the day before, foolish and alive beat smart and dead all to pieces.

Preacher went to his belly as he heard voices whispering nearby. Uncle Dan and Dog followed suit. The three of them lay there, listening intently.

The voices were too soft for Preacher to make out all the words, but what he understood was enough to make him stiffen in anger.

". . . in position?"

"Yeah . . . around the camp."

"Good. We'll attack . . . Buckhalter gives . . . signal. Them pilgrims . . . never know . . . hit 'em."

". . . smart plan. Did Buckhalter . . ."

". . . figure it was really Beaumont's idea."

Preacher heard that plainly enough, and so did Uncle Dan. The old-timer's hand reached over to Preacher's arm and clenched on it. Preacher nodded and breathed, "Yeah, I heard."

Beaumont! Somehow, Preacher wasn't surprised that the man had his finger in this. These would-be robbers worked for Shad Beaumont, and so did Buckhalter. Beaumont had it in his mind to control everything crooked west of the Mississippi, and if nobody stopped him, he might just pull it off. Grandiose schemes sometimes succeeded purely because folks didn't expect anybody to try something so big and audacious. Preacher wouldn't put anything past Beaumont, though.

The two men were still talking. One of them said, ". . . can do now . . . wait."

They would lurk there in the darkness until Buckhalter gave whatever signal they had agreed upon, and then they would rush into the camp, shooting and yelling, and gun down the menfolks. The women would probably be spared, at least the ones who were young enough to be taken back to St. Louis and forced to work in Beaumont's whorehouses. Everyone else would be killed, even the kids.

Preacher wasn't going to let that happen if there was anything he could do to stop it. The first step was to whittle down the odds a mite.

He put his mouth next to Uncle Dan's ear and whispered, "We're gonna take care of the two closest to us. The rest of 'em are probably spread out pretty good, so if we kill 'em quiet-like, the others won't know about it."

"Sure thing," the old-timer breathed. He reached down to his waist and drew his knife from its sheath.

Preacher did likewise, then told Dog to stay put. The big cur wouldn't like it, but he would obey.

Unfortunately, he wasn't able to fight without making a racket with all his growls and snarls.

Moving slowly and in utter silence, Preacher and Uncle Dan crept forward. After a few moments, Preacher made out the shapes of two men lying on their bellies at the edge of some brush. The wagon camp was visible about fifty yards away. The cooking fires had all died down, but glowing embers were still visible through the gaps between the wagons.

Preacher tapped Uncle Dan on the shoulder and pointed to the man on the right. The old-timer nodded in understanding.

Preacher crawled toward the man on the left. He knew he and Uncle Dan would have to strike quickly in order to kill the men before they could cry out. If the rest of the bandits knew something was wrong, they might go ahead and attack the wagon train without waiting for Buckhalter's signal. The gang had the men with the wagons outnumbered, and they were more experienced at fighting and killing, to boot. The defenders probably wouldn't stand much of a chance unless Preacher and Uncle Dan could somehow change the odds.

When they were close enough, Preacher silently rose to his feet. Uncle Dan stood up beside him. They lifted their knives.

Then, at a nod from Preacher, both of them lunged forward.

Preacher landed on the back of his man with both knees. He reached around the man's head with his left hand and clamped it over the man's mouth. At the same time, he brought the knife sweeping down and buried the blade in the man's back.

The man spasmed as the razor-sharp knife penetrated deeply into his flesh. Preacher jerked the weapon out, flipped it around so that he gripped it differently, and swiped it across the man's throat as he pulled the fella's head back. He felt the hot flood of blood over his hand, and then the man went limp.

Preacher looked over at Uncle Dan and in the faint starlight saw the old-timer wiping his blade off on the shirt of the dead man he knelt on. Uncle Dan had killed his man as quietly and efficiently as Preacher had disposed of his.

And with any luck, they were just getting started.

Chapter 7

Preacher and Uncle Dan split up, the old-timer skulking off to the right while Preacher made his silent, deadly way through the darkness to the left. Preacher made it clear through hand gestures that they were to locate and dispose of as many of Beaumont's men as they could in the time they had left before Buckhalter gave the signal to begin the attack on the wagon camp.

There was no way to know how much time that would be. The only thing Preacher was sure of was that it was running out with every second that went by.

He hoped that the robbers weren't clustered together. If they were, he and Uncle Dan were out of luck, and so, maybe, were the immigrants. They needed lone targets that could be handled without raising a ruckus and alerting the other bandits that all was not going as planned.

The sharp tang of whiskey came suddenly to Preacher's nose. One of the men must have brought along a flask, he decided, and the hombre was fortifying himself with some liquid courage before the attack.

Indulging that thirst was bad for a fella's health sometimes, Preacher thought as a fierce grin tugged at the corners of his mouth. He tightened his grip on his knife as he spotted the man kneeling beside the trunk of a tree, facing toward the camp. This time, taking a drink of whiskey was gonna be downright fatal.

A minute later, Preacher was moving away from that spot, leaving another dead man behind him with a slit throat. This wasn't the first time he had conducted such a deadly mission in the dark of night. In the past he had slipped among his enemies on numerous occasions, killing them swiftly and silently. Because of this ability, some of the Indian tribes in the mountains called him the Ghost Killer; others knew him as the White Death. But all of them, deep down, feared Preacher and what he could do.

The minutes ticked by, and with them went the lives of four more of the bandits. That made at least seven of them, Preacher thought, and chances were that Uncle Dan had disposed of a few more by now, too. They were whittling down the odds, just as he had set out to do.

But they wouldn't get a chance to do any more whittling, because as he rose from the corpse of his latest victim, two shots suddenly rang out from the camp, one right after the other. Preacher knew that had to be Buckhalter's signal.

Harsh yells came from dozens of throats as the men hidden around the perimeter of the camp leaped to their feet and rushed toward the wagons. They had no idea that there were fewer of them now than there had been a short time earlier.

Were there fewer enough to make a difference?

Preacher didn't know.

But he was going to take down a few more of them and see if that helped.

He was already on his feet. He shoved the knife back in its sheath and pulled both pistols from behind his belt. His thumbs looped over the hammers and pulled them back. As he ran forward, more shots sounded from the camp. That would be Buckhalter and whoever else was working for him, striking like vipers in the midst of the pilgrims they were supposed to be guiding to a new life, not an unexpected death.

Preacher ran up behind one of the attackers. He didn't waste time or breath calling out to get him to turn around. He just pointed his right-hand pistol at the man's back and blew a hole in the son of a bitch. The man fell, plowing up the dirt with his face.

The attackers began to open fire, probably thinking that one of their own had fired that shot. Preacher veered to his left and closed in on one of the other bandits as the man charged toward the wagons. The fella wore a coonskin cap with an especially bushy tail that bounced on his back as he ran.

He must have heard Preacher coming, because he turned his head to look just in time to catch both balls from the double-shotted pistol in the face. The coonskin cap flew in the air as the man's head was blown out from under it.

Preacher leaped past the falling body and headed for another of the attackers about twenty yards away. This one must have seen him shoot the other man, because he turned and brought up the rifle in his hands. Preacher went diving to the ground as flame gouted from the barrel.

He rolled and came back up on his feet, still

moving. The man was only a few feet away by now. He reversed his grip on the rifle, holding it by the barrel so that he could swing it like a club. Preacher went under it, lowering his shoulder and crashing into the bandit. The man went over backward, with Preacher landing on top of him.

The collision and the fall stunned the man long enough for Preacher to drop his pistols and grab the rifle instead. He wrenched the flintlock out of the man's hands and brought the butt down hard in the middle of his face. Preacher felt bone crunch under the impact. The man arched his back for a second, then sagged back to the ground in death.

Preacher dropped the rifle, snatched up his empty pistols, and tucked them behind his belt as he came to his feet. He loped toward the camp. Muzzle flashes lit up the night all around him. More shots came from inside the camp, but they were directed outward now. That meant the immigrants were putting up a fight.

Preacher had lost sight of Uncle Dan and hoped that the old-timer was all right. Dan Sullivan was a tough old bird, though, and could take care of himself. Preacher had problems of his own, such as the man he came up behind as the varmint knelt and aimed a rifle toward the wagons.

Before the man could fire, Preacher drew his knife and threw it. The blade went into the man's back to the hilt and drove him forward. The rifle slid from his fingers. Preacher grabbed the knife, ripped it free, and plunged it in again just to make sure, then ran on toward the wagons.

He saw a rifle spurt flame between two of the vehicles and heard the ball whine past his head. The

pilgrim who had fired the shot thought he was one of
the bandits!

That realization made Preacher pick up speed. The
rifleman would have to reload before he could fire
again. That delay gave Preacher a few seconds to
reach the wagons and let the defenders know who
he was. He hurdled the wagon tongue as the man
struggled with a ramrod, trying to get it down the
barrel. Preacher could see him by the dim light that
came from the embers of a nearby cooking fire.

"Hold on!" Preacher called. "I'm a—"

He was about to say "friend" when a gun blasted
close beside him. He felt the sting of burning powder
against his face. The roar was so loud it hit his ear
almost like a fist and made him stagger. He twisted his
head around and saw Lorraine Donnelly standing
there with a smoking pistol in her hand. He knew he
was lucky she had hurried her shot and missed him,
although the pistol ball must have come within a
whisker of him at almost point-blank range like that.

The man, who Preacher recognized now as Ned
Donnelly, had finished reloading the rifle. He started
to bring it up as Preacher yelled, "Hold your fire,
damn it! It's me, Preacher!" Half-deafened as he was,
his voice sounded strange in his ears.

Donnelly hesitated, giving Preacher the chance to
push the rifle barrel aside. "Preacher?" Donnelly said.

"That's right. You're under attack by bandits. Don't
let 'em inside the circle of the wagons, and you've got
a chance."

"You're not one of them?"

"Hell, no! I've been out there tryin' to stop them.
Where's Buckhalter?"

He thought that if he could bring down the gang's leader, the other bandits might not put up as much of a fight.

Donnelly just shook his head. "I . . . I haven't seen him. I heard him yelling something a little while ago. He's still around somewhere."

Maybe he was, and maybe he wasn't, Preacher thought. After firing that signal, Buckhalter might have slipped out of the camp to keep his own hide safe during the attack. Preacher wouldn't put it past the man for a second.

Lorraine stepped closer to him and said, "I'm sorry I shot at you, Preacher."

"You didn't know who I was," he said. "No harm done."

Other than the ringing in his ears, and she didn't have to know about that.

"Do you need powder and shot for your pistols?" She held out a powder horn and shot pouch toward him.

Preacher grinned and took them from her. "I dang sure do." With swift, practiced efficiency, he began reloading the weapons.

When both pistols were charged and ready, he handed the powder horn and pouch back to Lorraine and said, "You'd better hunt some cover, ma'am."

"I'm going to stay right here and reload for Ned," she declared without budging. "We have two rifles."

And they'd be liable to need them, Preacher knew. He nodded curtly and settled for saying, "Keep your head down as much as you can. Where are your youngsters?"

"In the wagon, between our trunks."

That was as good a place as any for the boys. Preacher nodded again and began loping around the circle to see how the rest of the defenders were holding up.

A frightened yell made him head for one of the gaps between wagons. As he approached, he saw one of the immigrants wrestling with a tall, hatchet-faced bandit who looked like a half-breed. The pilgrim had an ax, but as Preacher came closer, the bandit wrenched it away from him and swung it. With a grisly *thunk!* the blade split the immigrant's skull, sinking deep into his forehead.

The half-breed didn't have time to enjoy his triumph. His face turned into a crimson smear as Preacher fired one of the pistols into it. He stuck the empty gun behind his belt and reached down with that hand to pull the ax free, trying not to think about the sound it made as it came loose. Another bandit bounded up onto the wagon tongue and started over. Preacher met him with the ax, whipping it back and forth so that the razor-sharp blade opened up deep slashes across the man's chest. The man fell off the wagon tongue, and as he landed facedown on the ground, Preacher swung the ax up and brought it down in the back of the man's head.

He had lost track of how many members of the gang he had killed in the past ten minutes or so. He knew he had made a pretty good dent in their numbers, though, so it didn't really surprise him when the shooting began to die down. The attack had been blunted before it even began, and now it was losing the rest of its momentum.

Preacher saw one of the defenders go down with blood welling from a wound in his arm just as he finished reloading a rifle. Leaping to his side, Preacher took the weapon from him and said, "I'll put it to good use, friend." He lifted the rifle and aimed at another muzzle flash from the attackers. The rifle boomed as he pressed the trigger, and Preacher was rewarded by a howl of pain from his target that trailed off into a gurgling moan.

Several more shots sounded, and then a tense, eerie silence fell over the camp and the surrounding area. Preacher didn't know if any more of Beaumont's men were out there. Maybe they were all dead. It was possible, too, that the survivors had given up and lit a shuck out of there.

"Preacher!"

He looked around and saw Uncle Dan trotting toward him. The old-timer's beard was streaked with red from a bullet graze on his cheek, but other than that he seemed to be all right.

"I think they've rabbited," Uncle Dan said as he came up.

"I hope you're right. You think we should go have a look-see?"

"I don't know any other way to be sure, even though I ain't all that fond o' the idea."

Preacher chuckled. "Neither am I. We'd best reload all our guns before we venture out there."

"I'm going with you."

Preacher looked around and saw that Ned Donnelly had come up on his other side. He shook his head, saying, "I ain't sure you ought to do that."

"I am," Donnelly declared. "I'm the captain of this wagon train. The safety of its members is my responsibility."

Donnelly should have thought of that before he hired a skunk like Buckhalter, Preacher thought, then told himself that maybe he was being a mite unfair. Donnelly hadn't had any real reason to suspect Buckhalter of treachery until today.

"All right," he said. "Let's go."

As soon as their weapons were reloaded, the three men left the camp, moving warily through the darkness. Preacher whistled softly for Dog, and the big cur came loping up to him. Having Dog along would make it a lot easier to locate any two-legged varmints still lurking in the shadows.

The three men and the dog circled the camp several times, working their way farther out each time. They found numerous bodies, but no live bandits. The survivors might have taken some of the dead and wounded with them, but they hadn't lingered long enough to retrieve all of their fallen companions.

When Preacher was satisfied that the threat was over, at least for tonight, he led Uncle Dan and Donnelly back to the camp. As they walked through the gap between the wagons, he was surprised to hear a familiar blustery voice saying, "That man Preacher was behind the attack, I tell you! He and the old man were scouts for that band of thieves! They came in here and spun that cock-and-bull story about savage Indians being ahead of us so that we wouldn't suspect an attack was about to come from the other direction!"

Uncle Dan let out a low whistle. "That varmint don't give up easy, does he? He's tryin' to bluff his way through!"

"Let me handle this," Donnelly said. He stalked

toward the large group of immigrants gathered on the other side of the circle and raised his voice. "Mr. Buckhalter!"

Buckhalter stopped talking and turned to see who had hailed him. As he spotted Preacher and Uncle Dan following Donnelly, he grabbed for a pistol at his waist and yelled, "There they are! Get them!"

None of the pilgrims made a move, though. Donnelly was in the way. He raised his hands and called out, "Everyone listen to me! Mr. Buckhalter is mistaken! Preacher and Mr. Sullivan had nothing to do with the attack on us! They fought side by side with us and helped defend us against the robbers!"

Buckhalter's beard jutted out defiantly. "I didn't see that!" he declared. "And I don't believe it!"

Lorraine Donnelly stepped forward. "It's the truth," she said in a loud, clear voice. "I was about to speak up myself, but my husband beat me to it. With my own eyes, I saw Preacher and Mr. Sullivan battling the attackers."

"That's not possible!" Buckhalter blustered.

Donnelly stopped in front of him. "You'd better not be calling my wife—or me—a liar, Mr. Buckhalter. You're simply mistaken."

"No, he ain't," Preacher drawled. "He's lyin' . . . and for a good reason. He's the boss of the gang that's been trailin' you ever since the wagons left St. Louis. He set up the attack."

Buckhalter's face darkened in fury. "That's a bald-faced lie!" he bellowed.

"Give it up, Buckhalter," Preacher said. "I heard some of those varmints talkin' before *you* gave the signal for the attack to begin. And I know that all of you are workin' for Shad Beaumont, too."

At the mention of Beaumont's name, the flush disappeared from Buckhalter's face. He paled instead, because he had to realize now that the game was up. His hand moved toward the pistol at his waist. Preacher was ready to grab his own gun.

But before he could, a roar sounded behind him, and what felt like an avalanche crashed down on him.

Chapter 8

The crushing weight drove Preacher to the ground. What felt like an iron bar clamped itself across his throat, cutting off his air.

Even under attack like this, he was thinking straight enough to have a hunch that it was Mike Moran who had jumped him. Preacher was convinced that Moran was in on the scheme with Buckhalter. The big man must have been in the crowd of immigrants, heard Preacher's reference to Beaumont, and figured that he was done for.

He was going to try to kill Preacher first, though, before his own fate caught up to him.

Preacher drove his right elbow up and back and heard an animal-like grunt as it sank into his attacker's belly. He reached back with his left hand and tangled his fingers in the man's hair. A hard tug brought a howl of pain as Preacher came away with a handful of hair.

That distracted his opponent enough for Preacher to buck up off the ground and throw the man to the side. Preacher rolled the other way and came up on his feet. He saw that his hunch had been right. It was Mike Moran who clambered upright about ten feet away, blood running down the side of his face from his scalp where Preacher had torn out the clump of hair that he now tossed aside.

Uncle Dan raised a pistol and pointed it at Moran. "Hold it right there, big fella," the old-timer warned. "This here fight's gone on long enough."

Moran started to curse in a low, monotonous voice, but a muffled scream cut across his profanities. Preacher's head jerked around. He saw Buckhalter backing toward one of the wagons with an arm looped around Lorraine Donnelly's throat. His other hand held the muzzle of a pistol pressed against her head.

"Lorraine!" Ned Donnelly cried.

"Stay back!" Buckhalter warned. "I'll kill her!"

Preacher shook his head. "No, he won't. He knows that if he pulls that trigger, he'll be shot plumb full o' holes his own self before Miz Donnelly hits the ground. Might as well go ahead and give up, Buckhalter, because you ain't gettin' out of this."

Preacher started forward, but Donnelly said, "No!" and got in his way. The man put a hand against Preacher's chest. "I know you're probably right, Preacher, but I can't take that chance with Lorraine's life." He turned to the renegade wagon master. "What do you want, Buckhalter?"

"Safe passage out of here," Buckhalter replied. He had such a tight grip on Lorraine that she couldn't budge. "For me and Moran. And I want the money chest."

Preacher knew what Buckhalter was talking about. On a lot of these wagon trains, the immigrants pooled their funds and kept most, if not all, of their money in a chest in one of the wagons. That money would help them get started in their new lives when they got to where they were going. Many of the westward-bound pilgrims didn't have a lot of cash; it was expensive to buy a wagon and outfit it with a team and supplies. It might take most of a family's life savings to pay for such an epic journey.

But take those small amounts and multiply them by the number of families in a wagon train, and it could add up to a tidy little sum. Plus there were usually a few folks who were more well-to-do than the rest, and that would swell the total in the money chest even more.

"That's insane," Donnelly said in response to Buckhalter's demand. "We'll need that money when we get to Oregon. You can't expect us to give it up." He took a deep breath. "We'll let the two of you go, though."

Buckhalter shook his head. "Not good enough. After all we've risked, you can't expect us to ride away without a payoff." His mouth twisted in a sneer under the bushy beard. "Anyway, Donnelly, what will you need more in Oregon, the money or your wife?"

Donnelly didn't have an answer for that. He stood there, obviously tortured by fear for Lorraine, as well as the responsibility he felt toward the other members of the wagon train. He looked toward them, and one of the men said, "We're sorry, Ned, but we can't—"

"I know," Donnelly broke in. "I can't ask you to give up everything." He faced Buckhalter again. "Safe passage. That's all."

Several seconds crept by, the time drawing out painfully. Preacher heard a couple of owls hoot back and forth in the tense silence. Then Buckhalter jerked his head in a nod and said, "All right. Safe passage. Now tell that old man to stop pointing his gun at Moran."

Preacher motioned for Uncle Dan to put down his pistol. The old-timer complied with obvious reluctance. Grinning smugly—the only real expression Preacher had seen on the granite-faced renegade—Moran moved over to join Buckhalter.

"There's one more thing," Buckhalter went on. "Mrs. Donnelly goes with us."

Lorraine's eyes widened even more. Donnelly exclaimed, "You're mad!"

"Not at all. She'll be our guarantee of safety. Otherwise, what's to stop Preacher from coming after us as soon as we leave?" Buckhalter laughed. "You didn't know it, Donnelly, but you had a famous man in your midst. Preacher is known from one end of the Rockies to the other. In fact, my employer has placed a bounty on his head. I'm passing up a nice chunk of coin by letting him live."

Donnelly frowned over at Preacher. "Who's this employer he's talking about?"

"Fella name of Beaumont," Preacher drawled. "He planned this whole thing so Buckhalter, Moran, and those other fellas could loot your wagon train. He did his best to get rid of me so I wouldn't ruin the plan, but it didn't work."

Donnelly looked over at the other three guides, Stallworth, Jennings, and MacKenzie, who stood together at the edge of the crowd. Stallworth and Jennings appeared to have minor injuries from the battle.

"Did you men know anything about this?"

Stallworth shook his head and said, "Not a damned thing, Donnelly, and that's the truth. We just hired on as guides, that's all. Buckhalter and Moran double-crossed us as much as they did you."

One of the men spoke up. "I reckon he's telling the truth, Ned. I saw all three of them fighting those bastards who jumped us."

"Enough palaver," Buckhalter snapped. "We're leaving . . . and like I said, Mrs. Donnelly is coming with us." He told Moran, "Mike, saddle three horses for us."

In a choked voice, Lorraine forced out, "Ned, don't . . . let him . . . take me away . . . from my children!"

Buckhalter chuckled. "He doesn't have any choice, Mrs. Donnelly. Not if he wants to keep you alive."

Preacher said, "I hope you ain't forgot about those Pawnee, Buckhalter. They're still out there somewhere."

"That's why we're going east instead of west. You see, I believed you about them, Preacher, even though I couldn't admit that."

People got out of Moran's way as he went to saddle horses for him and Buckhalter and Lorraine. He had just lifted a saddle and turned toward the animals when there was a fluttering sound. Moran lurched to the side and dropped the saddle. He yelled in pain and reached up to clutch the shaft of the arrow that protruded from his shoulder.

"Pawnee!" Preacher shouted as he saw the arrow. "Everybody hunt cover!"

More arrows came flying out of the darkness around the camp. Preacher had suspected those owls he'd heard a few moments earlier weren't the real thing, and now he was sure of it.

Standing Elk and the rest of the war party must

have heard all the shooting and come to investigate it. Finding that the immigrants had their attention focused elsewhere, the Indians had decided it would be a good time to attack. Even though they didn't really like to fight at night, they would seize an advantage any time they could get it.

The Pawnee weren't Preacher's only worry, though. Buckhalter still had Lorraine as his hostage. Preacher had to get her away from him before something happened to her. He leaped toward the two of them as Buckhalter turned toward the wagons, hauling Lorraine around with him. The son of a bitch was using her as a human shield if any arrows came flying his way, Preacher realized.

Buckhalter still had the gun to Lorraine's head. The hammer was cocked, and all it was take was a little pressure on the trigger to send a heavy lead ball smashing into her skull at point-blank range. Preacher could see only one way to prevent that.

He drew his knife and let fly, putting every bit of skill and accuracy he possessed into the throw.

The blade flicked across the intervening space, turning over as it flew, and when it struck Buckhalter's wrist it landed perfectly, slicing deep into flesh and muscle and slashing the tendons. Buckhalter cried out in surprise and pain as his fingers opened, the digits splaying out instead of contracting. The pistol fell unfired from his hand.

Preacher crashed into Buckhalter's back a second later, driving the man forward and knocking him loose from Lorraine, who was shoved to the ground by the impact as well. That was a good thing, because arrows began to whip through the space the three of them had occupied a heartbeat earlier.

Preacher snatched up the pistol Buckhalter had dropped and slammed the butt into the back of the renegade wagon master's head. Buckhalter went limp.

Reversing his grip on the gun, Preacher tilted the barrel upward as a member of the Pawnee war party vaulted through the narrow gap between a couple of wagons. The warrior's feet had barely touched the ground when Preacher fired from a few yards away. The pistol ball, traveling in an upward path, caught the Indian under the chin and bored on up into his brain, flipping him backward so that he landed on the wagon tongue behind him. Blood gushed from the terrible wound as he lay there draped over the wooden shaft.

Preacher surged to his feet. He lifted Lorraine with him and hustled her toward the nearest wagon. "Stay under cover!" he told her.

Both his pistols were loaded. He pulled them from behind his belt as he swung back toward the fight. The Pawnee war party numbered about twenty men, he recalled, and even with the casualties the immigrants had suffered in the earlier battle, they still outnumbered the Indians. If they were cool-headed and kept their wits about them, they could win this fight.

Preacher was glad to see that the defenders had spread out, seeking cover behind the wagons. Shots roared all around the circle. Women and older children were reloading for the menfolks. It was asking a lot to expect these pilgrims from back east to fight for their lives and the lives of their families twice in one night, but it appeared that for the most part, they were meeting the challenge.

Preacher spotted an empty gap between wagons and knew the Pawnee were likely to realize there weren't any defenders there. He headed for it and got there just as three of the painted savages rushed the opening. They saw him too late to swerve aside. The brace of pistols in his hands boomed like thunder, spewing flame and smoke from their muzzles. Two of the Indians went down, driven off their feet by the deadly impact of the lead balls.

But that left the third Pawnee, and he came hurdling over the wagon tongue to crash into Preacher and knock him backward. The hard fall jolted the empty guns out of Preacher's hands. He looked up as the Indian screeched and brought a tomahawk sweeping down toward his head.

A rifle blasted somewhere close by. Blood and bone sprayed from the Pawnee's head as a ball smacked into it. Preacher heaved the body aside and rolled over, coming up onto hands and knees. He saw Uncle Dan standing there with smoke curling from the barrel of the rifle the old-timer held. Preacher grabbed the tomahawk the Indian had dropped and threw it as hard as he could.

The 'hawk flew past a startled Uncle Dan, missing him by mere inches. The blade embedded itself in the forehead of the warrior who had been about to fire a rifle at the old-timer from behind. Uncle Dan must have heard the Indian collapse, because he looked around and gaped as he saw how close he had come to death.

Preacher gave him a nod and scrambled to his feet.

Just as before, the shooting had begun to become sporadic. Indians were usually pretty quick to realize when they had bitten off more than they could chew, and they didn't have the same sort of stubborn, foolish pride white men often had that would make them keep fighting a losing battle. They would call off an attack and figure that they could fight again some other day. That appeared to be what was happening now, as the shooting trailed off and then stopped.

Preacher looked toward the spot where he had last seen Buckhalter. The renegade wagon master wasn't there now. Grimly, Preacher started in that direction, but he hadn't gotten there when he heard Ned Donnelly shout, "Preacher, look out!"

Twisting around, Preacher saw Mike Moran charging toward him, already practically on top of him. The arrow still stuck out of Moran's shoulder, but other than that he seemed to be unhurt. Moran yelled, "This is all your fault!" just before he rammed into Preacher.

For the second time tonight, Preacher landed on the ground with Moran's crushing weight on top of him. This time he was on his back, so he could look up and see the hatred and rage boiling in the man's eyes. Moran locked his hands around Preacher's neck and began trying to choke the life out of the mountain man.

Preacher knew that Uncle Dan or Donnelly would likely shoot Moran before Moran could kill him, but he didn't wait for somebody else to save his life. He reached up, got hold of the arrow sticking out of Moran's shoulder, and snapped off the shaft. Moran yelled in pain as that caused the arrowhead to shift in his flesh, but the yell dissolved into a gurgle as Preacher rammed the jagged end of the broken shaft into his neck. Blood flooded over Preacher's hand as he drove the makeshift weapon deep into Moran's throat.

Moran's hands came loose from Preacher's throat. He reached up to paw at the shaft of the arrow, but he didn't have the strength to pull it loose. By now, it wouldn't have mattered if he had. A sheet of crimson flowed down over his chest. He swayed back and forth for a second as his eyes rolled back in their sockets, and then he fell to the side. A final spasm went through his body as he died.

Preacher pushed the corpse to the side. Donnelly and Uncle Dan were there, and they both reached down to help him to his feet.

"You all right, Preacher?" the old-timer asked.

"Yeah, I'm fine," Preacher rasped as he rubbed at his throat. Moran hadn't done any real damage, but Preacher knew he'd have some bruises and soreness in his neck for a day or two. "Where's Buckhalter?"

"Gone," Donnelly replied, disgust evident in his tone. "I guess he slipped away during the confusion of the fight with the Pawnee."

Preacher wasn't surprised. Buckhalter seemed to have an instinct for self-preservation.

It might not save him this time, though, with the survivors of that war party roaming around. The Pawnee would be mad about what had happened, and while they might be too smart to attack the wagon train again, they wouldn't hesitate to take their frustrations out on a lone white man if they could get their hands on him.

"What about your wife?" Preacher asked Donnelly. "Was she hurt?"

Donnelly shook his head. "Lorraine is shaken up

some, of course, but she'll be all right." He paused, then asked, "Do you think we'll be attacked again tonight, Preacher?"

A grim chuckle came from Preacher. "Doubtful. I reckon you took a big enough toll on both bunches that they won't be lookin' for a fight for a while. There's probably not more than a handful left alive. Buckhalter's men will likely head back east as fast as their horses can carry 'em. The Pawnee will go back to their regular huntin' grounds and lick their wounds until they get ready to go raidin' again, with some young warriors to replace the ones you killed."

"I'm sorry that so many people had to lose their lives tonight."

"Better those varmints than you or the folks with you," Uncle Dan said.

"We lost several men," Donnelly said with sorrow in his voice. "They were killed during the fighting."

Preacher nodded. "I saw a couple of them go down. They were good men, fightin' right to the end."

"We'll give them proper burials, and leave markers for them."

"I reckon that's fine," Preacher said. He didn't mention the fact that in a few months, no one would be able to tell that any graves had been dug here. Chances were, the markers would be gone, too, claimed by the elements. They surely would be in a year or so, unless the words were carved in stone. And even if they were, the sun and the rain and the wind would wear those away in time, too. The memories folks had of a man were the only true legacy he left behind when he crossed the divide.

That was the way it had always been, the way it

would always be. As the years passed, there would be hundreds, if not thousands, of forgotten graves on these westward trails, Preacher reflected. Few of those who came after would know or care about the people who had died carrying civilization across the prairie.

But the country would be changed forevermore, anyway. For good or bad . . . ?

Well, Preacher didn't know about that part of it.

Chapter 9

More convinced than ever of the need to remain vigilant at all times, Donnelly doubled the usual number of guards for the rest of the night, but the hours passed peacefully and the sun rose the next morning without any more trouble having broken out.

Preacher and Uncle Dan were up more than an hour before sunrise, as usual, getting ready to ride as soon as it was light enough.

As they were having breakfast at the Donnelly wagon, Ned Donnelly asked them, "I don't suppose there's any way I could talk you men into coming to Oregon with us?"

Preacher shook his head. "I reckon not. We got business elsewhere."

"It's mighty temptin', though," Uncle Dan added. "That wife o' yours is one hell of a cook, Ned."

Donnelly laughed. "I know. She's brave and beautiful, too. I'm a lucky man, gentlemen, and don't think for a second that I don't know it!"

Preacher rubbed his bearded jaw and frowned in

thought. "You're gonna need a wagon master and chief guide to replace Buckhalter. Let's go talk to Stallworth. He strikes me as a good man."

Preacher let Donnelly do the talking. Pete Stallworth listened for a few minutes, then said, "I'm flattered, Ned, but I've never been all the way to Oregon."

"Buckhalter probably hadn't been there, either," Donnelly pointed out. "You can do a better job than he would have, Pete."

"Yeah, but he never intended to take the wagons all the way across the Rockies."

MacKenzie stood nearby. He spoke up, saying, "I've been through South Pass and on to the coast several times, Donnelly. I know the way . . . but I don't want the job of wagon master." The Scotsman gestured toward Stallworth. "Give that part of it to Pete, and I'll be your chief guide. Sound fair enough to you?"

Donnelly turned back to Stallworth. "What do you say, Pete?"

Stallworth shrugged, but then his friendly grin broke out over his face. "I say it sounds like a good deal to me. We'll need a few volunteers from the men with the train to serve as scouts and outriders, though. Three of us aren't enough."

"I'm sure that can be arranged," Donnelly agreed with a nod. He stuck out a hand. "It's a deal, then?"

"Between us, we'll get you folks to Oregon," Stallworth replied as he gripped Donnelly's hand.

Under the circumstances, Preacher thought that was the best arrangement the immigrants could have. He said as much to Donnelly a few minutes later as he and Uncle Dan were about to mount up.

"With a little luck along the way, you'll make it just

fine," he said. "Keep your eyes open, listen to Stallworth and MacKenzie, and don't forget why you're doin' this in the first place."

Preacher nodded toward Lorraine Donnelly and the two little boys, who were packing some of the family's gear in the wagon nearby.

"I know," Donnelly said. "Thank you for everything, Preacher. If not for you and Uncle Dan, those robbers would have taken us completely by surprise. They probably would have wiped us out."

Preacher nodded. "More'n likely."

"We'll have the wagons rolling as soon as we've taken care of the burying," Donnelly went on. "I don't know what to do about those other men who were killed. The robbers and the Indians, I mean. I suppose we could dig a mass grave . . ."

"Leave 'em where they fell, and I reckon the scavengers will take care of that problem for you."

Donnelly shook his head. "It doesn't seem right to just leave them."

"They wouldn't have wasted any sympathy on you folks. Anyway, you don't have to worry about the Pawnee dead. The ones who lived took all the bodies with them. I can tell you that without even lookin'. They'll be laid to rest the Pawnee way, the way they would have wanted."

"Well, that's good, I suppose. It still bothers me about those others, though."

"It's a harsh land," Preacher said bluntly. "Men die, and the ones who live move on. That's the way of it, and nothin' you can do will change that."

"I suppose you're right. I can't help but think about what those men would have done to my wife and children . . ." Donnelly took a deep breath. "But I'm not going to think about that. I'm going to think about the new life that's waiting for us in Oregon instead." He held out his hand. "Good-bye, Preacher. And good luck on whatever mission it is the two of you are on."

"Much obliged," Preacher said as he shook hands with Donnelly. He thought about the odds facing him and Uncle Dan in St. Louis, where they would try to destroy a beast of prey in his own lair. "Chances are, we're gonna need all the luck we can get."

For the next few days as they traveled eastward, Preacher kept an eye out for Buckhalter or any of the other members of the gang that had attacked the wagon train. As far as he knew, Buckhalter was on foot, and Preacher halfway expected to come across the renegade's scalped and mutilated body. He and Uncle Dan didn't see any sign of the man though.

As they drew closer to St. Louis, Preacher did a lot of thinking, and he let Uncle Dan in on some of it.

"If Beaumont's put a bounty on my head, he's got to be a mite worried about me comin' after him," Preacher mused as they rode along.

Uncle Dan grunted. "More'n a mite, I'd say. He's got to be scared plumb half to death. He knows you ain't a good fella to have for an enemy, son."

"As many pies as he has his fingers in, I reckon he's got folks scattered all over St. Louis who work for him," Preacher went on, thinking out loud. "That means if I just ride into town right out in the open, somebody's gonna see me and go runnin' to Beaumont to tell him I'm there. It won't be an hour before all the crooked varmints in St. Louis are tryin' to draw a bead on my back."

Uncle Dan scratched at his beard and frowned. "Yeah, that's a problem, all right. You got any ideas how to get around it?"

"Maybe," Preacher mused. He scratched his own beard. "I been thinkin' maybe it's time I got rid o' these whiskers."

"You mean to *shave?*" Uncle Dan sounded horrified. "Preacher, you've had a beard ever since I've knowed you."

"Which, as you pointed out your own self a few days ago, ain't been all that long. Listen, Uncle Dan . . . when folks think of Preacher, they think of a rangy fella in buckskins, with a beard and sort of long hair and a big ol' wolflike dog followin' along with him. If I shaved my beard off and cut my hair and dressed some other way, they wouldn't be near as quick to spot me."

The old-timer thought it over and began to nod slowly. "You're right. You could leave Dog with me, too, if'n he'd go along with that."

"He'll do what I tell him. Most of the time, anyway. And he knows you by now, which'll help."

"So you're gonna pretend to be somebody else when we get to Sant Looey?"

"I have to start pretendin' *before* we get there," Preacher said. "I'm gonna come at the settlement from a different direction, too. There's a ferry about fifty miles down the Mississippi. I'm gonna cross the river there, ride north, and then take one of the ferries at St. Louis like I just got to that part of the country from back east somewhere."

Uncle Dan laughed. "Preacher, that is plumb *sneaky!* Beaumont won't have nary a clue that you're in town."

"That's the idea," Preacher said with a nod.

"Where you gonna get different clothes, though? You ain't got any with you 'cept'n your buckskins."

"You'll have to help me out there. They ain't watchin' for you. When we get closer, I'll make camp, and you'll go on into the settlement and pick up a new outfit for me. While you're gone, I'll scrape off these bristles and hack off some of this hair, so I'll be ready to pretend to be somebody else when you get back."

Uncle Dan grinned. "Don't cut off too much of your hair. Remember what happened to ol' Samson in the Good Book."

"I don't reckon I'll have to worry about that. I don't expect to run into any Delilahs in St. Louis."

Uncle Dan shook his head. "I wouldn't count on that."

Preacher and Uncle Dan made camp about a day's ride west of St. Louis. Preacher didn't want to get any closer than that, because the closer he came to the settlement, the better the chances he might run into somebody who worked for Shad Beaumont.

"I'll see you in a couple of days," he said to Uncle Dan as the old-timer prepared to ride on eastward the next morning. Preacher had given him money to buy the new clothes, almost all the coins he had left from the last time he had sold some pelts. "When you get back, I'll be a whole new hombre." Preacher paused. "I'm countin' on you, Uncle Dan. Don't go gettin' drunk in

Red Mike's or any of those other waterfront dives and forget to come back out here with those new clothes."

"Don't you worry," Uncle Dan assured him. "I got a mighty big grudge against ol' Beaumont, too. There'll be time to wet my whistle later."

With a cheerful wave, Uncle Dan rode off, heading eastward. Preacher watched him go, then said to the big cur, "Might as well go ahead and take care of my part, Dog. That'll give me some time to get used to not havin' all this hair on my face."

He got a straight razor and a small piece of a broken looking glass from his pack and went to work. It was a painful task, scraping off months' worth of whiskers. By the time he was finished, he was bleeding from half a dozen nicks and cuts.

As he looked at himself in the glass, he realized that his plan had a flaw he hadn't thought of until now. The part of his face that the beard had covered was considerably paler than the rest of it, which bore a permanent tan from the outdoor life he had led for years.

Preacher grunted. "Reckon until it sort of evens out, I'll have to paint my face like an Injun. I ought to be able to make some paint to darken that part of it."

He did, using berries and mud. It wasn't a perfect solution, but he thought it would do. He wouldn't wear his hat during the two days he'd have to wait for Uncle Dan to get back, and that much exposure to the sun might help a little, too.

He used the razor to cut his hair, and when he was done, he looked at Dog and asked, "What do you think?"

The big cur stared at him as if puzzled, and after a

moment a deep, rumbling growl came from the dog's throat.

"What the hell!" Preacher exclaimed. "Don't you know me?"

Dog stopped growling and came forward tentatively to sniff at Preacher's hand. The mountain man laughed.

"I reckon if I can fool you, Dog, I can fool Shad Beaumont and his men."

Preacher was camped in a grove of trees not far from the river. He laid low when the occasional rider or wagon came by. Two days passed without incident, but Preacher was glad when Uncle Dan rode in on the second evening. Sitting around and doing nothing gnawed at his guts. Always had and, he supposed, always would. He was the sort of man who liked to stay busy.

Soon he would be busy, all right . . . figuring out the best way to kill Shad Beaumont.

Uncle Dan had a paper-wrapped bundle tied onto the horse behind him. He swung down from the saddle and cut the bundle loose, then tossed it to Preacher.

"Here you go," the old-timer said. "You're gonna look like you're from back east, Preacher."

"You didn't get duds that'll make me look like some sort of city fella, did you?" Preacher asked as he untied the cord holding the paper around the bundle.

"Nope. You said you wanted to look like a farm boy, so that's what I got."

Preacher unwrapped the bundle and found a pair of brown corduroy work trousers, a butternut shirt of linsey-woolsey, a pair of lace-up boots, and a funny-looking hat with a rounded crown. He frowned at the hat and asked, "What the hell is this?"

"Fella at the store where I bought the duds called it a quaker hat. He said farmers back in Pennsylvania wear 'em."

"Stupid-lookin' thing, if you ask me." Preacher put it on his head and looked at Uncle Dan. "What do you think?"

The old-timer's mouth worked under the white beard, and after a moment Preacher realized that Uncle Dan was trying hard not to bust out laughing. He managed to say, "I reckon with that hat and the rest o' the getup, and with those cheeks o' yours bein' as smooth as a baby's bee-hind, there ain't no way in Hades that Beaumont or his men ought to recognize you, Preacher."

"Good." Preacher tapped the quaker hat. "That's just what I want."

"What're you gonna call yourself? You're gonna need a different name, ain't you?"

Preacher frowned as he pondered that. He thought about calling himself Arthur or Art, since that was actually his name. He had even gone by Art for a while, during the early days of his fur-trapping career in the Rockies. He had been dubbed Preacher after he'd been captured by the Blackfeet and had to start preaching for hours on end, the way he had once seen a fella do in St. Louis, to convince the Indians that he was crazy so they would spare his life. After the story got around, he had been called Preacher ever since.

It was just barely possible somebody might remember that the man called Preacher had once been known as Art, so it would be better not to use that, he decided.

"Reckon I'll call myself Jim," he said after a minute.

"That's simple and easy to remember. Jim Donnelly, maybe, after those folks we met with the wagon train."

"All right, Jim Donnelly." Uncle Dan grinned. "Pleased to meetcha."

"Shad Beaumont will be, too . . . at first."

"What do you mean by that?"

"I've been thinkin' about it the whole time you were gone. And here's what we're gonna do . . ."

Chapter 10

A few days later, Preacher rode up to a ferry landing on the east bank of the Mississippi and looked across the broad, majestically flowing river at the settlement on the other side. St. Louis had grown into a sprawling, perpetually busy city in the seventy or so years since the fur traders Pierre Liguest and René Chouteau had founded it.

Preacher had heard it said that six or seven thousand people lived there now. It seemed hard to believe there were that many people in the world, let alone that many crowded into one town. Smoke rose from hundreds of chimneys over there, putting a stink in the air. At least, it stunk as far as Preacher was concerned. He was used to the crisp, clean air of the high country.

The old man who ran the ferry emerged from his shack on the riverbank and asked, "You lookin' to get across to St. Louis, son?"

Preacher nodded. "That's right. I don't see the ferry boat, though."

"That's 'cause it's on the other side. Be back soon,

and it'll be crossin' again prob'ly in an hour or so. You in a big hurry?"

"Nope," Preacher replied with a shake of his head.

Shad Beaumont would still be there when he got there. Beaumont didn't leave the city. He sent others west to the mountains to do his dirty work for him.

The ferryman, who was a tall, scrawny fellow with a black patch over his left eye, pointed over his shoulder with a knobby thumb. "I got a jug o' whiskey in the shack, if'n you'd like a drink whilst you wait. Won't cost you but a nickel."

"Kind of steep, ain't it?"

The man grinned. "It's good whiskey. Guaranteed not to give you the blind staggers."

"I don't reckon I can pass that up," Preacher said as he swung down from the saddle and wrapped Horse's reins around a hitching post near the wooden landing.

He wasn't particularly thirsty, but he had a hunch the old ferryman might prove to be talkative, especially if his throat was lubricated with a little Who-hit-John. Preacher followed him into the shack and sat down on a cane-bottomed chair. The ferryman took the jug out of a drawer in an old, scarred rolltop desk.

"You got business in Saint Looey?" the ferryman asked. He pulled the cork from the neck of the jug with his teeth, spat it into his other hand, and then held the jug out to Preacher.

"I reckon you could say that." Preacher took the jug, lifted it to his lips, and downed a healthy slug of the raw corn liquor it contained. The stuff burned like fire all the way down his gullet and lit a blaze in his belly. He gasped, then blew out his breath and wiped the back of his other hand across his mouth.

The ferryman cackled. "Told you it was good stuff. Packs quite a wallop, don't it?"

"Yeah," Preacher rasped. His throat had pretty much recovered from Mike Moran trying to strangle him, but now it felt as if the lining had been burned out of it. He went on, "I'm lookin' for a job. That's why I'm goin' to St. Louis."

The ferryman ran his gaze up and down Preacher's lanky frame in the drab clothes and quaker hat. "You look like you've spent some time behind a plow."

"Too damn much time," Preacher said with a disgusted snort. "That's why I lit out for the west. I had all the farmin' I could stand. Wanted to see some of the country before I got too old and wore-out to enjoy it."

The ferryman slapped his thigh. "I used to feel the same way, son!" he said. "Then, whilst I wasn't lookin', I got old and wore-out anyway! Now I spend my days runnin' this ferry and watchin' other folks come and go."

"You live here?" Preacher asked.

"Got a place over yonder in Saint Looey." The ferryman held out a bony hand. "Here, gimme that jug."

"I can pay," Preacher protested.

"Oh, hell, don't worry 'bout that. I've taken a likin' to you, son. You remind me o' me when I was a younker. And I like havin' somebody around to talk to whilst I'm waitin' for the ferry to get back. So I ain't gonna charge you for the whiskey. I just want a swig of it myself."

Preacher grinned and handed over the jug. He was glad the old man had decided not to take his money for the liquor. He didn't have very many coins left.

They passed the jug back and forth, and as Preacher had suspected, the ferryman got more garrulous with every drink. Preacher said, "St. Louis looks like a mighty big town. What's it like over there?"

"Big ain't the half of it. It's the biggest town in this whole part of the country. I don't reckon you ever saw anything like it back on the farm. Folks ever'where you look, and cobblestone streets, and buildin's all crowded close together . . . and some days, there are so many steamboats at the docks, you can't hardly see the town from here because o' their smokestacks."

"I don't know," Preacher said with a dubious frown. "I'm startin' to think it might not be safe over there for an ol' country boy like me."

"You got to be careful, all right. There's fellas who'll cut your throat for a nickel, or sometimes just because they feel like it. Once you've crossed, I'd get away from the riverfront if I was you. That's a rough patch down there, let me tell you."

"One of the fellas from back home came out here for a while," Preacher said. "When he got back, he told all sorts of stories. Said there are lots of taverns, and houses with fancy ladies in 'em, and that this one fella owned most of them—"

"Shad Beaumont." The old ferryman nodded sagely. "I've heard of him. I reckon everybody in Saint Looey has. It's only a rumor, though, that he owns most of the taverns and whorehouses. He has a fur tradin' company and a couple of emporiums and a livery stable. Hell, and who knows what else. He's a rich gent, that's for sure, and he's got friends in high places. The town's gettin' what they call society now, and Beaumont's part of it."

"Have you ever met him?"

"Me?" The ferryman tilted the jug to his mouth and

took a long swallow. The fiery stuff didn't seem to bother him. He had probably blistered his insides with it so much that he didn't even feel the burn anymore, Preacher thought. The old man wiped his mouth and went on, "Why would I have any dealin's with Shad Beaumont? I'm just a no-account old ferryman. I seen him drive by a time or two in his fancy carriage, though. He goes to a place called Dupree's. Some say he owns it, others claim he just likes to drink there." A frown formed on the ferryman's forehead. "Say, why are you so interested in Beaumont, son?"

"Maybe I'll see if he'd like to hire me," Preacher replied with a grin. "I told you, I'm lookin' for work."

The ferryman snorted. "I don't reckon you'll find any work with Beaumont less'n you're willin' to do some mighty shady things."

"I thought you said it was just rumors that he's some sort of crook."

"That's what some folks believe. I didn't say I was one of 'em."

"So you *do* think he's a criminal?"

"I don't know a damned thing about it, one way or the other." The old-timer put the cork back in the jug and pushed it down securely with the heel of his hand. "And that's just the way I want to keep it. I don't want it gettin' around that I'm shootin' off my mouth about Shad Beaumont."

Preacher held up his hands, palms out. "Don't worry. I ain't gonna say anything about it. What I'd really like to hear more about is those houses with the fancy ladies." He grinned. "It's been a hell of a long trip from Pennsylvania."

The ferryman, who had seemed to be getting

suspicious for a moment, now relaxed. He returned Preacher's grin and said, "What you want is a house called Jessie's Place. Friendliest gals in town, bar none. It's got a mite o' class to it, too. Tain't cheap, mind you, but like this here whiskey o' mine, it's worth it."

"All right," Preacher said, leaning forward eagerly. "Tell me how to find it."

The ferry returned to the east bank landing a short time later. It was a sturdy flat-bottomed boat large enough to carry two wagons and their teams, or a dozen riders. Preacher had to wait until several more men came along on horseback who wanted to cross the river before the ferryman would let them board. Four men who bore a definite resemblance to the one-eyed man and who were probably his sons worked the long, heavy sweep oars that guided the boat across the Mississippi's currents to the landing on the west bank.

During the crossing, Preacher stood at the boat's railing, holding on to Horse's reins, and unobtrusively studied the half-dozen men crossing with him. They appeared to be working men, much like he was pretending to be, except for one sandy-haired gent in a brown frock coat and beaver hat. He wore a ruffled shirt and a fancy cravat under the frock coat. His horse was a big black gelding, a fine-looking animal. The man appeared to be well-to-do. Preacher pegged him as a gambler, and a successful one, at that.

When the boat tied up at the landing about half a mile south of the long line of wharves that jutted out into the river, Preacher led Horse off onto solid ground again, which the rangy gray stallion seemed to appreci-

ate. The other men disembarked as well, including the
gambler. He swung up onto his expensive saddle and
rode off toward the main part of town. Preacher followed him, although he didn't care about the gambler.
He was going that way anyway, because the ferryman
had given him directions for how to find the whorehouse known as Jessie's Place.

Preacher had been to St. Louis many times before,
so he actually knew his way around the settlement fairly
well, although he was pretending to be a stranger. He
hadn't heard of Jessie's until today, though. It had
been a while since he'd been here, and things sometimes changed fast on the frontier. Although St. Louis
was civilized, it was right on the edge of a vast, untamed
wilderness, and some of that wildness had rubbed off
on it. There were a lot of different ways a man could
get killed on the prairie or in the mountains, but the
same was true here in the city.

Preacher thought maybe it was even *more* true here.

He had two possibilities for the first step in his plan:
the fancy saloon called Dupree's and Jessie's Place.
He was confident that if Jessie's was the best whorehouse in St. Louis, Shad Beaumont was bound to own
it. From what he knew of Beaumont, the man was involved in everything shady that went on in the settlement. He wanted to be sure that Beaumont heard
about "Jim Donnelly."

Unlike most of the houses of ill repute in St. Louis,
Jessie's wasn't located near the waterfront. Instead it
was in a quiet neighborhood on the north side of
town where trees grew around the houses and there
were flower beds full of brilliantly blooming flowers
in the yards. The house had two stories and wore

enough coats of whitewash that its walls gleamed. It looked like the sort of place where a wealthy merchant would live.

Which was exactly what it was, Preacher supposed. Jessie might not be the owner, but she was in charge here, and she definitely had merchandise for sale.

Preacher couldn't afford that merchandise, even if he'd been in a buying mood. He hadn't come to St. Louis looking for a woman, he reminded himself as he tied Horse at a hitch rail in front of the house. Several others were tied there, and Preacher frowned slightly as he recognized one of them. It was the big black from the ferry, the one that the sandy-haired gambler had ridden.

Well, that wasn't too much of a surprise, he told himself. A man who dressed that well and owned a horse like this would want to patronize the best whorehouse in town.

Preacher went up a flagstone walk bordered by flower beds to the front porch. There was a brass lion's-head knocker in the middle of the heavy door. He rapped sharply with it and waited.

The man who opened the door was tall, broad-shouldered, and black. He was bald except for a fringe of gray hair around his ears that trailed around the back of his head. Age didn't seem to have withered him any, though. The muscles in his arms and shoulders bulged against the coat he wore.

He took one look at Preacher, got a superior sneer on his face, and said, "If you've brought those barrels of wine from the boat, you need to take them around back."

"You see a wagon full of wine barrels out here?" Preacher asked.

The man frowned and looked past him. "No. What do you want?"

"This is Jessie's Place, ain't it? What do you think I want?"

Preacher started to push past the man, who put a hand on his chest to stop him. Preacher felt the strength coming from the man's arm and shoulders.

"This ain't your kind of place, mister. You need to go back down to the waterfront. The girls in the cribs there'll be more than happy to accommodate you."

Preacher sneered right back at the man. "You talk mighty fancy for a slave."

"I ain't a slave," the man said with a shake of his head. "I'm a freedman, and I ain't afraid of you just 'cause you're white, mister. The law around here ain't gonna blink an eye if I whup your ass."

Preacher returned the man's cold, level stare. "So you're a freedman, eh?" He turned his head and spat. "That's just a fancy word for a darky who's got too big for his britches. I got money, damn your black hide."

"Not enough," the man said. "I can tell by lookin' at you. Now, are you gonna leave peaceable-like, or—"

Preacher didn't let him finish. He swung a wild punch at the man's head instead.

The man ducked under the blow and lunged forward, wrapping his arms around Preacher's waist. Suddenly Preacher felt himself jerked up off the ground. He let out a startled yelp that was completely genuine as the man hoisted him above his head.

With only a slight grunt of effort, the man heaved Preacher all the way off the porch and into the yard.

He came down hard enough in one of the flower beds to knock the breath out of him. As he rolled over and gasped for air, he looked up and saw the big man stomping toward him, a look of outrage on the black face.

Well, thought Preacher, it looked like this part of the chore was about to turn out to be a mite harder than he'd expected.

Chapter 11

"You son of a bitch!" the black man yelled. "You landed right in my nasturtiums! I'm gonna thrash you within an inch of your life!"

"Well, you threw me here, you damn fool!" Preacher shouted back as he leaped to his feet. "Nobody does that to Jim Donnelly!"

Preacher knew he couldn't take it easy in this fight. He had drawn an opponent who was too fast and strong for that. If he didn't put his best effort into it, he might wind up crawling away with broken bones, and he couldn't afford that.

So this time he waited for the other fella to throw the first punch, and when the big, hamlike fist came sailing toward his face, he slipped aside so that it barely grazed his ear as it went past and stepped in to hammer a right into the man's sternum.

That was a good move, or at least it would have been if Preacher's fist hadn't felt like it had just slammed into a brick wall. The man brought up a looping left that clipped Preacher on the side of the head and sent him rolling on the ground again as rockets went off behind his eyes.

"Damn it, you're in my flowers again!"

The man reached down and slapped his massive hands on Preacher's shoulders. As he hauled Preacher upright, Preacher sent his right fist whistling skyward in an uppercut that caught the big man on the jaw. Preacher had hoped that anybody as solid in the middle as the black man might have a glass jaw, but that hope was dashed as the man shrugged off the blow and started shaking Preacher like a terrier shaking a rat.

The big son of a bitch had to have a weak spot *somewhere*, Preacher thought, so he went for the most likely area.

He kicked the fellow in the balls.

Finally, something went right. The man's eyes widened, and the black face turned an ashen shade of gray. His hands slipped off Preacher's shoulders. He didn't double over in agony as most men would have done, but at least he hunched his shoulders and bent over a little as he clutched at his injured groin.

Preacher clubbed his hands together and swung them against the corded muscles on the left side of the man's neck. That sent the man staggering to his right. While the man was off balance, Preacher kicked his right knee. That leg collapsed, dumping the man on the ground. Preacher landed on top of him and swung his clubbed fists again, back and forth, slamming them into the man's face twice.

"That'll be enough."

The cold, dangerous voice spoke from the porch. Preacher twisted his neck to look back over his shoulder. He saw the sandy-haired man from the ferry standing there, a small but deadly pistol in his hand. The gambler pointed the gun at Preacher. It was cocked and ready to fire.

While the gambler held the pistol rock steady, a woman rushed past him and hurried off the porch into the yard. "Brutus!" she cried. When she reached Preacher, she struck at him with a small fist and said, "Get off him, you bastard!"

"Jessie," the gambler said in a warning tone, "don't get between me and—"

It was too late for that warning. Preacher grabbed the woman's wrist and pulled her in front of him as he stood up. Using a woman as a shield really rubbed him the wrong way—hell, that was what Buckhalter had done with Lorraine when the Pawnee war party attacked the wagon train—but Preacher thought it might be something "Jim Donnelly" would do in circumstances like this.

"Take it easy, mister," he said as he jerked the woman against him. He had twisted her so that her back was to him, and he felt the enticing curve of her hips as he pressed against her. "Just put that gun down."

"I'll kill you for this," the woman spat furiously. "I'll kill you myself. And if you've hurt Brutus, I'll make sure you take a long time to die!"

"You take it easy, too," Preacher rasped in her ear. "Everybody needs to just settle down, damn it. I didn't come here lookin' for trouble."

On the ground, the black man called Brutus groaned, but he didn't show any signs of getting up soon.

"Jessie," the gambler said, "what do you want me to do?"

"Put your gun away, Cleve," she told him. She

glared back over her shoulder at Preacher. "I'll deal with this . . . gentleman."

She might as well have called him the most obscene name in the book, judging by her tone. Even though the gambler lowered his gun, Preacher didn't let go of Jessie. He said, "This is your place?"

"That's right."

"Call off your dogs, then. I don't want to hurt nobody, least of all a gal as pretty as you."

She *was* stunning, no doubt about that. Even though Preacher hadn't really gotten a good look at her yet, he was sure about that much. She was tall and slender— coltish would be a good word to describe her—and yet her body had plenty of womanly curves. Long, light brown hair swept around her face, over her shoulders, and down her back. The part that covered her ears had been curled into tight ringlets. She wore a fine, light blue gown that hugged her body. If she was a whore, she was one of the prettiest Preacher had ever seen. She looked more like she ought to be a rich man's wife.

She said to the man on the porch, "Cleve, go back inside and send Terence and Micah out here to help Brutus."

The gambler frowned. "You're sure?"

"I'm certain."

Cleve shrugged. "It's your house."

He tucked the gun away under his coat and disappeared through the door, which he left open behind him.

"Are you going to let me go?" Jessie asked Preacher, her voice cold with scorn.

"That depends. Are you gonna sic more of your men on me?"

"No. Not unless you cause more trouble."

Preacher still had hold of her wrist, so that her arm was doubled behind her back. He released it and stepped away from her. She turned to glare at him as she used her other hand to rub the wrist he'd been gripping.

"Sorry," he said. "I didn't mean to hurt you."

"Do you want to tell me what's going on here?" She had green eyes, Preacher saw now, and they were flashing with the emerald fire of anger. "This is a respectable neighborhood. I can't have people brawling on my front lawn."

"Wasn't my idea," Preacher snapped. "Your darky grabbed me and threw me in the flower bed, and that seemed to make him go loco."

"Brutus takes great pride in his flowers," Jessie said with a nod. "What were you doing coming to the front door, anyway? Tradesmen are supposed to go to the back."

"I'm not a tradesman. I'm a customer."

Jessie smiled. "Dressed like that? I don't think so. You couldn't afford to be a customer here, Mister . . . ?"

"Donnelly," Preacher said. "Jim Donnelly."

"Well, Mr. Donnelly, this is the most exclusive, and might I add, expensive house in St. Louis. Unless you've saved everything you've earned from your farm in the past, say, five years, I seriously doubt that you can afford to pay us a visit here."

"But you don't know that, and neither did he." Preacher nodded toward Brutus.

Before Jessie could respond, two more men came out of the house and hurried across the lawn. They were white, and although they weren't as big and burly as Brutus, they looked plenty tough. One of them asked, "You want us to run this varmint off, Miss Jessie?"

She shook her head. "No, just help Brutus inside and make sure that he's all right. I can deal with Mr. Donnelly."

"Are you sure?" the other man asked.

The angry look she gave him at the question made him step back and hold up his hands.

"Sorry, ma'am," he muttered. "Come on, Terence, let's do what the lady says."

Together, they helped Brutus to his feet. He seemed to be regaining his senses to a certain extent. He sent a murderous scowl in Preacher's direction as the two men helped him into the house.

"You've made an enemy," Jessie commented.

"Wasn't my intention. But I wasn't gonna let him toss me around like a rag doll and stomp me, neither."

She ignored that and continued in a haughty tone, "I think we've established that this isn't the place for you, Mr. Donnelly. Why don't you just move on? There are places down at the riverfront—"

"Yeah, I know. I ain't interested in those soiled doves. I want somethin' better."

A chilly smile curved her full, red lips. "We can't always get what we want, Mr. Donnelly."

"Why don't you let me talk to the fella who owns this place?" Preacher shot back at her. "We'll see what he says about it."

Her face remained cool and unperturbed, but he caught the flicker of surprise in her eyes. "I'm the owner," she declared. "That's why it's called Jessie's Place."

Preacher snorted. "Women don't own businesses. Not even whorehouses."

"That's where you're mistaken. And you've just become even more offensive. I have to ask you to leave now."

Her hand came up from the folds of her dress gripping a little pistol that must have been stashed in a hidden pocket. The barrel was short but big enough around to tell Preacher that the gun still packed a potent punch despite being undersized. Jessie thumbed back the hammer as she raised the weapon.

"I assure you," she went on, "at this range, this *will* blow a suitable hole in you."

Preacher didn't doubt that for a second. He was also aware now that she had been armed the whole time and could have pulled out that pistol and shot him any time she wanted to. That made a cold finger go down his backbone.

"All right," he said with ill grace. "I'm leavin'. But you remember my name. It's Jim Donnelly."

"I'm not liable to forget it soon, after all this commotion you've caused."

"And remember somethin' else," Preacher went on. "That big fella Brutus, who I reckon is supposed to handle any trouble around here . . . I beat him. Whipped him good. Maybe what you need is somebody tougher."

Jessie's eyes widened in surprise. "You're talking about yourself, I suppose?"

"I'm just sayin' he was a lot bigger'n me, but it was him who wound up goin' down and stayin' down."

"Good-bye, Mr. Donnelly. Don't come back here again."

Despite her flatly spoken words of dismissal, Preacher knew he had seen a flicker of interest in her eyes. He had made a good point, and she knew it. He let a smile play briefly over his face, but only after he had turned away so that she couldn't see it.

This was a start, anyway.

Dupree's was next.

The saloon was closer to the waterfront than Jessie's Place, but it wasn't a dive, either. It stretched along an entire city block, with the entrance at the corner. Preacher lingered at a hash house across the street, keeping an eye on the place from a table by the window. He had used up a few more of his precious coins buying some supper, but he had finished that a while back and now the proprietor was casting some hard looks at him from behind the counter.

He was about to stand up and wander out of the place, figuring he would take up a position in an alley and watch from there, when a carriage pulled up in front of Dupree's. The sun had set, but enough light remained for Preacher to make out the shiny brass fittings and expensive dark wood of the vehicle. A team of four fine black horses was hitched to the carriage, and a black driver in a top hat was perched on the high seat. It sure looked to Preacher like the sort of carriage that a man such as Shad Beaumont would drive around in.

Preacher stood up and strolled out of the hash house so that he could see better as the driver climbed down nimbly from the seat. The man opened the carriage door and then stepped back deferentially. The

man who climbed out of the vehicle was tall and wore
a beaver hat. A cape was draped over his shoulders.
That was all Preacher could tell about him at first.

Then the man turned around and held out a hand
to help someone else disembark from the carriage.
The light spilling through the big front windows of
Dupree's revealed the man's face to Preacher in sil-
houette. It was a handsome face sporting a close-
cropped dark beard. The man was smiling.

He had good reason to smile, Preacher saw a
moment later as the second passenger stepped down
from the carriage. She was a blonde with a mass of
curly hair under a stylish hat. Not too tall, but very
well shaped and expensively dressed. She said something to the man, who laughed and linked his arm
with hers. They went up the steps to the boardwalk
and into Dupree's.

Preacher had continued ambling across the street as
if he had no particular place to go and was in no hurry
to get there. When he reached the other side, he
stepped up onto the boardwalk and looked through
the window. The two new arrivals were being ushered
to a table in the back by a man in a dark suit who was
probably the proprietor.

But likely not the owner, Preacher thought. He was
convinced that Shad Beaumont really owned Dupree's,
just as he felt sure Jessie's Place belonged to Beaumont.

And what about Jessie? Did *she* belong to Beaumont, too?

Preacher frowned slightly as that thought crossed his
mind. Why should it matter to him what sort of arrangement Jessie had with Beaumont? The only reason she

might be important was if he could use her to get to his quarry.

He turned toward the carriage, where the driver had climbed to the seat again and was packing chewing tobacco into his cheek. Preacher gave him a friendly nod and said, "Evenin'."

The man didn't return the greeting. He was old and wizened and didn't look like he was in the habit of talking to riffraff on the street.

"Mighty nice carriage you got here," Preacher went on.

The driver sniffed. "Tain't mine, and you know it."

"Yeah, but you get to drive that fine team of horses. I got to say, that's some of the best horseflesh I've seen in a long time. I guess Mr. Beaumont don't want nothin' but the best."

"What Mr. Beaumont wants or don't want ain't for the likes o' you to be talkin' about."

That was easy, Preacher thought . . . and about time, too. He said mildly, "Didn't mean any offense, old-timer."

Then he turned, pushed the door open, and stepped into Dupree's.

Chapter 12

The place was a saloon. There could be no mistake about that. Not with the long, hardwood bar that ran all the way down the left-hand wall and then turned to run along the back wall, as well. Round tables covered most of the floor space to the right, although there was an open area toward the rear where people could dance if they wanted to. Some of the tables were topped with green felt for poker playing. There was a roulette wheel as well, although no one was playing at the moment. The air was hazy with smoke from cigars and pipes and filled with talk and laughter from the customers. Chandeliers made from wagon wheels hung from the ceiling. The candles in those chandeliers cast a yellow glow over the big room. The soft light gave the place a certain air of elegance. Even the laughter was subdued, not raucous as it always was in the crude taverns to which Preacher was accustomed.

The bar was crowded, and drinkers occupied most of the tables. A couple of poker games were going on. Preacher found an open place at the bar and bellied up to the hardwood, which had been polished to a high gleam.

A bartender as bald as a billiard ball came over to him. Preacher ordered a beer.

"Let's see your money first, pilgrim," the bartender replied.

Preacher slid a coin onto the bar. The bartender picked it up, studied it for a second, and then nodded.

"All right, farm boy. I'll be back."

Preacher waited while the bartender filled a pewter mug with beer from a keg. When the man brought it back to him, he nodded and said, "Much obliged."

"New in town?"

Preacher took a sip of the beer, which was good, and nodded. "That's right."

"Then you probably don't know that Dupree's caters to a higher class of customer than you. You can finish your drink, then you'd better be moving along."

Preacher felt a surge of anger but didn't show it. He didn't like people who put on airs, even bartenders. But unlike at Jessie's Place, where he had deliberately taken offense, he played this hand differently.

"Sorry, mister," he said. "Didn't mean to butt in where my kind ain't welcome."

The bartender got a look of magnanimous superiority on his florid face and said, "That's all right. You didn't know any better. Anyway, your money spends as well as anybody else's, I reckon."

"Like his over there?" Preacher asked, inclining his head toward the table where Shad Beaumont sat with the blonde. They were sharing a bottle of brandy. No buckets of beer for them.

The bartender laughed. "No, Mr. Beaumont's money

is better than anybody else's around here. Or rather, I reckon you could say that it's no good in Dupree's."

"You mean he don't have to pay for anything just 'cause he's some fancy swell?"

"I mean drink up and get out of here," the bartender said, his face and voice hardening. "What Mr. Beaumont pays for or don't pay for is none of your damn business."

"No, sir, it's sure not," Preacher said quickly. He lifted the cup to his lips and drank some more of the beer.

That was more than enough confirmation. He was certain now of Beaumont's identity and had gotten a good enough look at him in here that he knew he would recognize Beaumont the next time he saw the man. He would be able to describe Beaumont and his carriage to Uncle Dan, too, which was important to the plan.

"Is it always this crowded in here?" he asked the bartender, trying to sound idly curious.

"Dupree's is the best place in town," the man replied, pride in his voice.

"Does that fella Beaumont come in here every night?"

"*Mister* Beaumont is a regular customer, yes. And again—"

"I know, I know," Preacher said. "None of my business."

"That's right. You gonna finish that beer?"

Preacher drained the last of the liquid from the cup and set the empty back on the bar. "Much obliged," he said again.

"From now on, do your drinking in the taverns down

along the waterfront, with the river men and the rest of the farm boys who've come west looking for adventure."

"Yes, sir, I'll sure do that."

Preacher practically had to force the words out, when what he really wanted to do with ram that smug smile down the bartender's throat with a knobby-knuckled fist.

But that would be jumping the gun. Maybe he'd have a chance to teach the fella a lesson later.

He'd be coming back to Dupree's.

When he was ready.

That thought was going through his head as he turned to walk out of the saloon. His gaze roved briefly over the room and then stopped suddenly when he spotted a familiar face at one of the poker tables. The gambler called Cleve was dealing a hand. Preacher wasn't particularly surprised to see him. The man obviously had a taste for the finer things in life. He patronized the best whorehouse in St. Louis, so there was no reason he wouldn't do his gambling and drinking in the best saloon, too.

Cleve glanced up, and for a second his eyes locked with Preacher's. Then Preacher continued walking out.

He hoped this wasn't going to be an added complication. He had enough on his plate just figuring out what he was going to do about Shad Beaumont.

Horse was tied at the hitch rail. Preacher untied the reins and swung up into the saddle. He rode out of St. Louis, on his way to meet Uncle Dan.

The old-timer was camped about a mile west of the city. He and Preacher had agreed on the general area where they would meet, so Preacher just rode along in the darkness until he heard an owl hoot. The sound came from the deep shadows within a grove of trees. He reined in and returned the call. A moment later, Uncle Dan stepped out from under the trees and waved Preacher on into camp.

As Preacher dismounted, Uncle Dan asked, "Anybody follow you out here?"

Preacher chuckled.

"Well, it could'a happened, I reckon," Uncle Dan went on. "You ain't got eyes in the back o' your head."

"No, but I've got ears, and so does Horse. I trust him even more than I do my own self. Nobody followed us."

"I didn't figure they would. You find Beaumont?"

"I did. Got any hot coffee left?"

"I been keepin' it warm for you. Sit down."

Preacher sat on a log while Uncle Dan picked up the coffeepot from a small fire that had sunk down to little more than glowing embers. The old-timer had piled rocks around the fire so that not even that faint glow could be seen unless a person was within a few feet of it. He poured coffee in a cup and handed it to Preacher.

"I don't know where Beaumont lives yet," the mountain man said after he'd taken a sip of the strong black brew, "but I know where I can find him. He'll be at a saloon called Dupree's, or if we can't catch up with him there, we can try at a fancy whorehouse called Jessie's Place."

Uncle Dan laughed. "A saloon or a whorehouse. What a choice for a feller to have to make."

"From what I was able to find out, he's at Dupree's almost every night. Here's what he looks like."

Preacher described Beaumont, the blonde who'd accompanied him, and the fancy carriage that had brought them to Dupree's. For good measure, he told Uncle Dan everything he knew about Jessie's, too. It wouldn't hurt anything for the old-timer to know everything that he knew . . . just in case.

When Preacher was finished, Uncle Dan scratched at his beard and said, "You know . . . you could just climb up on the roof o' the buildin' across the street from that saloon with a rifle and shoot the son of a bitch."

"I know," Preacher said. "Don't think I haven't considered it. But then I thought about all the innocent folks who've died because of Beaumont, like your nephew, and somehow . . . it just didn't seem like shootin' him down like a dog was good enough."

"Been some not-so-innocent folks died because of him, too, like that Mallory woman."

Preacher nodded as his fingers tightened on the tin cup holding his coffee. Uncle Dan was right about one thing: Laura Mallory hadn't been innocent. But she hadn't deserved to die, either, and she wouldn't have if not for Shad Beaumont.

"Yeah," he mused, "I guess what we're doin' is for all the folks whose blood is on Beaumont's hands."

"Good enough for me. Say, you didn't happen to bring a jug back from town, did you?"

"Afraid not."

Uncle Dan sighed. "Well, I reckon we'll have to do without, then. Got a couple of biscuits and a little bacon left, if you're interested."

"Now you're talkin'," Preacher said.

* * *

He spent the night at the camp and rode back into St. Louis early the next morning, well before sunup so that he could slip into town without anyone seeing him. It would be better, he thought, if no one knew he had left the settlement the night before.

With nothing to do until evening, Preacher found a small livery stable and used the last of his money to rent a stall for Horse. Then he asked the proprietor if he could muck out the place in return for something to eat and the right to sleep in the loft that night. He was pleased when the man agreed. That arrangement accomplished two goals. It kept him off the street for most of the day—as much as he had changed his appearance, he didn't think anybody in St. Louis would recognize him, but why take extra chances?—and if anyone asked about "Jim Donnelly," it established that he was broke and willing to do just about anything, no matter how nasty a job it was.

Preacher didn't know how long he might have to stay here. The next step in his plan might work out that very night, or it might take several more days to come to fruition.

At midday, the liveryman shared a meager lunch with him, then Preacher went back to his work. By nightfall, he had the place about as spotless as a livery barn could ever get.

"You done a good job, son," the proprietor told him. "O' course, that's what I'd expect from a feller right off the farm. You're bound to be good at shovelin' dung."

Preacher nodded his thanks. He had the liveryman fooled, along with everyone else he had encountered in St. Louis. They all took him for some sort of bumpkin, just as he intended.

"You're welcome to have supper with me," the livery-man went on.

"I'm much obliged," Preacher said, "but that was thirsty work. I thought I'd go have a drink somewhere."

The liveryman sighed. "Young folks . . . Well, don't get drunk and forget where you left your horse."

"Not likely," Preacher said, and meant it.

He used the water trough to clean up a little, then headed for Dupree's. Beaumont's carriage wasn't parked out front. Preacher stood in the mouth of an alley across the street and watched, hoping that Beaumont would show up later.

An hour passed as night settled down over St. Louis, and Preacher began to think that the plan might have to be postponed until the next night or possibly even moved to Jessie's Place. But then Shad Beaumont's carriage came rolling along the street. Preacher stepped out from the alley and began walking toward the entrance to Dupree's.

The driver brought the carriage to a halt in the same place where he'd stopped it the night before. With the same alacrity, he hopped down from the seat and opened the door. Beaumont climbed out of the vehicle, and this time he didn't turn back to help a companion disembark. Evidently he was alone tonight. That was good, Preacher thought. It made things easier that way.

Beaumont stepped up onto the boardwalk as the driver closed the carriage door behind him. At the same time, Preacher circled in front of the team and came up onto the boardwalk, too, about twenty feet to Beaumont's left. Beaumont didn't even glance in his direction. The man sauntered toward the doors of

Dupree's, his beaver hat cocked at a rakish angle on his head, his long, elegant cape swirling around his knees.

Suddenly, Preacher lunged at him, shouting, "Look out!" He covered the distance between them in a heartbeat, and as he slammed into Beaumont and knocked him off his feet, a gun boomed somewhere nearby, the muzzle flash lighting up the night.

Chapter 13

The collision sent Beaumont crashing to the board-walk with Preacher sprawled on top of him. The rifle ball chewed into one of the posts holding up the awning over the walk and sprayed splinters down on the two men. Preacher shoved himself up on one knee, yanked a pistol from behind his belt, and fired into the shadows farther up the boardwalk, at the corner of the building.

Then he looked down at the clearly stunned Beau-mont and asked, "You hit, mister?"

Beaumont swallowed. "No, I . . . I'm all right—"

"Stay here, then," Preacher told him. "I'll go after that son of a bitch who tried to bushwhack you!"

He leaped to his feet and dashed down the board-walk toward the mouth of an alley. As Beaumont called, "Wait!" behind him, Preacher rounded the corner of the building and ducked into the alley. Another shot roared, the muzzle flash lighting up the night for a second. In that flicker of light, Preacher saw the big grin on Uncle Dan's face as the old-timer fired into the air.

Then the two of them ran along the alley, ducking in

and out of the shadows as they entered a rat's warren of darkened side streets and lanes.

They didn't stop until they were several blocks away from Dupree's. Uncle Dan was breathing a little hard, but that didn't stop him from chuckling.

"Hope I didn't come too close with that first shot," he said.

"It was just right," Preacher told him. "You had to come close, otherwise Beaumont wouldn't believe it."

"He'd better believe it. I damn near parted your hair with that ball. That would've played hob with the whole plan, wouldn't it?"

Preacher grinned in the darkness. "Yeah, if you'd blown a hole in my head, you'd have had to finish the job by yourself."

"Not hardly," Uncle Dan said with a shake of his head. "I ain't that crazy. I'd've just bushwhacked the son of a bitch for real."

"Let's hope it don't come to that," Preacher said. "Reckon I'd better get back now. Beaumont's probably wonderin' what happened to me. You headin' back to the camp west of town?"

"Yeah, I suppose it's as good a place as any to wait. You'll get word to me if you need me?"

Preacher nodded. "Yep. I'll try to get out there in a few days to let you know what's goin' on."

Uncle Dan extended his hand. "Good luck to you, son," he said as he and Preacher shook. "I reckon you're the one who ought to be named Daniel, since you're about to waltz right into the lion's den."

Preacher thought about that as he made his way back toward Dupree's. He was taking a big chance, all right, no doubt about that. But he had to run the risk if he wanted to give Beaumont a taste of his own medicine and bring the man's empire crashing down around him.

When Preacher emerged from the alley next to the fancy saloon and started along the boardwalk toward the entrance, he saw Beaumont standing there talking to a man with a badge pinned to his coat. That would be the local constable, Preacher thought, who'd likely been summoned because of the shooting. St. Louis was still enough of a frontier town that the law wouldn't come a-runnin' every time some shots broke out, but it was different when the intended victim was a man as rich and important as Shad Beaumont.

Beaumont caught sight of Preacher approaching and exclaimed, "There's the man now!"

The constable turned toward Preacher and reached for the pistol at his waist, causing Beaumont to continue hurriedly, "No, not the one who shot at me. The one who saved my life." He came along the boardwalk to meet Preacher. "Are you all right?"

"Yeah, I'm just sorry I couldn't catch up to that varmint," Preacher said. "How about you, mister? That damn bushwhacker missed you, didn't he?"

"Yes, thanks to you." Beaumont put out a hand and smiled. "And I mean that. Thank you."

Up close, the man was big, handsome, and charming. Preacher began to understand how Beaumont got folks to do what he wanted. Couple that persuasive charm with greed and a complete lack of scruples, and what you got was a man who was as dangerous as a diamondback rattlesnake.

Preacher clasped Beaumont's hand anyway and didn't allow the revulsion he felt to show on his face. This was all part of the plan.

"How did you know someone was about to take a shot at me?" Beaumont went on.

Preacher shrugged. "I was just walkin' along and saw a rifle barrel poke around the corner at you. Figured nobody does somethin' like that unless they intend to shoot."

"So you risked your own life to push me out of the line of fire."

"Don't make me out to be some sort o' hero," Preacher said with a frown. "To tell you the truth, I didn't really think all that much about what I was doin'. I just saw the gun and jumped."

"And I'm glad you did. But then you gave chase to the man. Why did you do that?"

"I don't like a damn bushwhacker. Back where I come from, folks get into feuds now and then. I've had kin shot down from ambush. Can't stomach it. I say, if you've got somethin' against a fella, it's better to come at him head on."

The irony of his words wasn't lost on him. Truthfully, he would have been more comfortable walking up to Beaumont, telling the man who he was, and shooting it out right then and there. But as he'd told Uncle Dan, that just didn't seem like a fitting punishment for all the misery Beaumont had inflicted on people from here to the Rocky Mountains.

"What happened when you ran into the alley?" Beaumont went on. "I heard another shot."

"Yeah, I reckon he'd had time to reload. He took a shot at me but rushed it. When he missed, he lit a shuck. He was so nimble, I never even got a good look at him." Preacher narrowed his eyes. "You got any idea who'd want to bushwhack you like that, mister?"

The question drew a laugh from Beaumont. "I'm a successful man, and no man becomes successful without making enemies along the way. I've made my share. Maybe more than my share. But there aren't many who'd have the guts to come after me like that. Most of them know better."

"Sounds to me like you need somebody watchin' your back trail."

"That might not be a bad idea. I'm Shad Beaumont, by the way."

"Jim Donnelly," Preacher said.

He thought he saw a flicker of vague recognition in Beaumont's eyes, as if the man knew he'd heard the name before but couldn't place it. Beaumont said, "Under the circumstances, I'm very pleased to meet you, Jim. Come inside and have a drink with me."

Preacher cast a dubious glance toward the saloon entrance. "I don't know," he said slowly. "I went in there last night and had a beer, and the bartender told me it ain't really my sort of place."

"That was before you were my friend." Beaumont clapped a hand on Preacher's shoulder and went on heartily, "Come on. I'll see to it that you're treated right."

"Well, in that case . . ." Preacher grinned. "I'm much obliged."

"Not as much as I am," Beaumont said as he ushered Preacher through the doors into Dupree's.

The same baldheaded bartender was behind the bar tonight. His eyes widened in surprise as he saw Preacher come in with Beaumont. The dark-suited man stood at the end of the bar. He hurried forward with an eager-to-please smile on his face.

"I heard that there was some trouble outside, Mr. Beaumont," he began. "You have my most sincere apologies—"

"It was nothing to do with you, Wallace," Beaumont cut in. "Send a bottle of brandy back to my usual table."

"Of course, sir."

Beaumont looked over at Preacher. "Or if brandy isn't to your taste, my friend, you can have anything you like."

"Well, I don't really know," Preacher drawled. "Don't reckon I've ever had any brandy. Just beer and corn squeezin's."

Beaumont laughed. "Then you're in for a treat. Come along."

He led Preacher to the big table in the back of the saloon, where they could see the whole room before them. Beaumont put his beaver hat on the table and draped his cape over one of the empty chairs.

One of the women who worked there came over to the table from the bar, carrying a tray with a bottle and two wide glasses on it. She was a tall, lanky blonde wearing a gray dress cut low enough to reveal a generous portion of her high, full breasts. She leaned over as she placed the tray on the table, and that made the creamy swells of female flesh even more prominent.

"Will there be anything else, Mr. Beaumont?" she asked as she straightened.

"That depends on my new friend here," Beaumont smirked. "What do you say, Jim? Do you see . . . anything . . . that you'd like?"

"Maybe," Preacher said. "I'll think on it."

"A man who prefers to keep his options open! I like that."

Beaumont motioned the blonde away. She was pretty, Preacher thought, and likely the man he was pretending to be would have taken Beaumont up on the thinly veiled offer. Hell, Jim Donnelly probably would have jumped at the chance to have a little slap-and-tickle with the blonde.

For some reason, though, Preacher still had an image of Jessie's face in his mind that made him hesitate. He wasn't sure why that was true, but he wanted a chance to figure it out.

Beaumont poured the brandy and handed one of the snifters to Preacher. "Once again, thank you for saving my life," he said as he lifted his own glass.

Preacher clinked his glass against Beaumont's and nodded. "Glad I was able to lend a hand," he said.

He took a healthy swallow of the brandy. It went down smooth but kindled quite a fire in his belly when it landed. Preacher's breath hissed between his teeth.

"Try sipping it next time," Beaumont advised with a smile. "I imagine it's a bit more potent than what you're accustomed to."

"I don't know. I've had some corn whiskey that'd peel paint right off a wall." Preacher took another drink, sipping this time as Beaumont had suggested. "This is mighty fine stuff, though."

"Only the finest for me in all things. That's how I live my life." Beaumont leaned back in his chair. "You know, Jim, your name is familiar to me for some reason. How long have you been in St. Louis? We haven't met before, have we?"

"I just got into town yesterday. And like I said, I was in here last night. If you were here, maybe you saw me."

"I was here, all right, but that wouldn't explain

why I've heard your name. And I'm sure I have. I—" Beaumont stopped and snapped his fingers. "I have it now. You got into some trouble yesterday afternoon at a house on the north side of town, didn't you?"

Preacher tried to look embarrassed and uncomfortable. "How the hell did you hear about that?"

Beaumont made a sweeping gesture and said, "I hear about everything important that goes on in St. Louis. I have friends and business associates all over town."

"What *is* your business, if I ain't pokin' my nose in where it ain't wanted?"

"Whatever makes me a profit," Beaumont replied. "And nearly every enterprise I undertake *does* make a profit, if I do say so myself."

Preacher nodded. "You must be a mighty smart man, then."

"I like to think so. What were you doing at Jessie's Place?"

"I heard tell it was the best whorehouse in town," Preacher said with a shrug. "It's been a long, lonely trip from Pennsylvania."

"That's where you're from?"

"My family's had a farm there for a long time. I ain't cut out for farmin', though." Preacher took another sip of the brandy. "So I left and come west. Figured I'd make my fortune out here."

"How are you doing on that?"

Preacher let a little bitterness creep into the laugh he gave. "Not too good so far. I spent the day shovelin' shit out of livery stable stalls in return for somethin' to eat and a place to sleep."

"Well, your luck has changed this evening." Beaumont reached inside his coat.

Preacher said quickly, "If you're about to give me a reward or somethin' like that, then no offense, Mr. Beaumont, but you can keep it. I was raised not to ever take charity, and even if I don't pay much attention to what my folks taught me, that's one thing I still abide by."

"A reward isn't charity, Jim. It's something you've earned."

Beaumont brought out a purse and took a five-dollar gold piece from it. Preacher let his eyes widen at the sight of the coin, as if he couldn't help it. Beaumont put the coin on the table but didn't take his finger off of it.

"Tell me about what happened at Jessie's," he said.

Preacher shrugged. "I reckon that was just one more case of me pushin' in where my kind ain't wanted. The big darky who come to the door took me for some sort of delivery fella and tried to run me off. We got in a little squabble."

"The way I heard it, you knocked Brutus senseless."

"You know him?"

"Like I told you, I know people all over town . . . and they know me."

"Then that Miss Jessie's a friend of yours?"

"She is."

Preacher took a deep breath. "I sure was sorry for the trouble I caused her. She struck me as a mighty fine lady."

"She is," Beaumont said again.

"But I wasn't gonna let that fella Brutus push me around, neither," Preacher went on, his voice hardening. "When the Good Lord made me, he didn't put much backup in me. That's just the way it is."

"I understand," Beaumont said, nodding. "I'm the same way myself. And it's quite impressive that you were able to handle Brutus like that. He's practically broken men in half on a number of occasions, whenever there was trouble at the house."

"Well . . . I didn't exactly fight fair. After I'd walloped him in the belly and the jaw and he didn't even blink, I figured I'd best kick him in the balls as fast as I could."

Beaumont laughed loudly and reached for the bottle of brandy. "By God, Jim, I like the way you think." He used his other hand to push the coin across the table to Preacher. "Here."

Preacher frowned. "I told you—"

"It's not a reward," Beaumont said as he poured more brandy in their glasses. "It's an advance on your wages."

"Wages?"

"That's right. You said I needed a man to keep an eye on my back trail, didn't you?"

"Well, yeah."

"I have a feeling you're the man for the job." Beaumont raised his glass again. "Unless, of course, you'd rather go back to mucking out that stable."

Preacher hesitated, but only for a second. Then he grinned, reached for his glass, and said, "I reckon you've just hired yourself a new hand, boss."

Chapter 14

They polished off the bottle of brandy before they left Dupree's. Preacher was a little drunker than he'd intended to be, but he was still thinking clearly enough. The plan had worked perfectly. He had established himself as a tough man who needed a job, and then he'd provided an excuse for Beaumont to give him one.

He was on the inside now, in a position where he could do the most damage.

Beaumont led Preacher outside, with all the employees and many of the customers smiling and bidding them good night as they left. Preacher had known that Beaumont wielded a lot of power in this town, but even he was a little surprised at the apparent extent of it. Nobody wanted to get on Shad Beaumont's bad side. Everyone wanted to stay in his good graces.

As they emerged onto the boardwalk, Beaumont said, "Since you decided not to take me up on my offer to have Margaret spend some time with you, Jim, why don't we go to Jessie's? I'm sure you can find something to your liking there."

"I don't know," Preacher said. "That fella Brutus might not take kindly to it if I was to show up again."

"Brutus will take kindly to what he's *told* to take kindly to. And everyone there needs to get used to seeing you around, since I visit the place frequently myself and you're going to be with me in the future."

Preacher shrugged. "All right. Sounds good. I'm obliged to you."

The driver had gotten down from the seat to open the carriage door, but Beaumont paused before climbing into the vehicle.

"We're going to have to get you some better clothes," he said to Preacher. "Something more suited to your position. And we're definitely going to have to get rid of that hat."

Preacher grinned. "Fine by me, boss. I never did like it."

Beaumont nodded toward the driver's seat. "Climb up there with Lorenzo. You can get acquainted with him on the drive over to Jessie's."

Preacher nodded. He wasn't surprised by the order. Beaumont had sat and drank with him in the saloon, but that was when he was still thanking Preacher for saving his life. Now that Preacher was working for him—was, in effect, one of Beaumont's servants—there had been a subtle shift in the man's attitude. There would always be a certain divide between them now.

That was all right with Preacher. He sure as hell hadn't come to St. Louis to make friends with the son of a bitch, he thought.

He swung up onto the driver's seat while Beaumont got into the carriage. Lorenzo closed the door and climbed up beside Preacher. As the wizened old black man took up the reins, Preacher said, "So you're Lorenzo."

"Hmmph," Lorenzo sniffed.

"Jim Donnelly," Preacher introduced himself. "I'm gonna be workin' for the boss, too. Or are you a slave?"

"I'm a freedman," the driver said proudly, reminding Preacher of Brutus. "Mr. Beaumont, he don't keep no slaves. Says it ain't fittin'." He paused. "If'n you ask me, he knows that you can own a man just as good with wages as you can with a whip."

Preacher knew exactly what Lorenzo meant.

The air was sticky this close to the river, but at least it was a little cooler than it had been earlier in the day. The ride up to Jessie's Place helped clear Preacher's head. He was still a little fuzzy from the brandy when the carriage rolled up to the house, but he felt better than when they'd left Dupree's.

When Lorenzo brought the carriage to a stop, Preacher said, "I'll get the door."

"The hell you will! I don't know what *your* job is, boy, but anything to do with this here carriage is *my* responsibility. You just get out'n my way."

Grinning, Preacher said, "Fine with me." He jumped down from the box and stepped back to give Lorenzo room.

Beaumont climbed down from the carriage and motioned for Preacher to follow him. As they went up the walk, Beaumont said, "You never made it inside yesterday, did you?"

"Nope. The front door was as far as I got."

Beaumont grinned. "Then you're in for a treat, Jim. This is the finest sporting house west of Chicago."

Someone must have been watching from inside,

because the door swung open before they even reached the porch. A big man stepped out, and in the light from inside, Preacher recognized him as Brutus.

"Mr. Beaumont!" Brutus greeted them. "It's good to see you, as always, sir." He turned toward Preacher. "And this is—" Brutus recognized him and stared at him in surprise. "You again!"

"Yes, I believe you and Jim here have met," Beaumont said with an amused tone in his voice. "Jim works for me now, Brutus, so you'll be seeing a lot of him."

"Is that so?" Brutus said, then went on hurriedly and not too sincerely, "Well, that's just fine. You know, Mr. Beaumont, that any fella you say is all right is always welcome here."

"That goes without saying," Beaumont responded. "Is the parlor empty?"

"Uh, no, sir, there are several gentlemen in there right now, makin' up their minds—"

"Then empty it." Beaumont gave the order in a curt tone that allowed for no argument. "Empty it of customers, anyway. The girls stay. And tell Miss Jessie that I'm here."

"Yes, sir, right away. If you and . . ." Brutus's jaw visibly tightened. "If you and this gentleman want to wait in the sittin' room, I'll be right back when they're ready for you in the parlor."

"That's fine."

Brutus ushered them into a small room furnished with a divan and two comfortable armchairs. There was an unlit stone fireplace on one wall. Everything in the room, even the smallest item, looked like it would cost more than he made in a year of fur trapping, Preacher thought.

Beaumont motioned for Preacher to have a seat, then indicated a tasseled bellpull on the wall. "Do you want me to have someone bring us something to drink?"

"Not on my account," Preacher said. "I'm still a mite dizzy from all that brandy," he added, even though he really wasn't.

"I understand. With the treat you have awaiting you, you don't want your faculties to be impaired. You want to enjoy this experience to the fullest."

Preacher managed to put a smile on his face. "Yeah, I reckon."

He'd been able to dodge the issue back at Dupree's when he'd refused Beaumont's offer to have that blond serving girl go with him. He sensed that he wouldn't be able to get away with that again. Like it or not, he was going to have to go upstairs with one of the girls who worked here at Jessie's Place.

Not that he wouldn't enjoy it, more than likely, he reminded himself. He had the same appetites as any other man, and probably healthier than most, when you got right down to it. He had enjoyed the intimate company of a number of women in his life. And he had nothing against gals who worked in houses like this. In fact, his first love had been a whore.

He felt a slight pang as he remembered Jennie and the tragic fate that had awaited her. Jennie . . . Jessie . . . Preacher wondered if the similarity in names was one thing that drew him to the woman who ran this house. In addition to her beauty, of course, and the fact that she hadn't hesitated to point that little gun at him. She would have used it if she'd needed to, as well. He felt sure of that.

Beaumont slid a cigar from his vest pocket and put

it in his mouth. He didn't light it, but rather said around the tightly rolled cylinder of tobacco, "Whatever you like in a woman, Jim, you'll find it here. Jessie has more than a dozen girls working for her, and every one of them a true beauty. Redheads, blondes, nigger wenches . . . I believe there's even an Indian squaw, if you're looking for something more exotic. I don't think any of them are younger than fifteen, but if you'd like something of a more tender age, say twelve, I'm sure that can be arranged by the next time we visit."

Preacher fought down the impulse to step across the room and strangle the sick, evil son of a bitch. He forced himself to say, "No, I reckon just a, uh, regular gal will do just fine for me, Mr. Beaumont."

Beaumont took the cigar out of his mouth and gave a casual wave with that hand. "Suit yourself."

Figuring it would be a good idea to continue to make conversation, Preacher asked, "You go with the gals who work here, too?"

"Me?" Beaumont laughed. "I told you, Jim, only the finest things in life for me. And the finest thing in this house . . . is Miss Jessie herself."

That answer didn't surprise Preacher, but it made his jaw clench again. He was saved from having to respond to it by the arrival of Brutus, who stepped into the sitting room and said, "The parlor's ready for you, sir."

Beaumont put the cigar in his mouth again and bit down on it. "Thank you, Brutus." He held out a hand for Preacher to go first. "After you, my friend. After what you did, you're the man of the evening, after all."

That comment caused Brutus to give Preacher a narrow-eyed glance, and Preacher knew he had to be wondering what Beaumont was referring to. Preacher didn't enlighten him. Instead, he followed Brutus down a hallway with an expensive rug on the floor. Paintings of nude women and various scenes of debauchery hung on the corridor's walls.

Preacher felt a little leery about having Beaumont at his back, but the man seemed to have accepted everything that had happened tonight. Preacher had to proceed as if that were true, anyway. He was in too deep to back out now.

Brutus opened a pair of double doors and stood aside to let Preacher enter the parlor first. Again Preacher felt a twinge of unease. There was nothing dangerous waiting for him in the elegantly furnished parlor, however.

Not unless you counted more than half a dozen nearly naked women as dangerous, he corrected himself.

Behind him, Shad Beaumont chuckled and said, "What did I tell you, Jim? And this is only a sampling of the delights available to you here."

The women were all good looking, all right, no doubt about that. Thankfully, all of them were grown, too. Preacher figured the youngest one was nineteen or twenty. The others were all within a year or two of that age. One had auburn hair flowing around her shoulders, two were blondes, and the others had varying shades of brown hair, from a light chestnut to a deep mahogany. Some were tall, some were short. All of them were well shaped, although there was variation in that, too, from slender and lissome to plush and rounded.

Each and every one of them wore a practiced smile

of welcome that hinted at all sorts of carnal delights to come.

Beaumont draped an arm around Preacher's shoulders and stood beside him, grinning and chewing the cigar. "What do you think?" he asked. "See anything that appeals to you? Nothing like that back on the farm, is there?"

Preacher swallowed hard. He didn't have to pretend. And maybe this wasn't going to be such a chore after all, he thought.

"I appreciate this, boss," he said.

"Well, go ahead. Take your pick." Beaumont laughed. "Hell, take two or three of them if you want. I'm sure they won't mind."

"No, I reckon one will do."

Preacher ran his eyes over the women. Three of them sat on a divan, and the others had arranged themselves around it. The gauzy shifts they wore revealed just about all the details of their bodies. Preacher would have enjoyed romping with any of them, but his gaze was drawn back to one of the blondes. She was giving him the same sultry smile as all the others, but he thought he detected a trace of impishness in the expression. Her face was rounded and pretty. She had a scattering of freckles across her nose and a little dimple in her chin, which was a little too prominent for her to be classically beautiful. He lifted a hand to point at her and said, "I'd admire to make the acquaintance of that lady right there."

She stood up from where she had been sitting on the divan and came toward him. Beaumont said, "Ah, you picked our little Cassandra. An excellent choice, Jim."

Cassandra came to a stop in front of Preacher and held out her hand. "Hello," she said. "Jim, is it?"

"Yes'm." Preacher seized her hand and gave it an awkward shake. He knew that probably wasn't what she was expecting, but "Jim Donnelly" was fresh off the farm and probably didn't have that much experience with women. "I'm mighty pleased to meet you."

"You will be," Cassandra said. "Come with me."

She started to lead him out of the parlor, but before they could leave the room, Jessie came through the door. She looked every bit as lovely as she had the day before, and the sight of her made Preacher's heart slug a little harder for a second.

She stopped in front of him and smiled at him. "So it really *is* you," she said. "When Brutus told me, I wasn't sure whether to believe him. And you work for Shad now."

"Yes'm."

"Then you're welcome here. Just behave yourself." She gave him a stern look, and he could tell she wasn't joshing. "No more brawling."

"No, ma'am," he said with a shake of his head.

Jessie's smile came back. "Enjoy yourself, then. Cassandra, make sure Mr. Donnelly is well treated."

"Don't worry, Jessie." The blonde turned her impish smile on Preacher again. "I intend to."

With a swish of skirts and a whiff of some delicate perfume, Jessie moved past them. Preacher heard her say, "Hello, Shad," and her voice had an intimacy in it that must have made his muscles react, because Cassandra laughed and said, "The way you're squeezing my hand, Jim, you must be really eager to get upstairs."

"Yes, ma'am."

They were in the hallway now. Cassandra turned to him and leaned closer so that her breasts pressed warmly against his arm.

"By the time this night is over, you won't be calling me ma'am," she predicted.

Chapter 15

She was right. Sometime during the next couple of hours—Preacher was a mite vague about when it was, exactly—she told him to call her Casey, so that's what he did from then on.

He was lying there in her bed, holding her as she dozed with her head on his shoulder, when a knock sounded on the door. The single candle in the room had burned down to where it cast only a faint, flickering glow. Casey stirred sleepily as the knock was repeated.

"Donnelly." The hoarse rasp of Brutus's voice came from the other side of the door. "Mr. Beaumont says for you to get your ass outta that whore's bed and get downstairs. He's ready to leave."

Preacher would have been willing to bet that Beaumont hadn't phrased the order quite so crudely. On the other hand, maybe he had. Preacher didn't really know Beaumont all that well yet.

All he really knew was that the man was responsible for the deaths of a lot of people Preacher cared about.

Preacher threw back the sheet and started to get out of bed, but Casey woke up enough to clutch at him and murmur, "Don't go, Jim. You're so sweet, and it feels so good just lying here."

Preacher knew better than to put much stock in whore-talk, but he had to admit, Casey sounded sincere. She snuggled against him with an urgency that seemed real, too.

"Sorry, darlin'," he told her as he reached up to stroke a work-roughened hand over her blond hair. "When the boss says it's time to go, I reckon it's time to go."

She sighed. "I know. It's just that I . . . well, Jim, you're not really—"

"You ain't about to say that I ain't like all the other men, are you?"

The words came out harsher than Preacher intended, and as soon as he said them, he wished he could call them back or at least soften them a little.

But it was too late for that. Casey stiffened, and even though a brittle laugh came from her lips, he sensed that he had hurt her feelings.

"Of course not," she said. She rolled over so that her back was turned toward him. "Good night, Jim."

"Casey, I didn't mean—"

"You'd better go. You don't want to keep Mr. Beaumont waiting."

That was true enough. And Preacher had learned over the years that once a fella said the wrong thing to a gal, it was damned near impossible to fix it right then and there. It took a little time for her to cool down and stop being so het up.

But chances were that he'd be coming back to

Jessie's Place fairly often with Beaumont, so he'd have the opportunity to see Casey again. Maybe he could make it right with her next time.

He stood up and started pulling on his clothes. "I had a mighty fine time," he told her.

She didn't roll over and look at him as she said, "I'm glad." She didn't particularly sound like she meant it, either.

Preacher gave a mental shrug and clapped the funny-looking quaker hat on his head. "Be seein' you," he said as he went to the door.

Before he could get there, Brutus's heavy fist fell on the panel again, and he rumbled, "Donnelly!"

Preacher jerked the door open. "I'm comin'," he said. "Hold your horses."

Brutus bared his teeth in a grimace. "You'll learn not to keep Mr. Beaumont waiting."

Preacher eased the door closed behind him and said, "For what it's worth, Casey agrees with you."

"Who?"

Preacher looked over at Brutus and saw that the man wore a puzzled frown. He jerked a thumb at the door and said, "Casey. Cassandra."

"Never heard her called Casey before. 'Round here she's always been just Cassandra."

Preacher said, "Huh." He looked at the door again and thought about the young woman on the other side of it. Had she revealed something to him that she hadn't shared with anyone else here in St. Louis? If that was true, why would she do such a thing?

Preacher didn't have the answers to those questions. Maybe he would learn them in time, he told himself as he followed Brutus downstairs.

The parlor was empty now except for Beaumont, who stalked back and forth on the rug with a drink in his hand. When Preacher and Brutus walked in, he stopped, threw back the liquor, and then said, "It's about time, Donnelly."

Evidently Beaumont considered the debt between them squared now. He and Preacher weren't friends anymore. Beaumont's voice held a definite tone of employer talking to employee. He handed the empty glass to Brutus and went on, "Let's go."

They stepped out into the parlor, where Brutus handed Beaumont his beaver hat and then draped the cape over his shoulders. Brutus was about to open the front door when Jessie called from the top of the stairs, "Good night, Shad."

Preacher turned to look up at her. She wore a long, flimsy gown and robe, and with the light from the landing behind her, the lines of her body were clearly revealed. Her hair was loose and appealingly disheveled.

Preacher wasn't sure if he had ever seen a lovelier woman in his life.

"Good night, my dear," Beaumont told her.

"Did you have a pleasant time with Cassandra, Mr. Donnelly?" Jessie asked. Beaumont frowned, as if she shouldn't even be speaking to Preacher.

Snatching his hat off his head, Preacher held it in front of him and said, "Yes, ma'am, I sure did. She's a right nice girl."

"I'm glad. You have a pleasant evening, too, what's left of it."

"Yes'm."

Beaumont glared at him for a moment as they left

the house. "Don't get used to Jessie paying so much attention to you," he said. "She was just being polite."

"Yes, sir, I never doubted it."

Inside, though, Preacher was laughing. Beaumont was jealous! Jessie had spoken barely a dozen words to Preacher, and yet Beaumont was jealous of him. That was rich.

And it was one more way to get at Beaumont. Not that he would ever take advantage of a woman just to strike back at an enemy, Preacher told himself. Some things just went too much against the grain, and that was one of them.

But a moment such as the one that had just occurred in the house, a moment that was not of his making . . . well, Preacher didn't see anything wrong with enjoying that.

Lorenzo had the carriage door open. Preacher figured it was sometime after midnight, but the elderly driver didn't even seem tired.

"Headin' home, Mr. Beaumont?" he asked.

"That's right," Beaumont said. "Home. And when we get there, Donnelly, Lorenzo can show you your quarters. I'll expect you in the main house at seven o'clock in the morning."

"Yes, sir," Preacher said. Looked like he was bound for the servant quarters. That was all right with him. He had a lot more in common with folks who actually worked for a living than he did with a rich, powerful crook like Beaumont.

Once Beaumont was inside the carriage, Preacher and Lorenzo swung up onto the driver's box, and Lorenzo got the team moving. After a few moments, in a tone of smug satisfaction, he noted, "I see you ain't Jim anymore. You just Donnelly now."

Preacher chuckled. "The boss can call me whatever he wants."

"You ain't as special as you thought you was."

"Trust me, I never thought I was special."

And yet he was special, Preacher mused, because he was the man who, sooner or later, was going to kill Shad Beaumont.

But not right away. Not over the next week, during which Beaumont kept his promise and saw to it that Preacher got a new outfit. He sent Lorenzo with Preacher to one of the stores in downtown St. Louis that sold men's clothing, where Lorenzo picked out and paid for a couple of gray tweed suits, half a dozen shirts, two cravats, a pair of high-topped black boots, and a beaver hat. None of the garments were as fine and expensive as what Beaumont wore, of course, but they were probably the fanciest duds Preacher had ever had. He felt a little like a damned fool, too, when he saw himself in the store's looking glass.

"You know what they say 'bout the silk purse and the sow's ear," Lorenzo commented sourly. "You still look like a big ol' farm boy to me, even if you *is* duded up some."

"Don't tell the boss, but that's the way I feel, too," Preacher said with a grin. He liked the little carriage driver, despite Lorenzo's habitually gloomy disposition. He figured working for Shad Beaumont would make anybody feel that way.

Although Jessie hadn't seemed unhappy, he

reminded himself, and neither did the folks who worked at Dupree's. He supposed that was because Beaumont paid well.

The two of them visited one place or the other every night, and sometimes they made it to both. Preacher didn't see Casey again, and when he asked Brutus about her, the big man said that she hadn't been feeling well.

"These whores get like that," Brutus said. "They're more fragile than you'd think they'd be."

Preacher managed to avoid going with any of the other girls, and Beaumont didn't press the issue. While he was upstairs with Jessie, Preacher usually stayed in the kitchen and sometimes played cards with Brutus and Lorenzo. Brutus didn't seem to hate Preacher quite as much as he had at first. At least, he tolerated the mountain man being around.

During the days, Beaumont rose late, had a leisurely breakfast, and then set out in the carriage from the big, whitewashed house on the south side of town that reminded Preacher of plantation houses he had seen down around New Orleans when he was a young man. As Beaumont's bodyguard, Preacher went with him, of course, while Beaumont made the rounds of his businesses in St. Louis, both the legitimate ones—and the not-so-legitimate. They stopped at taverns and lower-class brothels and dusty warehouses where the merchandise stored in them was probably stolen, Preacher thought.

During that week, Preacher didn't get a chance to slip away and pay a visit to Uncle Dan's camp. He hoped the old-timer wasn't getting too worried about him.

Then one evening, Beaumont stayed home and sent

Lorenzo with the carriage to fetch Jessie back to his house, instead of him going to her place. "I'm not leaving the house tonight, so you won't have to stay around, Donnelly," Beaumont said. He took a coin from his pocket and flipped it to Preacher. "You've been doing a good job . . . not that you've really had anything to do. Why don't you go out and find a woman or a poker game and enjoy yourself?"

Preacher caught the coin, deftly plucking it out of the air. He stuck it in his pocket and said, "Thanks, boss. Reckon I'll do that."

Beaumont was in his study, sipping some brandy that he didn't offer to share with Preacher this time. He took a drink and said, "You know, I put the word out that I wanted to know who took that shot at me, the night you saved my life. People have been asking around on my behalf all over town, because it's hard to keep a grudge quiet if it's bad enough to prompt an ambush. But no one seems to have any idea who could have done it."

For a second, Preacher thought that Beaumont was getting suspicious and was about to accuse him of something. But then the man went on, "If you could turn up that information, Donnelly, there'd be a bonus in it for you. I don't like the idea that there's some mysterious stranger out there somewhere who wants me dead."

You just don't know the half of it, you son of a bitch, Preacher thought.

But he nodded and said, "I'll see what I can find out, boss."

Chapter 16

Preacher had reclaimed Horse from the livery stable where he had kept the stallion temporarily, and now Horse had a stall in the stable behind Beaumont's house where the carriage and the team of fine black horses were kept. Lorenzo had been impressed by the rangy gray stallion, proving that he was a good judge of horseflesh. That had probably raised his opinion of Preacher somewhat, too, although Preacher knew that Lorenzo wouldn't admit that to save his life.

Preacher walked out to the stable and saddled Horse, then rode toward the center of town, just in case Beaumont was watching. When he was out of sight of the house, he turned west and headed out of St. Louis toward Uncle Dan's camp.

When he neared the grove of trees, he reined in and hooted like an owl. A moment later, an answering hoot came, telling him that the old-timer was still there, just as Preacher had hoped. He rode into the trees and found the camp, which had been moved a short distance from where it had been the last time Preacher was here.

"Too fiddle-footed to stay in one place for a whole week, eh?" he asked with a grin as he swung down from the saddle. Dog reared up, put his paws on Preacher's shoulders, and licked the mountain man's face.

"That ain't it at all," Uncle Dan replied. "This campsite's just a mite better, that's all. Better firewood, and a little closer to the crick that runs through these trees."

"Sure," Preacher said, knowing full well that Uncle Dan's restless nature had had something to do with it, no matter what the old-timer said. He knew that because he was the same way. His feet always began to itch after a few days in the same place. He had already experienced that in St. Louis, although the desire for revenge on Shad Beaumont that drove him made it easy to suppress those urges.

"I been keepin' the coffee warm for you ever' night," Uncle Dan went on as he took the pot from the embers of the campfire. "Figured you'd be showin' up before now."

"Beaumont's been keepin' me pretty busy. He's still spooked from that bushwhack attempt, so I've had to stay close to him whenever he leaves the house."

Uncle Dan clucked his tongue. "Must be a terrible chore, havin' to visit saloons and whorehouses ever' night."

Preacher laughed. "It ain't as entertainin' as you might think it'd be."

With the exception of the time he had spent with Casey, he told himself. And he'd managed to mess that up at the end and hadn't seen her since. He hoped she was all right.

The two men sat on logs and sipped coffee while Dog lay at Preacher's feet. Preacher reached down with his free hand and scratched between the big cur's ears.

Uncle Dan asked, "Now that you're workin' for Beaumont, what do you figure on doin'? Want me to take another shot at him, so's he'll know he's still got somebody gunnin' for him?"

Preacher shook his head. "No, we got away with that once, but I don't want you runnin' that risk again, Uncle Dan. I'm waitin' for Beaumont to come up with some new scheme, so I can ruin it for him."

"How long you gonna keep that up?"

"Don't know. Depends on what happens, I reckon."

"You know . . . you could kill the son of a bitch just about any time now, and be halfway back to the mountains 'fore anybody knowed what happened."

"Yeah, but there's one problem with that." Preacher took another sip of coffee. "I ain't a murderer. When I kill Beaumont, it's gonna be head-on, and he's gonna know why he's dyin'."

"Well, I didn't never say to strangle the son of a bitch in his sleep, now did I?" Uncle Dan grumbled. "Tell him who you are. You can even give him a chance to get his paws on a gun if you want. I reckon you could still kill him."

"It may come to that. But not yet."

Even though the embers of the fire didn't cast much light, Preacher could feel Uncle Dan studying him. After a moment, the old-timer said, "This ain't like you, Preacher. I may not have knowed you all that long, but I've heard plenty about you. You ain't the sort o' fella to pussyfoot around. What's all this sneakin' and pretendin' to be somebody else gonna accomplish?"

That very question had been gnawing at Preacher's brain, too. When he had first come up with the plan, he'd thought that it would be fitting to give Beaumont a taste of his own medicine. To take away the things that the man cared about and put him through the same sort of suffering that he had inflicted on so many others.

Yet as the days had gone by, Preacher had begun more and more to doubt the wisdom of this course. Uncle Dan was right. It wasn't like him, and knowing that he had fooled Beaumont wasn't as satisfying as he'd hoped it would be. But the plan had proceeded so far that to change it now seemed like a mistake, too.

"I don't know," he said in reply to Uncle Dan's question. "I'll think on it. I can tell you this, though . . . it ain't gonna go on too much longer."

"I hope not. I'm gettin' anxious to see the mountains again."

So was Preacher. He could only stand civilization for a short time.

He finished his coffee, then stood up and said his good-byes to Uncle Dan. As he started out of the trees, he heard something that caught his attention. It was the muffled whicker of a horse, somewhere nearby in the thick shadows under the trees.

Preacher stiffened in the saddle. That sound hadn't come from Uncle Dan's horse, which meant there was another animal somewhere close to the camp. And where there was a horse, there was usually a rider. This one could be a stray, but Preacher's gut told him that wasn't the case.

He didn't react visibly to the sound but kept Horse moving at a steady pace instead. As he emerged from the trees, he turned the big stallion onto the trail that led back toward St. Louis. He didn't look back.

Every instinct in his body told him that someone was following him, though.

The lights of the town glittered in the darkness ahead of him. They were bright enough, and there were enough of them, so that a faint glow filled the sky over the settlement. Preacher didn't slow down when he reached the streets of the town. He rode on through St. Louis toward the riverfront. The sound of raucous laughter and scraping fiddles came from the taverns he passed. Somewhere a woman cried out, but it sounded more like a scream of pleasure rather than one of pain or fear. A man cursed. Another shouted a question. The smell of the river filled the air.

Preacher turned into a narrow lane and slipped out of the saddle as soon as he was around the corner. He gave Horse's rump a soft slap that kept the stallion moving forward. Horse wouldn't go too far before he stopped and waited for Preacher to summon him back. It shouldn't take long for him to find out what he needed to know, though, Preacher thought.

Sure enough, only a minute or so had gone by when another rider rounded the corner and started along the lane, following the steady clip-clop of Horse's hooves on the hard-packed dirt. By that time, Preacher had drawn back into the impenetrable shadows that clogged the deep, recessed doorway of an abandoned building. The man who rode past never even glanced in his direction.

Even though the light in the lane was bad, Preacher's eyesight was keen enough to tell him that the man was familiar. After a second, Preacher recalled his name. The man following him was the gambler Cleve. Preacher had seen him at both Dupree's and Jessie's Place. As far as Preacher knew, there was no connection between Cleve and Beaumont except for the fact that the gambler patronized places owned by Beaumont.

It seemed likely, though, that Cleve had picked up Preacher's trail at Beaumont's house. Was he a spy for Beaumont? Did Beaumont really suspect Preacher of some sort of treachery after all?

There was only one way to find out, Preacher thought as he slipped grim-faced out of the shadows.

He went after Cleve. The man was riding slowly enough so that Preacher had no trouble keeping up with him on foot. Preacher stayed back about a hundred yards and haunted the shadows so that he could duck out of sight if Cleve happened to look back. After a few minutes, though, Cleve reined in and stood up in the stirrups to look around. He must have realized that he'd lost his quarry, Preacher thought.

Preacher had already spotted Horse standing in front of a darkened livery barn across the street, and he recognized it now as the barn where Horse had spent one night. The stallion must have recognized the place, too, and was waiting there for Preacher to come for him.

Cleve hadn't noticed Horse when he rode past the livery, though. That much was obvious from the way the gambler yanked his own mount around and rode up the street, moving quicker now. Preacher waited until Cleve was almost out of sight, then gave a low whistle that brought Horse trotting over to him. He mounted up quickly and rode after Cleve.

The hunter had become the hunted now.

Preacher knew that by staying well back, he ran the

risk of losing Cleve. He had confidence in his own ability to trail the gambler, though. He was maybe a little less confident here in town than he would have been in the wilderness, but he still thought he could keep up with the man.

Anyway, it wasn't long before Preacher had a pretty good idea where Cleve was going.

The man seemed to be headed straight toward Jessie's Place.

That turned out to be the case. Cleve rode around to the back of the house. Preacher brought Horse to a stop under some trees and dismounted, then went after Cleve on foot. He reached the rear corner of the house in time to see that Cleve had led his horse into a shed at the rear of the place and left the animal there. The gambler stood at the back door, evidently having just knocked on it. When the door opened, light spilled from inside, and Brutus's voice rumbled, "Did you find out what you went after?"

"I'll speak to Jessie about it," Cleve replied curtly.

"She ain't back from Beaumont's yet. She said for you to come in and wait."

Cleve nodded. "All right."

He went inside and the door closed, leaving the rear of the house in darkness again. Preacher stood at the corner of the building, frowning in thought.

Was *Jessie* the one who had sent Cleve to follow him? She had known that she was visiting Beaumont's house tonight, instead of the other way around, so she could have figured that Beaumont might dismiss Preacher for the night.

On the other hand, she could have simply been acting on Beaumont's orders and serving as an intermediary between him and Cleve, although Preacher couldn't really see why Beaumont would go to that much trouble.

The best way to find out the truth was to wait until Jessie got back, so that's what Preacher settled down to do.

About an hour later, he heard the clatter of carriage wheels in front of the house. Several vehicles had passed by on the street while he was standing in the shadows, waiting, but this one came to a halt. Preacher ventured to the front corner of the house and watched as Lorenzo opened the door of Beaumont's fancy carriage and helped Jessie climb out.

"Thank you, Lorenzo," she told him.

The driver tipped his hat. "My pleasure, Miss Jessie."

Then Jessie came up the walk to the house. Preacher could see well enough to tell that she had a shawl draped around her shoulders.

Brutus met her at the door. "Cleve's back," he said, his deep voice carrying in the still, quiet night. "He's waitin' for you in your office."

"Thank you, Brutus." Jessie's tone was brisk and businesslike now. As she disappeared into the house and Brutus shut the door, Preacher turned and hurried along the whitewashed side of the house. He had never been in Jessie's office, but he had been around the house enough in the past week to have figured out that it was in the rear of the house.

Only one window back there had the glow of lamplight showing through it. Preacher headed for it. The night was warm, and he hoped that the window would be open, at least a little.

It was. He crouched underneath it and was able to hear clearly as Jessie came in and said, "Hello, Cleve."

A chair scraped as the gambler stood up. "Jessie," he said. "You're looking as lovely as ever."

"Just tell me what you found out. Were you able to follow Donnelly?"

"Yes, your hunch was right. Beaumont told him he could leave the house tonight, since you were coming over there."

"Where did he go? Some dive down by the river?"

"Hardly." Cleve paused. "I followed him to a spot about a mile west of town. He met someone there, under some trees, and talked to them for a while. I couldn't get close enough to see who it was, though, or to hear what they were saying."

"Then he *is* up to something! I knew it!" Jessie's voice was breathless with excitement. "But what?"

"I don't know, but I think we need to keep an eye on him. If he really had something to do with that shot at Beaumont, as you suspect, then he's planning something and wanted to get close to Beaumont for a reason."

From the sound of it, Preacher thought, Jessie hadn't sent Cleve to follow him on Beaumont's behalf. If anything, it almost sounded like the two of them didn't like Beaumont any more than Preacher himself did.

That was confirmed a moment later when Jessie said, "We have to find out who Donnelly is and what he's after. We don't want him getting in the way when we make our own move against Shad."

"I agree."

"Where did he go when he got back to town? To Beaumont's house?"

"I don't know, damn it," Cleve replied with a note of bitter disappointment in his voice. "I hate to admit it, Jessie, but I lost him somewhere in town."

"Lost him!" Jessie sounded upset, and maybe a little scared. "He didn't know you were following him, did he?"

"I don't see how he could have. I was very careful."

In the darkness outside the window, a grin tugged at Preacher's mouth. Cleve might be a good gambler and able to take care of himself in town, but he was no frontiersman.

"We'll have to figure out some other way to find out what we need to know," Jessie mused. "Maybe Cassandra could get it out of him. He seemed to like her."

Preacher's interest perked right up at that comment. He hadn't seen Casey in a week, and he was starting to get a mite worried about her.

Evidently with good cause, too, because Cleve asked, "How's she doing?"

"She hasn't recovered from what Beaumont did to her," Jessie said, "but she's getting better. Another week and she might be all right.

Preacher stiffened, and a cold finger ran along his spine. What the devil could Beaumont have done to Casey to make her keep out of sight for two weeks? He must have hurt her pretty bad to do that.

Maybe what he ought to do, he thought, was march right in there and put his cards on the table with Jessie and Cleve. If they were out to bring Beaumont down, too, they could prove to be valuable allies.

But what if it was a trap of some sort? he asked himself. What if they knew somehow that he was out here, eavesdropping on their conversation, and were testing his loyalties?

Preacher gave an abrupt shake of his head. He couldn't rule out that possibility completely, but it was far-fetched enough so that he couldn't take it seriously.

He didn't have time to ponder the question any more, because at that moment, he heard the metallic clicking of a gun hammer being cocked behind him, and in a voice like the rumble of distant drums, Brutus said, "Don't you move, mister, or this old blunderbuss of mine will blow a hole in you."

Chapter 17

Preacher stayed right where he was, although for a second he considered trying to leap out of the line of fire, twist around, and jerk his own pistol from behind his belt.

But maybe this was exactly what he wanted, he realized, so he said, "Take it easy, Brutus. It's just me, Jim Donnelly."

"Donnelly!" Brutus boomed. "What the hell are you doin', skulkin' around out here? Damn it, man, I was just startin' to trust you."

Before Preacher could answer, the window above his head was thrust up, and Cleve leaned out with a gun in his hand. "What's going on out here?" the gambler demanded. "Who's that standing there?"

"It's that fella Donnelly," Brutus replied. "I just caught him skulkin' around. Looked like he was eavesdroppin' on you and Miss Jessie."

And that was why he hadn't heard Brutus until it was too late, Preacher thought. He'd been concentrating on what Jessie and Cleve were saying inside the office and had missed the small sounds Brutus must have made as he came around the house. That had to be how the man had approached, because Preacher was certain the back door hadn't been opened.

"Donnelly!" Cleve exclaimed. "By God, I was just—"

He stopped short, probably because he didn't want to admit that he had been following Preacher tonight. Preacher wasn't going to let him get away with that, though.

"I know what you were doin'," Preacher said, allowing some harsh anger to creep into his voice. "I heard you and Miss Jessie talkin' about it. You were followin' me, because you don't trust me."

Jessie came up beside Cleve at the window and said tensely, "Evidently with good reason. Bring him into the house, Brutus. We have to find out how much he knows."

Brutus came closer with the old, short-barreled musket. From the way the muzzle flared out, Preacher knew the weapon was old, probably from colonial days. But if it had been well cared for—and from the looks of it, it had—and still worked properly, the heavy ball the blunderbuss fired could indeed blow a fist-sized hole all the way through him at this range. Preacher didn't want to risk it, and besides, this gave him a good excuse to talk to Jessie and Cleve. He kept his hands half-raised and in plain sight as he walked to the back door with Brutus behind him.

Once they were inside, they used a rear hallway to reach Jessie's office, avoiding the parlor where customers were talking and laughing with the women who worked here. Preacher could hear them. Jessie and Cleve waited in the office, and both of them wore

grim expressions when Preacher walked in ahead of
Brutus. Cleve's pistol was still in his hand.

"Close the door, Brutus," Jessie ordered.

"You want me to stay, Miss Jessie?"

She shook her head. "No, I think we can handle
Mr. Donnelly."

"You sure?"

"Yes. Go tend to the house."

"Yes'm. But you just holler if you need me." Brutus
put his face close to Preacher's and glared murder-
ously. "You best behave yourself, Donnelly."

He turned and stalked out, taking the blunderbuss
with him.

Jessie nodded toward an armchair in front of the
big desk that dominated the room. "Sit down," she
told Preacher.

He did as she said. She went behind the desk and
sank into the big, leather-upholstered chair there.
Cleve stood beside her, the pistol still pointing in
Preacher's general direction. Preacher felt pretty
good about his chances of taking the gun away from
the gambler any time he wanted to . . . but right now,
he didn't want to.

"How much did you overhear?" Jessie asked as she
gave Preacher a stern, level stare. Even at a moment
such as this, when she was angry and maybe even a little
scared, she was still stunningly beautiful, he thought.

He said, "Enough to know that the two of you are
plottin' against Shad Beaumont."

Cleve's lips drew back from his teeth in a grimace.
"I say we go ahead and kill him. Brutus can get rid of
the body so that no one will ever find it."

Preacher didn't wait to see how Jessie would respond

to the suggestion. He said, "If you do that, you'll be losin' an ally."

That statement put his opposition to Beaumont right out in the open. If they really were trying to trick him into admitting that, the next few seconds might prove to be extremely dangerous. He was ready to lunge across the desk at Jessie if he saw Cleve's finger tightening on the trigger. He figured the gambler would be less likely to shoot if he thought Jessie might be in the line of fire.

Instead, Cleve just frowned in puzzlement, and Jessie's lips thinned. "What are you talking about?" she asked.

"I reckon you must have some sort of grudge against Beaumont. Well, you ain't the only ones."

Cleve asked, "Are you saying that you're his enemy, even though you work for him?"

Preacher smiled slightly. "An old Chinaman called Sun-tzu once said it was a good idea to keep your friends close but your enemies closer."

Cleve stared at him. "How does a farmer hear about Sun-tzu?"

Preacher shrugged. He wasn't sure he wanted to reveal who he really was, just yet, but if he had, he could have explained that many of the men who came to the Rocky Mountains as fur trappers were educated, well-read men. Some of them could quote Shakespeare, Milton, and other poets for hours on end. As it happened, Preacher had heard another mountain man named Audie talking about Sun-tzu, and the name and the quote had stuck in his head.

Instead of going into all that, though, he said, "I

reckon I must've heard it somewhere. It makes good sense, don't it?"

"What do you have against Beaumont?" Jessie asked sharply.

"I reckon that's my business."

"And how do we know that you're telling the truth? You could be lying just to save your skin."

"You ain't told me why you're pretendin' to be his friends while you're really working against him," Preacher pointed out.

Jessie leaned back in her chair and continued giving him that cool, level stare for several seconds. Then she said, "You're right. But I'll do better than tell you. I'll show you." She got to her feet. "Wait here. Cleve, you'll keep an eye on him?"

"Be glad to," the gambler replied, hefting his pistol slightly.

Jessie came out from hehind the desk, went around Preacher's chair, and left the room. As she did so, Preacher caught a hint of her perfume. It smelled mighty good, sort of like a meadow full of wildflowers on a spring morning in the high country.

"I still say it would be simpler to kill you," Cleve said when Jessie was gone. "I could tell her you tried to escape, and I had to shoot you."

"Reckon she'd believe you?"

"I think so."

Preacher's eyes narrowed. "I wouldn't advise tryin' it."

Cleve tried to meet him stare for stare but couldn't quite do it. As the gambler's eyes flicked away, he said, "Jessie generally knows what she's doing. I'll string along with her . . . for now."

A couple of minutes later, the door into the office opened again. Preacher looked around, saw that Jessie was coming back into the room. She had someone with her, and when she stepped aside, Preacher realized that the woman behind her was Casey. The blonde wore a robe and had her head down so that Preacher couldn't see her face, but he knew it was her.

"You said you wanted to know what we had against Shad Beaumont," Jessie told him. "This is just one thing, among many."

She reached out, cupped a hand under Casey's chin, and gently lifted the blonde's head so that Preacher could look into her face.

Preacher had seen a lot of bad things in his life. He'd been in a war and seen men blown apart by cannon fire. He had seen whole families, including the youngsters, killed and mutilated by Indians. What he was looking at now was nowhere near as bad as those things.

But it was bad enough to make him come up out of his chair, his hands clenching angrily into fists as he surveyed the damage that had been done to Casey's face. Both eyes were blackened and still swollen half-closed. Her nose had been broken and reset, but it would probably never look like it had before. Bruises mottled her cheeks and her jaw. Her lips were puffy and had healing cuts on them. More bruises on her neck showed where a big hand had brutally strangled her.

"Beaumont," Preacher breathed.

"That's right," Jessie said. "He held her down and nearly choked the life out of her while he beat her again and again with his other fist. He did this with his bare hands, Mr. Donnelly, and it's not the first time he's treated . . . one of my girls . . . this way."

Preacher caught the slight hesitation in Jessie's voice and wondered if Beaumont had ever beaten her like that. When Beaumont was around, she seemed friendly and flirtatious, more like a lover than an employee. Obviously, that was just an act.

Casey said in a hoarse voice, "Can I . . . go back to my room now?"

"Of course, dear," Jessie told her. "I'm sorry I had to bring you in here. But Mr. Donnelly wanted to know why we feel the way we do about Shad Beaumont."

Casey looked at Preacher before she left. She seemed embarrassed that he had seen her this way, but at the same time, he thought he recognized a hint of a smile on her puffy lips, as if she were glad to see him again. He hoped things would work out so that they could spend some more time together, one of these days.

Once Casey was gone, Preacher asked Jessie, "What did she do to set Beaumont off?"

"Nothing. Nothing that she could remember, anyway. He just flies into these rages sometimes, for no apparent reason. I think it's because he's so full of vile hatred and scorn for everybody in the world that from time to time he can't hold it in behind that smooth façade he puts up." She paused and drew a deep breath. "He's an evil man, Mr. Donnelly. A truly evil man."

"I know. It's because of him that a bunch of innocent folks I know are dead."

"I don't doubt it for an instant."

Preacher looked over at Cleve, who had finally lowered his gun, although he hadn't put it away. "How about you? What's your part in this?"

"You mean, what grudge do I bear against Beaumont?" Cleve shook his head. "None, really. I just think that someone else would be better suited to run things around here."

"In other words, you. You're just ambitious."

"Not *that* ambitious," Cleve said with a laugh. "I was speaking of Jessie. She's the one who should be in charge, not Beaumont. I'll be quite content just to help her achieve that goal."

And cash in for himself at the same time, Preacher thought. He didn't say it, though, because he figured that Jessie was smart enough to have figured it out for herself by now.

She was regarding him with a curious, intent look. "You had something to do with that attempt on Shad's life, didn't you? It must have been a friend of yours who shot at him, so you could pretend to save him and get him in your debt."

"That'd be a tricky thing to do," Preacher said, impressed that she had figured it out so easily.

"It was a smart thing to do. He trusts you now, because of that. I began to wonder about it when neither Cleve nor I could find out anything about who it might have been that shot at him. Shad has plenty of enemies in St. Louis who'd like to see him dead, but if any of them had worked up the courage to actually try something like that, the word would have gotten around. That meant it almost had to be a stranger. And since *you* were a stranger in town as well . . ."

Preacher shrugged. It was an admission that she was right.

"And you're not a farmer from Pennsylvania, either," she went on. "There's a sense of danger that seems to follow you around. I don't believe I've ever seen a man who's always so alert for trouble. You didn't learn that trudging along behind a plow."

Preacher still didn't say anything.

Jessie smiled. "I can make a guess who you really are. There's a man that Beaumont's afraid of, so afraid that he's put a bounty on his head. A man from the Rocky Mountains who has ruined several of Shad's plans and killed dozens of his agents. I think *you're* that man, Mr. Donnelly."

Cleve stared at the mountain man. "You mean that this fellow is—"

Jessie cut him off with a nod. "That's right," she said. "I believe that this is the famous Preacher."

Chapter 18

There didn't seem to be any point in denying it. Jessie probably wouldn't believe him, anyway.

"There's another old sayin' about a cat bein' out of a bag, but I don't believe a Chinaman said it."

"So you admit that you're Preacher?"

"Yeah, might as well."

"Wait a minute," Cleve said. "I've heard of Preacher. He's just one of those ignorant, unwashed mountain men—"

Jessie silenced him with a look. "Just because a man doesn't have much education doesn't mean that he's unintelligent. I haven't been to school all that much myself, and I believe I'm fairly smart."

"Yeah, but you're a . . ."

"Woman? Is that what you were about to say?"

Preacher chuckled and said to Cleve, "I may be ignorant, but I know enough that when I'm neck-deep in a hole, I stop diggin'."

Cleve frowned and muttered something, then said, "Sorry, Jessie. I didn't mean anything. And of course, you're right. The question is, what are we going to do about him now?"

"We'd be fools to pass up this opportunity to have him on our side," Jessie said, as if Preacher were no longer in the room. "You know his reputation. You know there are good reasons why Shad fears him."

Preacher jerked a thumb at the door. "If you folks want me to step outta the room, I reckon I could go out to the parlor. I bet I could find a gal there willin' to keep me company for a while."

"I'm sure you could," Jessie said, "but you don't need to leave, Preacher. I think we should all work together. We have a common enemy, after all."

Preacher looked at Cleve. "You feel the same way, gambler?"

"Of course, if Jessie does," he said with a nod. He opened his coat and put away his pistol, slipping it into a holster somewhere under the garment.

Preacher wasn't sure he completely believed or trusted Cleve. The gambler had teamed up with Jessie to overthrow Beaumont's reign because he wanted power and money. Those were mighty good motives.

But they weren't as pure as the hatred that Preacher and evidently Jessie, too, felt for Shad Beaumont.

For the time being, though, Preacher's best course of action was to cooperate with them. As he always did, he would just keep his eyes open and be ready for trouble at any time. That way, if Cleve tried to double-cross him somewhere down the line, he'd be ready.

"We're agreed, then?" Jessie said. "We'll all work together?"

"Suits me," Preacher said. "Just one question . . . what do you plan on doin' next?"

Jessie went back behind the desk and sat down, motioning for Preacher to resume his seat in front of the desk. Cleve remained on his feet, still watchful. His hand didn't stray far from the place where the pistol was tucked away under his coat.

"How much do you know about Beaumont's business?" Jessie asked.

"I know he really owns this place and Dupree's and a lot of other places in St. Louis," Preacher replied. "Some of 'em are pretty shady, but some of them are real businesses."

Jessie nodded. "That's right. Does he let you in on his plans?"

"Nope," Preacher said with a shake of his head. "He tells me to come with him when he goes somewhere, and I go. That's it."

Jessie clasped her hands together in front of her. "One of the businesses he owns is a cotton brokerage. A riverboat is supposed to dock tomorrow with a load of cotton from New Orleans that's bound for Shad's warehouse. But it's not going to make it. River pirates are going to take it over, run it aground, and steal the cotton."

Preacher had run into river pirates before. He knew how cunning and vicious they could be. "These here pirates . . . they'll be workin' for you?"

"Not at all," Jessie said. "They work for Shad."

Preacher frowned. "Wait a minute. He's gonna steal his own cotton?"

"That's right. The cargo is insured, you see. Shad's men will deliver the cotton to one of his other warehouses here in St. Louis, so he'll still have the shipment and can dispose of it discreetly, but he'll collect the value of it from the insurance company, too."

"That's mighty tricky," Preacher said. "Most robbers I've ever heard about just stick a gun in somebody's face and tell 'em to stand and deliver."

Cleve said, "That's penny-ante stuff. Beaumont operates on a bigger scale than that. At the rate he's going, he'll soon be one of the richest men in the entire country, and most of it will have come from ill-gotten gains."

"So you plan to stop this riverboat hijackin'?" Preacher asked.

"That's right," Jessie said. "Anything we can do to put a crimp in Shad's plans . . . is really less than what he actually deserves."

Preacher couldn't argue with that. "What can I do to help?"

"You go with Beaumont every time he goes out?"

Preacher nodded. "That's right."

"But on a night like this, where he stays home . . . he didn't have anything for you to do?"

"Nope." Preacher didn't want to think about the reason Beaumont had stayed home tonight. He could see her for himself, sitting right across the desk from him.

Knowing what she knew about Beaumont, how could Jessie act around him like she did? How could she—

Preacher shoved those thoughts out of his mind. The answers to those questions were none of his business.

"If he was going to be at home tomorrow, maybe he would send you with the men who are supposed to rob the boat," Jessie mused as she leaned back in her chair. "I can arrange for him to be busy, and you could tell him that you want something else to do, something bigger than just guarding him."

"You reckon that would work?"

"Shad admires ambition . . . as long as he doesn't think anyone who works for him is getting *too* ambitious. I think it's worth a try."

"And if I go with those so-called pirates . . . what then?" "We're going to have men waiting for them," Cleve said. "Having a man on the inside who could take them by surprise might make it easier to deal with them."

"To bushwhack them, you mean," Preacher said heavily.

"You can't very well claim you have some sort of moral dilemma when it comes to killing Beaumont's men," the gambler shot back at him. "You've done plenty of that yourself."

What Cleve said was true, of course, but there was a vital difference, Preacher thought. His previous battles against Beaumont's agents had been fought out in the open. There hadn't been any sneaking deception involved.

But wasn't something like this exactly what he'd had in mind when he decided on this masquerade? he asked himself. He'd wanted to get on the inside of Beaumont's organization so he could wreak havoc.

"I reckon what you're sayin' might work, Miss Jessie," Preacher admitted grudgingly.

She smiled across the desk at him. "I hoped you'd see it that way."

"The fellas who work on the riverboat . . . they don't know anything about this?"

"Not a thing," she said. "And it's very likely that

some of them will be killed when Shad's men attack the boat. So if you help us ruin his plans, you may well be saving the lives of those boatmen."

Preacher couldn't argue with that conclusion. He gave a grim nod and said, "All right, I'll go along with that plan. Beaumont may not, though."

"I know," Jessie said. "If he doesn't, we'll bide our time and wait for our next opportunity to make use of you. The one thing we can't afford to do at this point is to make him suspicious of you." Her lips curved in a smile. "You're our secret weapon, Preacher."

"Just don't misfire," Cleve added.

Preacher's eyes narrowed as he got to his feet. "Ain't likely," he said.

"Where are you going?" Jessie asked.

"We're done here, ain't we?"

"I suppose."

"There *is* one more thing," Preacher said. "I'd like to see—" He started to say "Casey," then recalled that no one here used that name for her. "I'd like to see Cassandra again before I go."

"I'm not sure she'd like that," Jessie said with a frown.

"Well, I don't want to upset her, but I've got somethin' I want to tell her."

Jessie thought it over for a moment, then nodded. "All right. I suppose it would be all right. You can knock on her door, anyway, and find out if she'll see you. However, I don't know if she'll be up to—"

Preacher stopped her with a gesture. "It ain't about that. I just want to talk to her."

"All right."

"And you might tell Brutus that we're all friends

again, in case he sees me wanderin' around the house and decides to use that ol' blunderbuss on me."

"I'll take care of that," Cleve offered.

They left the office together after Preacher said good night to Jessie. Once they were in the hallway, the gambler went on in a low voice, "You'd better not be planning on double-crossing us, mister. I can tell you right now, you'll regret it if you do."

"Don't worry about me," Preacher said. "Just tend to your own rat-killin'."

They parted company, Cleve heading for the parlor while Preacher took the rear stairs to the second floor. He found the room where he had been with Casey before and rapped quietly on the door.

"Who . . . who's there?" The tentative question came from the other side of the panel.

"Jim Donnelly," Preacher said, since that was the name she still knew him by.

"Oh! Jim." He heard soft footsteps on the other side of the door. "I . . . I don't think I feel up to seeing you right now, Jim."

"I just want to talk to you for a minute," Preacher said.

"Really, I—"

"Won't take long."

She sighed. "All right. But wait just a minute."

He stood there in front of the door as a few seconds passed. Then Casey told him, "You can come in now."

He twisted the knob and opened the door. The room was dark, and when he saw that, he knew that's what had caused the delay. She had blown out the lamp so that he couldn't get a good look at her. He could barely see her standing on the far side of the room.

Preacher closed the door, shutting out the light

from the corridor. "Casey, you don't have to worry about what you look like," he told her. "Not with me. It ain't your fault, what Beaumont done to you."

"It wouldn't have happened if I . . . if I hadn't been with him."

"Well, now, you didn't have a whole heap o' choice about that, now did you?"

"No," she whispered. "None at all."

"So, like I said, it ain't your fault. It's that bastard Beaumont's fault, and I'm here to promise you . . . he's gonna pay."

Her gown rustled as she came closer to him. "But I don't understand. You . . . you work for Beaumont, don't you?"

"Well, that's a mite complicated." Obviously, Jessie trusted the girl, or she wouldn't have brought her into the office and showed Preacher her injuries the way she had. But Preacher wasn't sure just how far they should trust her. "All I can say is that things ain't always what they seem."

"Are you going to . . . kill him?"

"We'll have to wait and see about that."

He heard a soft, swishing sound as she came still closer to him. "If you do, Jim, I want you to know that I'll be so—"

"You don't have to say anything else. I just wanted you to know that justice is gonna catch up to Beaumont, sooner or later."

"Jim." She reached out in the darkness and found his arm with her hand, stopping him as he started to turn toward the door. "Jim, you don't have to go just yet, do you?"

He felt her lean against him, and as his arms

instinctively went around her, he realized the last sound he'd heard had been her robe falling to the floor. Her nude body was soft and warm in his embrace.

"You'll have to be gentle with my face," she whispered, "but as for the rest of it . . . you don't have to be gentle at all."

Chapter 19

Preacher hadn't asked Jessie how she was going to keep Beaumont from making his usual rounds the next afternoon. He didn't want to know.

But whatever she did—sending word to Beaumont that she wanted to come to his house again that afternoon, Preacher supposed—it must have worked, because shortly after Beaumont rose late in the morning and had a leisure breakfast, he sent for Preacher and told him, "I'm not going to need you until this evening, Donnelly."

Preacher put a frown on his face. "Boss, if I've done somethin' that don't suit you, and that's why you don't need me around as much all of a sudden—"

Beaumont stopped him with a curt gesture and said, "That's not it at all. I don't intend to go out this afternoon, and I'm not worried about anyone bothering me here in my own house. If you think I'm going to dock your wages for the time I don't need you at my side, you can ease your mind about that. I still intend to pay you the same."

"Oh." Preacher nodded but kept the frown on his face. Beaumont didn't know it, but he had just played right into Preacher's hands. "No offense, boss, but I ain't sure I like bein' paid when I ain't doin' anything to earn those wages. That ain't the way I was raised. You got anything else I could do to help out?"

Beaumont took a sip of the brandy-laced coffee he had at the end of every breakfast and began impatiently, "No, you can do whatever you— Wait a minute." A thoughtful look appeared on his face. "You've done very well at your job, Jim. Would you be interested in perhaps trying something other than being my bodyguard?"

Preacher gave a nonchalant shrug, but he allowed interest to flicker in his eyes. "I'll do whatever you say, boss. I always figured to move up in the world, though."

"I'll bet you did," Beaumont said with a laugh. "I have some men doing a job for me this afternoon, and I can always use another good man to help out. Plus, it might not hurt to have someone else there to look out for my interests. There are a lot of men who are willing to work for me, but that doesn't mean I can fully trust all of them."

Again, Preacher had an uneasy suspicion that Beaumont had seen through his ruse and was just toying with him. That was one more reason Preacher didn't like this damned playacting. He preferred to have everything out in the open, so that he always knew where he stood.

Beaumont seemed to be completely sincere, though, so Preacher nodded and said, "You say the word, boss, and I'll be glad to take care of whatever chore it is you got for me."

"Excellent. You go down to Red Mike's and find a man named Dugan. Tell him I said that you're to go along on the job this afternoon."

Preacher nodded again. "Red Mike's. Dugan." He didn't like the idea of paying a visit to that particular waterfront dive, since he had patronized it on previous visits to St. Louis. He looked totally different now, though, and he would try to disguise his voice a little as well.

"Oh, and Jim," Beaumont said, "you'd better take a rifle with you, and an extra pistol as well."

Preacher let a grin spread slowly over his rugged face. "Sounds to me like there's gonna be some excitement."

"Well, let's put it this way," Beaumont said. "I don't think you're going to be bored."

Then, as Preacher turned away, Beaumont added something under his breath that he would have just as soon not heard.

"And as soon as Jessie gets here, neither will I."

Red Mike's was the kind of place where a man could get his throat cut, and the only thing anybody would worry about would be not getting the blood on them. Preacher had been there before on previous trips and also with Beaumont. Until a year or so earlier, Preacher had never even heard of Shad Beaumont, and he wouldn't have guessed that the man owned Red Mike's. Preacher had always assumed that the red-bearded giant who tended bar there and gave the place its name was the proprietor. It turned out that wasn't the case, however.

Preacher tied Horse to one of the hitch rails in the

next block. It was possible that one of the regulars at the tavern might recognize the rangy gray stallion and say something about it belonging to the mountain man called Preacher. Of course, there were a lot of gray horses in St. Louis, and without Dog around, and without his buckskins and beard, Preacher thought there was a good chance he could continue pulling off the pose as Jim Donnelly.

With his long-barreled flintlock rifle cradled under his arm and a pair of double-shotted pistols tucked behind his belt, he walked into Red Mike's. All the guns didn't draw a second glance. Even at midday like this, the windowless place was gloomy inside, lit only by several candles. The air was heavy with the mingled smells of smoke, unwashed flesh, stale beer, whiskey, piss, and puke.

In other words, it smelled like civilization to Preacher.

He was used to it, though, or at least as used to it as he was going to get, so he ignored the stench and went to the bar, which was nothing more than rough-hewn planks laid across whiskey barrels. With a nod to the hulking, redbearded figure on the other side of the boards, Preacher said, "Howdy, Mike. Dugan around?"

"Who's askin'?" Red Mike rumbled. Then he squinted at Preacher and went on, "Oh, yeah, you're that new fella who works for Mr. Beaumont." The bartender's attitude changed subtly. Beaumont commanded respect, and to a lesser extent, so did the men who worked for him. Mike jerked a thumb toward a door at the back of the room. "Back yonder."

"Obliged," Preacher said with a nod.

Several men stood at the bar with cups of whiskey or

buckets of beer in front of them. A few others were at the tables scattered around the tavern. The place would be busier later on. There weren't even any serving girls in here now to deliver drinks and let themselves be pawed by the rough, drunken patrons. None of the men paid any attention to Preacher as he walked past, heading for the room at the rear of the building.

He opened the door and walked in without knocking. Instantly, the four men sitting at a rickety table passing around a bottle turned toward him and lifted pistols, cocking the weapons as they rose.

Preacher's instincts told him to duck back out the door and start blazing away with his own guns, but he checked the impulse and managed to just look startled instead.

"Take it easy there, boys," he said. "I ain't lookin' for trouble."

"What *are* you lookin' for?" one of the men asked. He was an ugly, lantern-jawed man with black hair under a tattered coonskin cap.

"I was told to ask for a fella name of Dugan."

"And who told you that?" Coonskin Cap demanded.

Preacher smiled thinly, but his eyes remained cold. "I reckon if you're Dugan, you know the answer to that as well as I do."

Coonskin Cap studied him intently for a few seconds, then said, "Yeah, this is the fella that Beaumont told us to look for. Put your guns away." As he lowered the hammer on his own pistol and slid the weapon behind his belt, he went on, "I'm Dugan."

"Donnelly," Preacher introduced himself. He hadn't known that Beaumont was going to tell the men he was coming.

"Yeah, I know." Dugan waved a bony hand at the other three men. "This is Wilkins, Schrader, and Troy."

Preacher nodded to them. He didn't want to seem overly friendly.

And the truth was, he didn't feel the least bit friendly toward these men. They were about to go out and attack a riverboat and probably murder some of the crew members, as well as helping Beaumont swindle an insurance company. Preacher had heard vaguely of insurance, and while he didn't fully grasp the concept of it, it seemed a little like a swindle to him, too. But not as bad as the sort of things Beaumont did, that was for sure.

Reminding himself that he wasn't supposed to know anything about a riverboat or a shipment of cotton, he said, "The boss didn't tell me what we're doin' this afternoon. I supposed one of you fellas would explain it to me."

"All in good time," Dugan said as he pointed to an empty chair. "We're waitin' on some other fellas. Sit down and have a drink with us, Donnelly."

Preacher sat and took the bottle when one of the other men handed it to him. The rotgut inside it was vile stuff, Preacher thought, and he knew that his tastes weren't exactly what anybody would call refined. He downed a healthy swig of it anyway and then wiped the back of his other hand across his mouth as he passed the bottle along.

Over the next half hour, three more men showed up. Dugan introduced them as Marshall, Statler, and Hellman. Once they were there, Dugan said, "All right, I reckon we can go."

Preacher was a little puzzled. Eight men, counting

him, weren't enough to take over a riverboat. They
ought to have at least twice that many for such an attack.
He couldn't very well say anything, though, since he still
wasn't supposed to know what the plan was.

"Where's your horse?" Dugan asked as they emerged
from the tavern.

"Up yonder," Preacher replied with a nod toward
the hitch rail where Horse was tied.

"What did you leave him 'way up there for?" Dugan
wanted to know.

Preacher grinned. "You think I'd leave my horse in
front of a place full of cutthroats and thieves like this?"

Dugan frowned at him for a second, then suddenly
grinned and laughed. "Yeah, you might have a point
there," he said. "I reckon we're lucky our horses are still
here."

"I believe in bein' careful," Preacher said.

He walked up to where he had left Horse, untied
the reins, and swung up into the saddle. It took only
a moment to rejoin the other men. They rode south
along the riverfront and eventually left the settlement
behind them.

It was peaceful out here, Preacher thought, with the
river flowing majestically to their left. They passed several jetties, on one of which a couple of boys were fish-
ing with cane poles. Preacher wouldn't have minded
joining them for a while if he hadn't had a job to do.
A job that would probably turn into a killing chore
before the afternoon was over, he reminded himself.

They had covered several miles, and St. Louis was
well out of sight behind them when Preacher spotted several riders coming toward them.

"That'll be the rest of the boys," Dugan said with a

note of satisfaction in his voice. "The boss didn't want us to all get together in town. Thought we might draw too much attention if we did. The boss is mighty smart that way."

Preacher couldn't argue that Shad Beaumont was smart. It was too bad the man didn't have even an ounce of scruples to go with his intelligence.

There were seven men in the second group. Dugan didn't bother telling Preacher their names. He just greeted them and then asked, "You got the boats?"

"Yeah, just like you said," one of the men replied. "Four canoes. We'll hit the boat right at the bend, where the channel brings it close to the shore." The man grinned. "Come paddlin' out there like a war party o' damn redskins."

Preacher looked around at the men. They had the look and stink of towns and cities about them. They might be tough, but they weren't frontiersmen. He doubted if any of them had ever even seen an Indian who wasn't tame. They didn't know anything about war parties.

He kept that opinion to himself, though, and instead asked Dugan, "Don't you reckon it's about time you told me what we're doin' here?"

"Yeah, I guess you're right," Dugan replied with a nod. Before he could go on, though, a high-pitched whistle came from somewhere downstream. Dugan grinned and continued, "Hear that, Donnelly?"

"Yeah. What is it?"

"Steamboat 'round the bend," Dugan said, "and when it gets here, that's when the shootin' starts."

Chapter 20

"Let me get this straight," Preacher said to Dugan as they and the other men rode hurriedly toward the bend in the Mississippi about a quarter of a mile downstream. "We're gonna take over that riverboat?"

"That's right. It's just a cargo boat, no passengers, and it's the cargo we want. We'll pick off the pilot and the captain in the pilot house by shootin' from shore, then board her, get the drop on the rest of the crew, and run the boat aground on the bank. We got wagons and drivers waitin'. Won't take long to unload all the cotton the boat's carryin' and cart it away."

Preacher let out a low whistle. "That'll be worth a pretty penny, I reckon. Did Mr. Beaumont put you up to this?"

"Damn right. I told you he was smart."

Preacher didn't say anything about the cotton already belonging to Beaumont. He didn't know if Dugan was aware of that part of the scheme and didn't want to raise even a hint of suspicion that he might know about it.

The steamboat's whistle sounded again, closer this time. It was almost at the bend when Preacher and the other men reached the four canoes pulled up on the bank.

"Three men to a canoe!" Dugan ordered as they dismounted. "Donnelly, you'll be the fourth man in the first canoe. Troy and I will stay here on shore and pick off the captain and the pilot."

"I'm a mighty good shot with a rifle, if I do say so myself," Preacher said. "You might want me to stay here with you, Dugan."

"Do what I told you!" the leader of the robbers snapped. "Unless you want to back out of the deal completely, and I'll tell the boss if you do."

"Take it easy, take it easy. I'll go along with your orders. I was just tryin' to help."

"Then move! Here comes that damned riverboat!"

It was true. The big sidewheeler was coming into view around the bend, close to the near shore because of the way the channel ran. The would-be robbers hurriedly climbed into the canoes and shoved off. Preacher found himself right up front in the lead canoe, the most dangerous spot to be when the attack got underway.

He didn't care about that. He knew that the men working for Jessie and Cleve had to be somewhere close by, and no doubt they would strike at any moment. In the meantime, though, the pilot and captain of the riverboat were in deadly danger.

Preacher had snatched up one of the paddles in the bottom of the canoe, laid the flintlock across the narrow boat in front of him, and dug the paddle in the water like the other men. Their efforts sent the canoe cutting across the river's surface toward the steamboat. Preacher saw the name *Harry Fulton* painted on the boat's bow, with *St. Louis, Mo.* underneath it. Smoke billowed from the top of the tall, round smokestack that ran down to the firebox in the vessel's engine room. The whistle blew again, loud enough now to hurt the ears, and Preacher saw the big paddle wheels on the sides of the boat suddenly lurch to a halt. Somebody on board must have spotted the river pirates approaching and ordered the engines stopped.

It was too late. The boat's momentum carried it forward against the current for a moment as it slowed. The canoes arrowed toward it.

Preacher dropped his paddle at his feet, snatched up his rifle, and stood up as he turned back toward the shore. One of the other men in the canoe yelled, "Hey! What the hell do you think you're—"

The canoe rocked back and forth, thrown off balance by Preacher's movements, but he ignored that and drew a bead on Dugan as he eared back the flintlock's hammer. Neither Dugan nor Troy had fired yet at the pilot house. Preacher didn't give Dugan the chance to do so. He pressed the trigger.

The flintlock roared and kicked against his shoulder. Fifty yards away on shore, Dugan's coonskin cap leaped in the air as the ball from Preacher's rifle smashed into his head and dropped him like a rock.

The other men in the canoe were shouting at him now, some of them yelling curses while others warned him not to upset the little craft. Preacher saw the man nearest him clawing at the butt of a pistol behind his belt and didn't hesitate. He drove the butt of his rifle into the center of the man's face as hard as he could and felt bone crunch under the impact.

At that moment, rifles began to bang on the far shore. Powder smoke spurted from a clump of trees that grew down close to the water. On the near bank, Troy went down, still without firing a shot. Preacher heard the hum of rifle balls passing through the air not far from his head and put one foot on the side of the canoe, shoving off with it as he leaped out into the river. That tipped the canoe over behind him. The men in it spilled out into the water.

Preacher hauled as much air into his lungs as he could before the Mississippi closed over him. He dove deep and kicked hard to get away from the area where the shots from the far shore were cutting into the water. Jessie and Cleve might have warned their men to try not to kill him, but in the heat of battle, sometimes it was hard to be careful. He stayed under as long as he could, then began kicking toward the surface.

That wasn't easy, since he was fully dressed and weighed down with two pistols and a rifle, but he wasn't willing to give up any of the weapons if he didn't have to. His legs were powerful enough to propel him to the surface. As his head broke out into the air, he gratefully gulped down a breath. That eased the pounding inside his skull.

He saw the *Harry Fulton* off to his left, now drifting slowly downstream with its engines stopped. Two of the canoes were overturned, and the other one appeared to be sinking, probably shot full of holes. Several bodies floated in the river near the canoes. Two of Beaumont's men were trying to swim to the near shore.

More shots doomed their efforts. They jerked in

the water and then slowed as reddish streamers of blood drifted away from them. The men came to a stop and began to float facedown.

That left Preacher as the only apparent survivor of the group that had tried to take over the riverboat. He swam slowly toward the *Harry Fulton* as a flat-bottomed skiff with several men in it pushed off from the far shore. The men paddled out to rendezvous with the riverboat.

Preacher was closer and got there first. Three men were waiting for him on deck—the captain and a couple of crewmen, all of them holding pistols. They covered him as he tossed his empty rifle onto the deck and then caught hold of one of the fenders and used it to help him climb on board.

"Don't try anything, you thieving bastard!" the captain ordered.

Preacher lay there for a moment, catching his breath as the water streamed off his sodden clothing. When he could talk, he looked up and said, "You may not've noticed, Cap'n, but I reckon I saved your life a few minutes ago. One of those fellas on the shore was drawin' a bead on you when I blew a hole in his head."

The captain looked confused. "But I thought you were one of the river pirates!"

"So did they," Preacher said.

The skiff reached the riverboat. One of the men in it called, "Howdy! Looked like you needed a little help there!"

The captain nodded toward Preacher and told his men, "Keep him covered," then turned to the men on the skiff and went on, "Indeed we did, sir! We are much obliged to you. Did you just happen to be traveling along and saw those scoundrels attacking us?"

"Nope." The man in the skiff raised a pistol and pointed it at the captain. "We're here for the same thing they were. Now put this boat ashore so we can start unloading that cotton you've got on deck."

The captain of the *Harry Fulton* stared goggle-eyed down the barrel of the pistol that menaced him. His mouth opened and closed a couple of times before he managed to say, "You're pirates, too?"

"That's right," the man in the skiff said. "And there are a dozen men on shore with rifles pointing at you and your men right now, Captain. You'd better do as you're told."

For a moment, the captain's bulldog-like face looked like he was going to put up a fight. But then his shoulders sagged in defeat. "Are you going to kill me and my crew?" he asked in a dull voice.

"Nope. All we want is the cotton."

"Very well." The captain motioned for his men to drop their guns, then cupped his hands around his mouth and called up to the man in the pilot house, "Ahead one-quarter! Put her ashore!"

Preacher had watched the exchange with interest. He was glad the men working for Jessie weren't going to murder the captain and crew. Now as he stood up, the man who seemed to be the leader said, "You're the fella we were supposed to watch out for, aren't you?"

Preacher was relieved that Jessie and Cleve hadn't told these men who he really was. The longer he could keep that information under wraps, the better. He nodded and said, "That's right. You came mighty near to hittin' me with some of those shots, too."

The man shrugged. "Hard to be too careful in the middle of a shootin' scrape. And you're not dead, are you?"

"No, I reckon not."

The riverboat captain glared at him. "You double-crossed the men you were with? That makes you even worse than them, and I don't care if you *did* save my life!"

"Think whatever you want, mister," Preacher snapped. He picked up his empty rifle. Along with his pistols, it would need a thorough cleaning and drying before he tried to use it again. "Just do what you're told and be grateful you're alive." He paused and then added truthfully, "I am."

It didn't take all that long to run the boat aground and unload the cargo. Some of Jessie's men had crossed the river before the attack even began and gotten the drop on the drivers Beaumont had hired. Those drivers had been sent packing, and they had been glad to be given the chance to flee and save their lives. So it was Jessie's men who brought the wagons to the riverbank and unloaded the cotton onto them. Then they drove off, taking the valuable cargo with them.

Preacher didn't know what Jessie planned to do with the cotton. She would probably sell it, although she would have to be careful not to let Beaumont get wind of the transaction. Preacher figured she was smart enough to be able to handle that.

Some of Jessie's men took the horses left behind by Dugan and the others. As Preacher got ready to mount up on Horse and ride back to St. Louis, the man who'd led Jessie's group asked, "What are you going to do now, mister? Go back to Beaumont's place?"

"That's right."

"What will you tell him?"

"The truth . . . some of it, anyway. We got bush-whacked. I'm the only one who got away."

Preacher had checked to make sure that was true. All of Beaumont's men were dead. Their bodies had been hauled out of the river and left on the bank in a grisly display.

"You reckon he's gonna believe that?"

"He won't have any reason not to," Preacher said, although he expected that Beaumont might be a little suspicious of his story. Beaumont wouldn't be able to prove any differently though.

"Well, I suppose it's your business. Seems to me like you're playin' a mighty dangerous game though."

Preacher just shrugged. The man was right. If Beaumont found out the truth, things could get bad in a hurry. But that was a risk Preacher was prepared to run. The danger had always been there, right from the start.

He said so long, swung up into the saddle, and rode north along the river. He had gone about half a mile when he heard a sudden flurry of shots behind him. Reining Horse to a stop, Preacher hipped around in the saddle to look back in that direction. He couldn't see anything. The bends of the river and the trees that grew along its banks hid the riverboat from his view.

But that was about where the shots were coming from, he realized as the reports continued, a steady, ominous booming that might have been mistaken for thunder if the skies hadn't been clear except for some high, fluffy white clouds.

Grim lines formed trenches in Preacher's cheeks as he listened to the shots die away. He turned Horse around and watched as black smoke began to rise in the sky, blooming and billowing. He dug his heels into Horse's flanks and sent the stallion racing back along the shore of the river.

As Preacher came around a bend a few minutes later, he saw that the riverboat had drifted away from the shore and into the middle of the river. It was burning, flames leaping up at the base of the column of smoke. The blaze stretched from one end of the vessel to the other, and it was burning so fiercely that Preacher knew the boat was doomed.

He knew as well that there was no one left alive on board to fight the fire. Those shots he'd heard had been Jessie's men gunning down the captain and crew. He didn't know why they would have done such a thing, but he was sure that's what had happened.

The men were all gone now, putting distance between them and the murders they had committed. There was nothing Preacher could do to stop them. It was too late.

Too late to do anything except turn Horse around and start again toward St. Louis with a bitter, sour taste filling his mouth.

Chapter 21

It was late enough by the time Preacher got back to the settlement that he didn't go to Jessie's Place. He headed straight for Beaumont's house instead.

When he got there and rode around back to the carriage house, he found Lorenzo waiting out there with a worried frown on his face.

"Something wrong?" Preacher asked as he swung down from the saddle.

"You damn right they's somethin' wrong, boy," the old man replied. "The boss is so mad he's fixin' to chew nails. Somethin' happened today whilst you was gone. I don't know what it was, but it was bad enough to make him half-crazy. I got my black ass outta there 'fore he decided to shoot it off."

"Nobody tried to kill the boss, did they? It's my job to stop things like that from happenin', but he's the one who told me to go do whatever I wanted to this afternoon."

"Naw, ever'thin' was fine until a little while ago. I brung Miss Jessie over here, and I reckon her and the boss had theirselves a fine ol' time. But when I got back from takin' her back to her house, there was a fella here I didn't know. I heard Mr. Beaumont yellin' at him, and then the fella, he went scurryin' outta here like the Devil his ownself was after him." Lorenzo grunted. "I reckon that's about the size of it, too. When I tried to ask the boss what was wrong, he 'bout bit my head off."

Lorenzo frowned as he looked at Preacher, who had started to unsaddle Horse.

"Say, boy, you look like you been dunked in the river."

"I have been," Preacher said. "And I've got somethin' to tell the boss that ain't gonna make him happy. I got a feelin' he's already heard about it, though, from the way you said he's been actin'."

One of those drivers who'd been chased off from the wagons must have come back here and told Beaumont what had happened, Preacher thought. The man might not have known all the details, but he would have been well aware that the theft of the cotton from the riverboat hadn't gone as planned. That by itself would have been enough to cause an explosion of Beaumont's hair-trigger temper.

Preacher took his time about tending to Horse, as if he were reluctant to go into the house. As a matter of fact, he was, but not because he was afraid of Beaumont, even though that's probably what Lorenzo thought was going on. He was reluctant because he thought that if he came face to face with Beaumont, he might pull out his knife and bury it in the man's chest just to end this terrible business right here and now.

All the way back to St. Louis, Preacher had struggled to come to grips with the fact that some of the blood spilled from the captain and the crew of the *Harry*

Fulton was on his hands. If he hadn't come to St. Louis and started this business of posing as Jim Donnelly, he wouldn't have thrown in with Jessie and Cleve. He wouldn't have gotten stuck in the middle of a war between the two of them and Beaumont.

Preacher knew the attack set up by Jessie and Cleve would have taken place today whether he was involved or not. But he had thought long and hard about it, and the only reason he could see for the murders of the captain and crew was to keep his secret safe. The drivers with the wagons who worked for Beaumont had been let go with their lives because they had never seen him and didn't know he'd betrayed Dugan and the other river pirates. But the captain and crew *had* seen him. Somebody, either Jessie or Cleve, had ordered that they be killed and the riverboat burned just to make sure there were no survivors who could talk.

All to keep Preacher safe so they could continue using him against Beaumont.

That knowledge was a damned bitter pill to swallow. Preacher didn't really blame himself for those murders. He hadn't pulled the triggers or set the riverboat on fire, but his presence had escalated things to the point that someone believed wholesale slaughter was necessary.

"You goin' in there?" Lorenzo asked.

"Got to," Preacher said. "Mr. Beaumont's expectin' me back."

Lorenzo folded his arms across his chest. "Well, *I'm* stayin' out here with the horses, where it's safe."

"Probably ain't a bad idea," Preacher said as he walked through the open double doors of the barn and started toward the house.

As he stepped in through the back door, he heard a crash from somewhere upstairs. It sounded like someone had just thrown something against the wall. There was another crash as he went up the stairs.

Beaumont was so mad he was throwing things, Preacher thought.

When he reached the upstairs hallway, he heard ranting and cursing coming through an open door at the end of the corridor. That was Beaumont's bedroom, Preacher knew, although he had never actually set foot in there. He approached the door carefully. It was possible Beaumont had a gun in there, and if he was loco enough, he might take a shot at anybody who poked his head inside.

Preacher stopped about a dozen feet from the door and called, "Hey, boss! It's me, Donnelly!"

Beaumont's cursing stopped abruptly. A second later, he appeared in the doorway, his collar askew, his hair disheveled, and his face flushed dark red with rage. Shards of broken crockery littered the floor behind him.

"Donnelly!" he roared. "What the hell happened downriver? I sent you to look out for my interests!"

Beaumont didn't have a gun in his hand, so Preacher came closer. "We were ambushed, boss. Riflemen were waitin' in the trees on the far bank when we tried to stop that riverboat. Their first volley wiped out Dugan and most of the rest o' the boys before we even knew what was goin' on, and then they picked off the rest of the bunch."

Beaumont stared at him and said, "But not you. You're still alive."

"Only because they figured I was dead, I reckon,"

Preacher said. "I can swim pretty good, so when the canoe I was in tipped over, I dove as deep in the river as I could go and swam underwater for a good ways. Those bushwhackers must've thought I was either hit by one of their shots, or drowned, or both. When I come up for air, I could still hear some shootin', but they weren't aimin' at me."

Beaumont's upper lip curled in a sneer. "So you hid like a coward while everyone else was killed?"

Preacher allowed some anger into his voice as he replied, "I didn't see how it'd do a damned bit of good to get myself killed, too. There were more'n a dozen of those bastards, maybe as many as twenty or twenty-five. One man wouldn't have stood a chance against them."

Beaumont glared at him for a moment longer, then finally shrugged and said, "I suppose you're right about that. What happened after the ambush?"

"I found a place downstream where a tree fell over in the water and used it for cover while I watched what was goin' on. Some of those fellas who'd been layin' in wait for us paddled out to the riverboat in a skiff and took it over. They had the captain at gunpoint, so he had to do what they said. He put the boat ashore, just like you planned for Dugan and the rest of us to do, and some wagons came up and they unloaded the cargo onto 'em."

Beaumont nodded. "I talked to one of the drivers I hired. He said some men with guns got the drop on them and stole the wagons from them. That's all he knew, because they had to either get out of there or be killed. I was hoping that not everything had gone wrong . . . but I had a feeling that it had."

"Sure enough," Preacher agreed. "Dugan and the

rest of the men dead, the cotton gone . . . and that ain't all of it."

"What else could there be?" Beaumont snapped.

Grim-faced, Preacher said, "After the wagons left with the cotton, those bushwhackers murdered everybody on the riverboat and set it on fire."

Beaumont just stared at him for a long moment, as if he couldn't believe what Preacher had just told him. He seemed genuinely shocked. Finally, he muttered, "My God. Why would they do such a thing?"

"Clean slate, I reckon," Preacher said with a shrug. "No witnesses left behind."

"I suppose. I've never worried about anyone getting hurt if they got in my way, but to wipe out a whole riverboat crew like that in cold blood . . ." Beaumont's voice trailed off as he shook his head.

Beaumont might like to believe that was worse than anything he had done in the past, but that wasn't the case, Preacher knew. Beaumont was responsible for scores of deaths, and he wouldn't hesitate to order multiple murders if they served his purposes.

But clearly he wasn't the only one who could be that ruthless.

"You have any idea who would do such a thing, boss?" Preacher asked.

Beaumont shook his head. "No, but I'm going to find out. Whoever they are, they can't keep something this big a secret for very long. I'll find out, and when I do . . . they'll pay. By God, they'll pay."

"If there's anything I can do to help . . ."

Beaumont came forward out of the room and clapped a hand on Preacher's shoulder. "Don't worry, Jim, I'll let you know. I'm sorry I sent you into that trap."

"You didn't know somebody was double-crossin' you."

"No." An insane light glinted in Beaumont's eyes. "And that's exactly what happened. Someone knew my plans and hired those men to steal the cotton right out from under me. That's the only way it could have happened."

Preacher didn't want to steer Beaumont's thoughts in that direction, but there wasn't much he could do to stop them. He could try to muddle the situation, though.

"Dugan or one of those other fellas could've talked too much in a tavern about what they were gonna do," he suggested. "Some fellas get a little too much whiskey in 'em, they don't know when to shut up."

"I suppose that's possible." Beaumont rubbed his jaw and frowned in thought. "And if that's what happened, they've already paid for their carelessness with their lives. But I'm not convinced, Jim. I think whoever planned this may still be out there, plotting against me."

There was more truth to that statement than Beaumont knew. He had all sorts of enemies who wanted to ruin him.

Beaumont put a hand on Preacher's shoulder again. Preacher managed not to pull away in revulsion. "I'm going to need your help looking into this. You and Lorenzo may be the only ones I can trust. And if there's something you want to do for me, Jim . . ."

"You name it, boss," Preacher said, trying not to be too obvious about the fact that he had to force the words out.

"Whenever I find out who's to blame for this, I'm going to give you the privilege of killing him . . . or her."

Chapter 22

Preacher didn't like the sound of that. Beaumont might already suspect Jessie.

But a second later, he went on, "Some of those whores at Jessie's Place are always sneaking around. There's no telling what they might have overheard. I don't trust any of them, especially that bitch Cassandra."

Preacher's jaw tightened. He suppressed his anger and said, "I still think it's more likely to have been Dugan or one of his men to blame."

"Leave the thinking to me," Beaumont chuckled. "I'm glad you survived, Jim. I've come to depend on you."

"I ain't done all that much."

"You saved my life, that first night. And you've done everything I've asked of you since then. Together we'll get to the bottom of this. In the meanwhile, why don't you go get cleaned up? Those clothes are probably still pretty clammy after you got dunked in the river like that."

"They're a mite damp," Preacher admitted. "Are you goin' out tonight, boss?"

"I think I could use a few drinks. We'll go to Dupree's later."

Preacher nodded. "I'll be ready."

He went to the servants' quarters in the rear of the house. He and Lorenzo were the only ones who lived there—Beaumont's cook and housekeeper just came in during the day—and the old black man wasn't there at the moment. He was probably still lying low, out in the carriage house. Preacher peeled out of the damp clothes and washed up, then dressed in fresh duds. He had lost his hat in the river and would have to see about getting a new one, but that could wait.

Then he began disassembling, drying, and cleaning his guns, spreading the pieces out on the bed as he did so. It was the sort of work he enjoyed, and he could lose himself in it, not really needing to think as he went about the process that he had carried out hundreds, maybe even thousands of times in his life.

Today, though, he couldn't keep unwelcome thoughts from crowding into his head. Most of them had to do with the wanton murder of the riverboat crew, but he also couldn't help but think of Jessie.

Had she actually ordered that slaughter? That seemed to be the most likely answer. She had the most to gain, at least potentially, by taking whatever steps were necessary to protect Preacher's identity. The fact that she was a beautiful woman didn't really mean anything.

Preacher had known beautiful women in the past who had turned out to be as treacherous and deadly as black widow spiders.

By the time he was finished with the guns and had them in good working order again, he still didn't have any answers to the questions that plagued him, but he knew he wouldn't get answers until he had a chance to talk to Jessie again . . . and maybe not even then, if she chose to lie to him.

Beaumont seemed to be his usual charming, affable self again by the time they were ready to go to Dupree's that evening. All traces of the furious, wild-eyed lunatic he had been earlier in the day had vanished.

As they went out to the carriage, which a still-nervous Lorenzo had pulled around to the drive in front of the house, Beaumont said, "We'll be stopping by Mrs. Hobson's house on the way to Dupree's."

Preacher nodded. He knew that Mrs. Luella Hobson was a wealthy widow Beaumont sometimes squired around town. She was the short, curvaceous blonde Preacher had seen with Beaumont the first night he'd watched his quarry visit Dupree's. He suspected that Beaumont was planning to swindle her out of her money at some point, and in the meantime, she was a woman with quite healthy—and sometimes unusual—appetites, according to the hints Beaumont had dropped.

As the carriage rolled through the streets of St. Louis, Lorenzo said quietly to Preacher, who sat beside him on the driver's seat, "Appears the boss ain't foamin' at the mouth no more."

"I reckon he's still plenty upset about what happened this afternoon, but you're right, he ain't out of his head about it no more."

"What 'zactly *did* happen this afternoon?" Lorenzo asked.

Preacher glanced over at the driver. "How much do you know about the boss's business?"

"More'n I want to, sometimes!"

"Then you probably don't want to know about this," Preacher said. "Let's just say he had something planned for this afternoon, and it went bad wrong."

"I believe it. I seen the boss lose his temper before, but this was one o' the worst times."

Lorenzo wouldn't think that if he had seen what Beaumont did to Casey, Preacher mused.

They arrived at Luella Hobson's house, and while Beaumont was inside picking up the attractive blond widow, Preacher asked, "What did the late Mr. Hobson do for a livin'?"

"He owned a bank," Lorenzo replied. "I never did see how a fella could make a livin' holdin' money for other folks. I'd be too tempted to take off for the tall and uncut with all that cash. That's why I keep all my money hid in a place nobody knows about 'ceptin' me."

Preacher laughed. "Bankers have been known to do that very thing. I don't have to worry about that, myself."

"You don't use banks, neither?"

"Never had enough money to bother puttin' it in one. Bein' a fella like me, I don't expect I ever will."

That was a true statement, in the midst of all the lies Preacher had been telling lately. As long as he had enough money to pick up a few supplies every now and then, that was all he needed. He didn't support anyone except himself and Horse and Dog, and all three of them could do just fine living off the land if they had to.

At least, that would be true again once they all got away from this damned town, Preacher thought.

When they reached Dupree's, the manager showed Beaumont to his usual table. Mrs. Hobson clung to Beaumont's arm so that her ample breasts in a gown with a low neckline pressed against his sleeve. She laughed too loud, and her smile was a little too bright. Preacher figured that deep down, she was a lonely woman, and having a handsome rogue like Shad Beaumont pay attention to her probably meant the world to her. She would be easy pickin's, once Beaumont finally decided to go ahead and pluck her clean.

Preacher sat at a table nearby to keep an eye on Beaumont and watch out for any trouble that might come their way. He had a mug of beer that he sipped from time to time. During the evening, a number of people approached Beaumont's table, but they were only interested in saying hello and currying favor with a rich, powerful man. Beaumont sat back like a king holding court and received them. Mrs. Hobson preened at his side.

They had been there about an hour when Cleve strolled into the place. Preacher saw the gambler come in the door. Cleve's gaze swept over the room. His eyes paused just for a second as they passed over Preacher, and then Cleve continued looking around the room as if he hadn't even noticed the mountain man.

In that brief second, though, Preacher had seen a flash of satisfaction in Cleve's eyes. The day had gone well, at least from the gambler's point of view.

Cleve found an empty seat at one of the poker tables and soon was engrossed in the game. Preacher wanted to talk to him, but he didn't see any way of doing so without running the risk of provoking Beaumont's suspicions.

After a while, Beaumont emptied the last of the brandy from the bottle that had been brought to him when he arrived. Preacher saw that and got to his feet.

"Need another, boss?" he asked.

"One of the girls can bring it," Beaumont replied offhandedly.

"They look like they're all busy," Preacher said. "No need to wait. I'll fetch it."

He went to the bar, which was crowded and busy. While he stood there waiting to ask one of the bartenders for another bottle of brandy, Cleve folded his hand and stood up, saying, "I believe I'll take a break, gentlemen." The gambler gathered up his winnings and ambled over to the bar, where he stood next to Preacher.

"Everything went well," Cleve said under his breath, quietly enough so that no one could hear except Preacher. "Good work, my friend."

"I got to talk to you."

"Not here. Not in front of Beaumont. Later, when he goes to Jessie's."

"He ain't said anything about goin' to Jessie's."

A smirk tugged at Cleve's mouth. "Trust me. He'll pay the place a visit later."

Preacher didn't know about that, but Cleve seemed to know what he was talking about. The bartender came up then, so they couldn't talk any more. Preacher asked for another bottle of Beaumont's special brandy, and the bartender handed it over without hesitation. Preacher took the bottle back to Beaumont's table.

Luella Hobson was already drunk, Preacher saw.

He wasn't quite sure why Beaumont continued to ply her with liquor. She was already at the point where she would do anything he wanted her to. She probably would have, even without the brandy, just to keep him interested in her.

He understood Beaumont's motives a little better once the carriage reached Luella's house a hour later. Beaumont called from inside the vehicle, "Give me a hand here, Jim."

The poor woman was as drunk as she could be, Preacher saw as he helped Beaumont lift her from the carriage. "Take her inside," Beaumont ordered. "I'm in no mood for her usual games tonight."

"That's why you kept pourin' that brandy down her throat?"

Beaumont's face hardened. "Why I do things is none of your business."

"Yeah, you're right," Preacher said. "Sorry, boss." He got an arm around Luella's waist and helped her make her unsteady way up the walk.

"Gonna . . . gonna make you so happy, Shad," she mumbled. "You'll see . . . do anything you want . . . you can have me . . . any way you like."

She leaned heavily against him so that her breasts rubbed on his arm. Preacher gritted his teeth. He had never cared for drunken, sloppy women.

"I ain't Mr. Beaumont," he told her as they reached the door. "You go on inside, Mrs. Hobson, and get some sleep. You need it."

She was going to be sick as a dog come morning, no matter what she did now, Preacher knew. Damn, but he hated this place! He needed to be back in the mountains, where folks didn't carry on like this, and if you had enemies, you fought them out in the open.

"You got a housekeeper?" he asked.

"Housekeeper? What do you need . . . a housekeeper for?"

Preacher knew he wasn't going to be able to get a straight answer out of her. He pounded on the door instead of trying to ask her anything else. After a few minutes, someone jerked open the door, and a heavyset black woman carrying a lantern peered out.

"What in heaven's name—Oh, lawsy mercy, what's wrong with Miz Hobson?"

"She's had too much to drink," Preacher said. "You work for her?"

"Reckon you could say that, since her husband done bought me five years ago afore he died."

Preacher practically shoved Luella into the slave's arms. "Well, you know how to look after her, then. Good night."

"Wait just a minute! Is that Mr. Beaumont's carriage I see parked there in the road?"

"Yeah."

"You tell him he ought to leave poor Miz Luella alone. She just a poor, lonely woman since her husband up and died, and he takin' advantage o' her."

"Sure," Preacher said. "I'll tell him."

The woman looked at him and sighed. "No, you won't. I know better."

"You just take good care of her. Maybe things'll get better."

"Not as long as that Shad Beaumont around. And you can tell him I said so!"

A look of fear came over the woman's face, though, as soon as the defiant words were out of her mouth.

"Don't worry," Preacher said. "I ain't gonna tell him that, either."

He went back to the carriage and swung up onto the driver's seat next to Lorenzo. Beaumont leaned out the window and asked, "Any problems?"

"None to speak of," Preacher said.

"Fine. Lorenzo, drive to Jessie's Place."

It looked like Cleve had been right about Beaumont going to Jessie's later. Preacher's gut told him this might not be good.

The carriage drew up in front of the big house a short time later. Beaumont climbed out of the vehicle as Preacher jumped down from the driver's box. "Keep your eyes open tonight," Beaumont warned as they went up the walk to the door. "That trouble this afternoon tells me that my enemies are getting bolder. They're not afraid to move against me now. We may be in for a war, Jim. Are you up for that?"

"I'm up for whatever I need to be up for," Preacher said.

"I hope so. Because even though they've started the war—whoever *they* are—I intend to finish it."

Brutus met them at the door. "Mr. Beaumont! Good to see you as always, sir." He turned his head and gave Preacher a curt nod. "Donnelly."

The freedman was treating him the same way he always had, and that was good, Preacher thought. He didn't know how much Jessie and Cleve had told Brutus about what was going on. It seemed likely, though, that Brutus was part of their campaign against Beaumont.

As he handed his hat and cape to Brutus, Beaumont said, "Tell Miss Jessie I'm here, will you?"

"Of course, sir. I—"

"Shad!" Brutus didn't have to tell Jessie, because she was coming along the hall toward them, a brilliant smile on her face. Preacher looked at her and wondered how a woman so beautiful could order the cold-blooded murder of approximately two dozen men, then reminded himself that evil sometimes came in pretty packages. Jessie went on to Beaumont, "I didn't expect to see you again so soon."

"I had a . . . business reversal this afternoon, and I thought spending some time here might be just the thing to lift my spirits," he said.

Jessie stepped up to him and ran her hand up and down his upper arm. She hadn't glanced even once in Preacher's direction. She was an icy-nerved gal, he had to give her credit for that.

"I'm sure we can find something pleasant to do that will make you forget all about any business problems, Shad," she murmured.

Beaumont shook his head. "No offense, Jessie. You know how I feel about you. But I think your charms aren't exactly what I need tonight."

"No?" she asked with a look of surprise. Her tongue came out of her mouth and ran enticingly along her full upper lip. "Are you sure? You know I'm . . . very good at what I do."

"Yes, but I had something else in mind. Some*one* else." Beaumont's right hand slowly clenched into a fist. "I thought I'd go up and see Cassandra. I had such a lovely evening with her the last time."

Chapter 23

Preacher was standing behind and to one side of Beaumont. When Beaumont said Casey's name, Preacher felt a wave of cold hatred go through him. The hell with this, he thought. His hand moved toward the pistol tucked behind his belt.

Jessie's eyes widened in apprehension as they flicked toward Preacher. He saw pleading in them, pleading for him not to give the game away. Beaumont must have been too caught up in the evil thoughts filling his head to notice Jessie's reaction, because he didn't look around at Preacher.

With a supreme effort of will, Preacher pulled his hand away from his gun before he ever touched the butt of the pistol. He felt the muscles in his arm tremble from the suppressed urge to kill Beaumont.

He wasn't made this way. The whole plan had been a mistake. He could see that now, but unfortunately, he wasn't the only one involved. The lives of Jessie and Cleve might well depend on him carrying on with the masquerade.

Relief shone in Jessie's eyes as she saw that he wasn't going to kill Beaumont right here and now.

"That's not a good idea, Shad," she said. "Cassandra is . . . indisposed."

"Oh? I'm disappointed." Beaumont sounded like he could barely comprehend the idea that someone would dare to disappoint him.

"It'll be better if you come upstairs with me," Jessie went on as she rested her hand on Beaumont's arm again.

"I suppose." Beaumont turned to look at Preacher. "We'll be here for a while, Donnelly. You can feel free to amuse yourself. After the day you've had, I'm sure you can use some diversion."

"Sure, boss," Preacher said.

Jessie moved to link her arm with Beaumont's, and for a second, he couldn't see her face but Preacher could. She mouthed the words *thank you* at him, then turned to go arm in arm toward the stairs with Beaumont.

Preacher heard laughter and talking from the parlor and knew he could go in there and pick any of the girls who were available to take upstairs. Right now, however, that wasn't what he wanted. He waited until Jessie and Beaumont had disappeared up the elegant, curving staircase, then turned to look for Brutus.

He didn't have to search. The big man must have been somewhere close by, waiting for his opportunity. He was already there in the hallway. He rumbled, "Mr. Cleve wants to talk to you."

"And I want to talk to him," Preacher said.

"He's in one of the card rooms. This way."

Brutus led Preacher to one of the small rooms that

opened off the corridor. Inside was a round table covered with green felt, lit by a lamp that hung from the ceiling above its center. The light was concentrated on the table and the chairs around it, leaving the rest of the room cloaked in shadows.

Only one of the chairs was occupied at the moment. Cleve sat at the table laying out a hand of solitaire. As Preacher and Brutus came in, he used his hands to sweep the cards together and left them in an untidy pile in front of him.

"I told you Beaumont would come here," Cleve said with a smile as he looked up at Preacher.

Brutus closed the door and remained in the room, leaning against the panel and crossing his arms over his massive chest. That was one more indication that he was aware of the plans Jessie and Cleve had made, as well as Preacher's involvement in them. Cleve wouldn't have allowed him to stay, otherwise.

"You figured he was so mad over what happened on the river he'd have to let it out by thrashin' some poor whore?" Preacher said.

"That's right. Who did he choose? Not Cassandra again, I hope. She's just now getting back to something approaching normal."

Preacher pulled out one of the chairs and sat down at the table without waiting for an invitation. "That's who he picked," he said, "but Jessie wouldn't allow it. She went with him herself."

Cleve had been idly straightening the cards. At Preacher's words, he stopped and frowned. "Jessie?" he murmured. He started to get up from his chair, then sank back down and went on, "Nothing to worry about. She won't let him get away with any ugly behavior."

"How's she gonna stop him if he loses control of himself?"

"She'll kill him," Cleve replied with a shrug. "We'd rather keep him alive, of course, so that we can ruin a few more of his plans and steal some more profits out from under him, but if she has to, she'll cut his throat, or perhaps blow his balls off with that little pistol she carries. That would be most appropriate. The one thing she *won't* do . . . is let him hurt her again."

"So he *did* whale on her before, the way he did on Cassandra?"

"That's right. What do you think turned her against him?"

"I don't know. Greed?"

Cleve shook his head. "Jessie's not a greedy person. Me, on the other hand . . ." His voice trailed off into a laugh.

"What does she want, then, if it's not the money?"

"Revenge? Power? Simply to be free of Beaumont, which she knows she never truly will be as long as he's alive?" Cleve went back to straightening the cards, picking up the deck in his long, slender fingers and tapping it on the table to even the edges. "I'd say that all of those things play a part in her actions."

"That's why she was willin' to have that riverboat crew murdered so they couldn't tell anybody about me double-crossin' Beaumont?"

"You found out about that?" Cleve seemed surprised. "The men we hired weren't supposed to take care of that part of the job until after you were gone."

"They didn't wait quite long enough," Preacher said in a grim, flinty voice. "I heard the shots and went back, saw the riverboat burnin'."

Cleve shrugged again. "Well, you have to admit, it was effective."

"Was the fire Jessie's idea?"

"What?" Cleve shook his head. "Jessie didn't know anything about that, Preacher. It was all my idea."

Preacher felt relief go through him. He hadn't wanted to believe that Jessie was capable of such a thing, but truly, he didn't really know.

"You didn't think Jessie came up with that, did you?" Cleve went on. The gambler shook his head. "Even if it had occurred to her that your secret needed to be protected, she wouldn't have given the order for those riverboat men to be killed."

"Then why did you?" Preacher asked.

Cleve sat up straighter. "Because someone had to! When I threw in with Jessie on this, I knew I might have to make some of the difficult decisions that she couldn't make."

"Like murderin' innocent men?"

"Beaumont has murdered innocent men. At least, he's been responsible for it, many times. And you saw what he did to Cassandra. A man like that is worse than an animal, because he *knows* what he's doing. He just doesn't care."

Preacher couldn't argue with any of that. He knew Cleve was right about how bad Shad Beaumont was. He still wasn't sure that justified sinking to Beaumont's level.

There was no way to go back and change things now though. He just said, "I don't like it," and left it at that.

Cleve chuckled. "Then it's a good thing you're not in charge here, isn't it?"

Preacher let that go, although it wasn't easy, and said, "What's next?"

"Jessie and I haven't decided yet. We were thinking that some of Beaumont's warehouses might just happen to burn down."

Preacher shook his head. "You do somethin' like that, you'll risk burnin' down the whole town, includin' this place. You don't want to take that chance. You'd be better off cleanin' out those warehouses instead and movin' the goods somewhere else."

"That would involve killing the guards. I thought you were opposed to that much bloodshed."

"I ain't gonna lose any sleep over somebody who takes money from Beaumont, knowin' the sort of varmint he is," Preacher said. "Anyway, you wouldn't have to kill the guards, just knock 'em out."

Cleve looked across the table at him. "Do you know anyone stealthy enough to accomplish something like that?"

"I might," Preacher said. "I just might."

Cleve thought about it for a moment and then began to nod. "I'll talk it over with Jessie, but it's not a bad idea. That way the merchandise isn't destroyed. The profits from it go into our coffers instead. Which makes me wonder . . . just how big a share are *you* expecting out of all this, Preacher?"

"I ain't all that interested in the money, either. I'm after a different payoff."

"Making Shad Beaumont's life a living hell and then killing him?" Cleve guessed.

Putting it like that made it sound even worse, Preacher thought, and yet that was exactly the goal that had brought him to St. Louis. Never again, he vowed. From here on out, whenever he had a score to settle with a man, he would do it right out in the open.

"Let's just figure out which of those warehouses you want to clean out first," he said.

Three nights later, in the dark of the moon, Preacher stole through an alley near the riverfront. He had a bandanna tied over the lower half of his face like a damned highwayman, which he didn't like, but it was necessary to conceal his identity because it was possible someone might see him and recognize him if he didn't wear it.

His destination was a warehouse full of stolen goods supplied by a ring of thieves working for Beaumont. Jessie had agreed with the plan Preacher and Cleve hatched, and now Preacher was carrying out his part of it.

He had waited until after midnight to slip out of his quarters at Beaumont's house and make his way here. According to what Jessie had been able to find out, there were two guards outside the warehouse and two more inside. She knew this because Beaumont's men sometimes patronized her house when they had been lucky at cards and were particularly flush. A whore could always find a way to make a man talk and never even realize just how much information he was spilling.

Evidently things had gone well three nights earlier when Jessie took Beaumont upstairs. Preacher didn't like to think too much about that, but clearly Beaumont hadn't given in to his rage while he was with her, and that was the important thing. Since the ambush during the attempted riverboat robbery, Beaumont had resumed his normal routine for the most part, although he spent some of the time asking questions in waterfront dives, trying to find out who was behind what had happened. Preacher accompanied him on those trips and saw firsthand how Beaumont wasn't having any luck with his investigation. Jessie and Cleve had done a good job of covering their tracks.

For a man who had crawled into Indian camps and slit the throats of several warriors without any of the other Indians knowing a thing about it until morning, sneaking up on these warehouse guards didn't pose much of a challenge for Preacher. Even though it was late, raucous laughter and the scraping notes of a fiddle came from a nearby tavern, helping to cover up any sounds he might make as he approached the big double doors of the warehouse. Two men sat on kegs near the doors, one on either side, and while they might be tough gents, their senses didn't come anywhere near being as keen as those of a Blackfoot or Crow warrior. Preacher slipped along the brick wall of the building until he was close enough to reach out and touch the nearer of the two guards.

He struck swiftly and without warning, his left arm shooting out to loop around the guard's neck and jerk the man to his feet. Preacher's arm closed so tightly that the guard couldn't let out a yell, couldn't even croak. The sound of the keg overturning alerted the other guard, though, so Preacher didn't waste any time. He rushed the guard he held across the twenty or so feet separating him from the second of Beaumont's men and rammed the first guard into the second one as that man leaped to his feet. Their heads cracked together, and both men went limp and slumped to the ground.

That left the two inside. Preacher knew the doors were barred on the inside, so he had to get the other two guards to open up. He left the two he had knocked out lying on the ground and used his fist to pound on one of the doors.

When he heard footsteps approaching inside the warehouse and saw the glow of lantern light seeping through the narrow crack between the doors, he bent and hoisted one of the unconscious men to his feet. He knew their names were Tompkins and Rice. There was a viewing slot cut into the warehouse door, and when it was thrust back and a bar of light shone through it, Preacher stood halfway behind the man he held, so that the guard inside the warehouse couldn't get a good look at him. He saw the gray-shot beard jutting out from the chin of the unconscious man and knew this was Rice he held.

"Something's wrong with Rice," he rasped, muffling his voice a little against the man's shoulder. "He just moaned and fell over. Might be his heart."

"Son of a— Hold on," the guard on the other side of the door said. Preacher heard the bar being lifted, and then the other door opened a couple of feet. "Bring him in here. Maybe one of us ought to fetch the sawbones."

Preacher kept his head ducked down as he lugged the limp form through the narrow opening. One of the inside guards swung it closed behind him and lowered the bar again.

"Better not tell the boss about this," he said. "We ain't supposed to open up for any reason. Rice still owes me two dollars from that last poker game, though, and by God, I don't want him dyin' before he pays me!"

A smile tugged at Preacher's mouth. Greed, like lust, was something that could bring a man down without much trouble.

"Well, here, see if he's got it on him," Preacher said. He gave the unconscious figure a hard shove toward the man at the door, then whirled and kicked the man with the lantern in the belly. The man doubled over and started to fall. Preacher grabbed the lantern before it could drop to the floor, shatter, and start that fire he wanted to prevent.

A harsh curse came from behind him. He swung around in time to see that the second guard had gotten tangled up with the man Preacher had knocked out, just as Preacher had hoped would happen. The guard had gone to one knee and was trying to get up. Preacher met him with a hard, looping right that stretched him out on the warehouse floor, out cold.

The man Preacher had kicked in the belly was still gasping for breath, but he was also trying to work a pistol out from behind his belt. Preacher brought the barrel of his pistol crashing down on the man's head, knocking him out as well.

The whole thing, start to finish, had taken less than three minutes.

Preacher set the lantern down on a crate, lifted the bar holding the doors closed, and went back outside for the other guard. When he had all four of them inside, he used some rope he had brought with him to tie their hands and feet, then pulled some more bandannas from his pocket and blindfolded them as well, so they wouldn't be able to see what was going on if they regained consciousness before the men hired by Jessie and Cleve finished cleaning out the stolen merchandise from the warehouse.

Then Preacher opened the door a little, stuck the lantern out, and waved it from side to side three times. That was the signal. A few moments later, he heard the creak of wheels as several big freight wagons rolled toward the warehouse. He swung the doors wide open to let them in.

He was surprised to see that Cleve himself was at the reins of one of the wagons. The gambler grinned at him and said, "Good work. You didn't have to kill any of them."

"Said I wouldn't," Preacher replied.

Cleve nodded and lifted a hand in farewell. "We'll handle it from here."

"Those fellas better be alive when you leave. They ain't any threat to you now."

"Fine," Cleve said as he hopped down from the wagon he had brought to a halt. "You have my word."

Preacher wasn't sure what that was worth, but for now he had to accept it. He nodded and left the warehouse, trotting away through the shadows.

A few blocks from the warehouse, he stopped in an alley and pulled the bandanna from his face. It felt good to have it off. He just wasn't cut out to be a thief, even though he was helping to steal from a thief and a murderer.

As he walked away into the night, he wondered how long he would have to be back in the mountains before he started to feel clean again.

Chapter 24

Beaumont was livid the next morning when one of his men came to the house to deliver the bad news about the warehouse robbery. Preacher and Lorenzo were having breakfast in the kitchen when they heard the furious shouting.

"Oh, hell," Lorenzo muttered. "Somethin' else gone wrong. Startin' to seem like this house got a hoodoo on it."

Preacher started to get up. "I reckon I'd better go see what it's all about."

The stocky, florid-faced Irish woman who did the cooking for Beaumont swung away from the stove and said, "Sit yourself right back down, Mr. Donnelly. 'Tis not finished with your breakfast you are, and no good will come of leavin' perfectly good food on your plate."

Preacher listened for a moment to the raving coming from upstairs, then grinned and sank back into his chair. "I reckon you're right, ma'am," he said. "I believe I'll finish these here flapjacks first."

Something crashed upstairs. Lorenzo shook his

head and muttered, "Man ain't gonna have a stick o' furniture left that ain't broken if this keeps up."

After breakfast, Preacher climbed the stairs and knocked on Beaumont's door, which was closed. "Come in," Beaumont called from the other side of the panel.

Preacher opened the door and stepped into the room. Beaumont stood by the window, wearing a dressing gown and holding a glass in one hand and a bottle of whiskey in the other. He tipped up the bottle, splashed liquor into the glass, then threw it down his throat. Preacher wasn't sure why he didn't just drink from the bottle. Too undignified, he supposed.

"Kind of early in the day for that Who-hit-John, ain't it, boss?" he asked.

"Not after the sort of news that I've had this morning," Beaumont snapped. "The time of day doesn't really matter right now."

"More trouble?"

"Someone broke into one of my warehouses last night, knocked out the guards, and emptied it of everything that was in it. They cost me five thousand dollars, maybe more." Beaumont poured more whiskey into the glass. "And I know who did it, too."

"You finally found somebody willin' to talk?" Preacher didn't see how that was possible, since he had accompanied Beaumont every time the man left the house and had been there for all the interrogations.

Beaumont shook his head. "No. But I've figured it out at last. There's only one person who could be to blame for everything that's happened lately." Beaumont drained the whiskey and licked his lips. Then his mouth twisted in a snarl. *"Preacher!"*

It took iron will not to react. Preacher realized after a second that Beaumont hadn't figured out who he was. Beaumont was just spitting out the name of the person he blamed for all his troubles.

Preacher shook his head. "I don't reckon I know who that is."

"You haven't heard of Preacher?" Beaumont asked with a frown. "He's some son of a bitch mountain man who's been taking great delight in ruining some of my plans over the past year or so. Every time I've tried to make any inroads into the fur trade in the Rockies, he's stopped me."

"And now you think he's come to St. Louis?"

Beaumont shrugged. "It makes sense. About six months ago I sent some agents to the mountains to take over a trading post and settlement that's gotten started out there, and Preacher made sure that didn't happen. Quite a few people were killed in the process, though, and I'm willing to bet that he holds a grudge against me because of it. That's the sort of thing an uneducated lout like him would do."

"Yeah, I reckon," Preacher said. "What's this fella look like?"

"Well, I've never seen him myself, you understand, but he's been described to me on several occasions. He's supposed to be almost seven feet tall, a giant of a man, with a black beard that comes halfway down his chest."

Preacher looked close to see if Beaumont was joshing him, but the man seemed to be completely serious. Somebody had exaggerated a mite while they were telling Beaumont about him. More than a mite, actually. Preacher was nowhere near that big, and his beard had been that long only on rare occasions when he had been up in the mountains for months at a time and hadn't bothered to trim it.

"Sounds like I'll know him if I see him," he said to Beaumont. "And you can bet I'll keep my eyes open for him, if you think he's the one causin' all the trouble."

Beaumont smacked his right fist into his left palm. "I'm convinced of it. I'm going to take steps to put a stop to it, as well."

Preacher didn't like the sound of that, but chances were, as long as he continued fooling Beaumont about who he really was, he'd be in a good position to foil any plan the man came up with.

"We'll be going out and making the usual rounds today," Beaumont went on. "I'm sure that Preacher is spying on me, and I'm going to show him that no matter what he does, he can't get the better of me."

If it weren't for the fact that Preacher was really here in St. Louis, working against Beaumont, he'd think that the fella was getting a mite loco on the subject, seeing enemies where there weren't any. But even though Beaumont had some of it wrong, he was actually right about who was behind his troubles. That almost brought a smile to Preacher's face.

He remained serious, though, as he said, "All right, boss. I'll be ready to go whenever you are."

The fact that Beaumont had someone to direct his rage at now seemed to have calmed him down a little. Later in the day, after checking on some of Beaumont's other illegal enterprises, the two of them went to the warehouse where Preacher had been the night before. Beaumont stood just inside the open doors with his hands on his hips, looking around at the empty space where thousands of dollars worth of stolen property had been stored.

The men who had been on guard duty at the warehouse the night before were waiting there, and for a moment Preacher worried that Beaumont intended to kill them for letting someone clean the place out.

Instead, Beaumont just questioned them, asking all four men how they had been taken by surprise and if they had gotten a look at the man who'd knocked them out.

Tompkins and Rice, the two men who had been on duty outside, both replied that they hadn't seen the man at all. He had knocked them out before they caught even a glimpse of his face.

Beaumont turned to the other two. "How about you?" he asked. "Did you see him? Was he a giant with a long black beard?" He put a hand about halfway down his chest to indicate the length he was talking about.

The men glanced at each other and frowned, as if they thought that their boss might be losing his mind. One of them shook his head and replied, "No, sir, he was a pretty good-sized fella, but he wasn't anywhere near that big. I couldn't really see his face, because he wore his hat pulled down low and had some sort of cloth tied across his nose and mouth. I think I would have seen a beard sticking out from under it, though, if it was as long as you say."

"How was he dressed? Was he wearing buckskins?"

"No, sir. Just normal work clothes, I reckon. I didn't see anything unusual about them."

"Maybe one of those caps made from the skin of a raccoon with the tail still attached to it?"

Both men shook their heads.

"Damn it, I was sure it had to be him!" Beaumont said to Preacher as they left the warehouse. "But even if he wasn't the one who snuck in here, he had to be involved. I can feel it in my bones."

"I'm sure you're right, boss," Preacher said. He opened the door to the carriage, which was parked in front of the warehouse. "Where do you want to go now?"

"Jessie's," Beaumont snapped. "I need to think about this. Jessie's smart . . . for a woman. Maybe she can help me figure it out."

Lorenzo pointed the carriage toward Jessie's Place. As it rolled through the streets, the elderly driver said, "The boss sure has been goin' on about this here Preacher fella. I reckon I'd sure hate to be him, if'n the boss ever gets his hands on him."

"From the sound of it, he's a pretty slippery gent. If he don't want to be found, the boss may not be able to find him."

Lorenzo snorted. "You say that 'cause you don't know the boss the way I do. He's like a ol' bulldog. Once he gets his teeth into somethin', they ain't no way to make him let go until he's good and ready."

Preacher didn't doubt that. Beaumont hadn't gotten the wealth and power he possessed by giving up easily.

When they reached Jessie's, Preacher jumped down from the driver's box and opened the carriage door for Beaumont. Lorenzo asked, "You gonna be here long enough for me to take the horses around back to the stable, boss?"

"I don't know how long I'll be here," Beaumont snapped. "Just wait right out front here."

"Yes, sir."

Beaumont marched up the walk to the front door.

Preacher followed a couple of steps behind him, looking around as he always did, as if on the alert for an ambush or anything else that might threaten Beaumont. There wasn't any real danger, of course, but Beaumont didn't know that.

And, come to think of it, Preacher realized that he couldn't rule it out entirely, either. Beaumont had other enemies in St. Louis. It was possible that one of these days, Preacher might actually have to defend Beaumont against a genuine attempt on his life. That would be a damned hard pill to swallow, but he wouldn't have any choice if he wanted Beaumont to continue believing that he was really Jim Donnelly.

Brutus was waiting for them at the door, as usual. As he swung it open and they came in, he bowed a little and said, "Good to see you, Mr. Beaumont. Would you like me to fetch Miss Jessie for you?"

"No, I'll just go back to her office if that's where she is." With the arrogant stride of a man who didn't expect to be denied anything he wanted, Beaumont started along the hallway that ran toward the rear of the house. He walked like a man who owned the place . . . which, of course, he did.

"Yeah, she's back there," Brutus said. "I can tell her you're here—"

"No need," Beaumont said.

Preacher started after him, only to have Brutus get in his way. The big man put a hand on Preacher's chest to stop him, saying, "Why don't you wait in the parlor, Mr. Donnelly? Got some good-lookin' gals in there to keep you company, if you want."

Preacher saw a worried look in the man's eyes that made him aware Brutus was trying to tell him something. He didn't know what it was, though, and he didn't get a chance to ask him about it, because Beaumont paused, glanced over his shoulder at the two of them, and said impatiently, "Donnelly, come with me. You can carouse with those whores some other time."

"Yes, sir," Preacher said. He started to move past Brutus, only to have the man shift position to block his path.

"Careful," Brutus breathed. "Turn your face away when you go past the parlor."

At that instant, Preacher realized there must be somebody in the parlor who represented a threat to him. Brutus hadn't really meant to take him in there when he'd made his suggestion a moment earlier. That had been strictly for Beaumont's benefit. If Beaumont hadn't insisted that Preacher come with him, Brutus would have hustled the mountain man off somewhere else in the house.

Preacher didn't know for sure what was going on and didn't have a chance to try to figure it out, because at that moment, two things happened. Jessie appeared at the far end of the hallway, perhaps having heard Beaumont's voice, and closer, between her and Beaumont, a man stepped out of the parlor into the corridor with his arm around the waist of one of the whores. The man was a tall, barrel-chested gent with a long, ragged brown beard that looked like it hadn't been trimmed in a while. He was laughing at something the girl with him had just said, but that didn't stop his eyes from turning toward Beaumont, Brutus, and Preacher.

The man's gaze landed on Preacher and froze. Recognition flashed in his eyes. Preacher knew him, too, but he hadn't expected to ever see the man again. The last time he'd laid eyes on him had been during that Indian attack on the wagon train. The man who had just come out of the parlor was Buckhalter, the renegade wagonmaster who'd been working for Beaumont.

And now Buckhalter jerked his arm up, pointed, and yelled, "Preacher! Damn it, there he is now! Preacher!"

Chapter 25

Beaumont stiffened and whirled around, his hand darting under his coat for a hidden gun. He stared toward the foyer, *past* Preacher, and snapped, "Donnelly! Preacher must have run back outside! Go get him!"

"Donnelly!" Buckhalter roared. "What the hell are you talkin' about? That's Preacher, *right there!*"

He clawed at a pistol stuck behind his belt.

Well, this bit of bad luck had blown things all to hell, Preacher thought as Beaumont's eyes widened in shock and understanding of what Buckhalter meant. There was nothing left to do now . . .

Except kill the man he had come to St. Louis to kill.

The problem was that Beaumont and Buckhalter both had guns in their hands now, and Preacher had only one pistol. Even though he was fast with it and probably could reload as swiftly as any man alive, there was no way he would be able to gun down either of the men and reload in time to stop the other one from

killing him. At this close range, he didn't think either
Beaumont or Buckhalter were likely to miss.

That meant if he killed Beaumont, Buckhalter
would undoubtedly kill him. The price was worth it,
though, for justice to finally catch up to Shad Beaumont, Preacher thought as he smoothly pulled the
pistol from behind his belt and brought it up. His
thumb looped over the hammer and drew it back.

A shot sounded, only it wasn't the boom of a large-
bore pistol but rather the sharper crack of a smaller
weapon. Buckhalter lurched forward, the barrel of his
gun drooping. The weapon roared and smoke and
flame spurted from the muzzle, but by then it was pointing down and the heavy ball smacked harmlessly into
the floor. Buckhalter fell to his knees and pitched forward, blood welling from a hole in the back of his head.

Preacher caught a glimpse of Jessie standing at the
end of the hall, powder smoke curling from the barrel
of the little pistol in her hand as she held her arm extended out in front of her.

Preacher was about to fire at Beaumont, when a big
shape suddenly leaped forward and got in the way.
Brutus lunged at Beaumont just as the man pulled
the trigger. Even over the blast of the pistol, Preacher
heard the meaty thud of lead striking flesh. Brutus
grunted in pain and reeled backward, crashing into
Preacher as he did so.

"A trap!" Beaumont yelled as he cast a furious, wild-
eyed glance over his shoulder at Jessie. "It's a damned
trap! You betrayed me, you bitch!"

Preacher had gone down under Brutus's massive
weight. It was like having a house fall on him. He was
stunned, the breath knocked out of him. He tried to

lift his pistol and shove Brutus aside so he could get a shot at Beaumont, but the man ducked through the parlor door and vanished.

Screams came from inside the parlor, and then a second later Preacher heard glass crash. He finally managed to get out from under Brutus, but by the time he reached his feet and hurried to the parlor door, Beaumont was gone. The front window, which had been covered by heavy curtains, was shattered and the curtains had been pulled down. As Preacher looked at the damage, he realized that Beaumont had dived through the window to escape.

Several of the girls who worked here were in the parlor, along with a couple of customers. They all stared fearfully at Preacher, who realized he still had the pistol in his hand. He was about to tell them that they were in no danger when a scream came from the hallway behind him.

"Brutus!"

He wheeled around and saw Jessie on her knees next to the big man. She put her trembling hands on either side of his face and turned his head so that he appeared to be looking at her, only his wide, staring eyes were empty and lifeless now. As Preacher watched, a large red stain continued spreading across the front of Brutus's white shirt.

Preacher didn't know what the hell Brutus had been trying to accomplish by leaping at Beaumont that way. Maybe he had thought that he could knock Beaumont's gun aside and keep anyone else from getting killed. Maybe it had been just instinct that made him move toward trouble instead of away from it, since his job was to keep ruckuses from breaking out here in the house. No matter what Brutus's motive, his actions had gotten him killed.

And maybe saved Preacher's life in the process.

That was just one more mark against Beaumont, Preacher thought as he saw tears rolling down Jessie's cheeks. One more score to settle with the bastard.

Preacher reached down and grasped Jessie's arm as she continued sobbing over Brutus's corpse. "We got to get out of here," he rasped. "You heard Beaumont. He thinks you're to blame for what just happened here."

"I . . . I am," Jessie choked out. "It's my fault Brutus is dead."

"No, it ain't, but we can worry about that later. Beaumont's got men workin' for him all over St. Louis. He won't have to go very far before he finds some of them and heads back here."

Jessie let Preacher tug her to her feet. She used the back of her hand to paw at her wet, red eyes.

"You're right," she said. "With his temper, he's liable to come back with a bunch of men and . . . and burn the place down. We have to leave, find some place to hide . . ."

Preacher nodded. "Where's Cleve?"

"I don't know. Maybe at Dupree's. Not here, though. He should be safe, at least for a while. Shad may not suspect him of being involved in this. We need to find him and warn him—"

"Later," Preacher said. "For now, let's just get you out of here." Something else occurred to him. "And Casey—I mean Cassandra—too."

Jessie stared at him. "Cassandra?" she repeated. "What does she have to do with this?"

"You saw how Beaumont was when he lost that shipment of cotton. He might've beaten her to death that night if he'd gotten anywhere near her. How mad do you reckon he's gonna be about you and me double-crossin' him?"

Preacher saw understanding dawn in Jessie's eyes. "You're right. He'll take out his rage on her. All the other girls should get out of here, too, just in case."

"Probably wouldn't be a bad idea," Preacher agreed.

Jessie turned to the parlor. Her voice was still strained with the grief of Brutus's death, but she managed to make her tone brisk and businesslike as she said to the customers, "I'm sorry, but because of all this trouble, we're closing down for the rest of the day. Please leave now."

None of the men argued with her. They didn't want to be around any more shooting, so they hurried out, averting their eyes as they stepped around Brutus's body in the hallway.

"You, too," Jessie told the scantily clad women in the parlor once the customers. "Pack up whatever you need and get out as quick as you can. The house is closed. When you go upstairs, pass the word to the rest of the girls, and any customers who are still up there, too."

"But, Jessie," one of the whores wailed, "what are we going to do? Where will we go?"

Jessie shook her head. "I'm sorry. You'll have to figure that out for yourself." Then she turned to Preacher and went on, "Come on, let's get . . . what did you call her? Casey?"

"Yeah, that's what she told me to call her," Preacher said as they left the parlor and headed for the staircase.

"I wonder why she never mentioned that to me."

Preacher didn't have an answer for that.

Jessie paused at the top of the stairs. "What are we going to do about Brutus?" she asked as she looked back down toward the hall where his body lay.

"Ain't nothin' we can do," Preacher replied. "We'll have to leave him there and hope that Beaumont gives him a decent burial."

"He won't," Jessie said with bitterness in her voice. "You know he won't."

"It ain't likely," Preacher agreed with a shrug. "But we can't tote his body with us."

Jessie sighed. "No, of course not." She started toward the door of Casey's room.

The door swung open before she got there. Casey must have heard the shots and the rest of the commotion downstairs and been watching fearfully through a narrow crack. Her face with its fading bruises was pale as she looked at Jessie and Preacher.

"What's wrong?" she asked. Her gaze went to Preacher. "Jim . . . ?"

He could explain later about how that wasn't really his name. Right now he said, "Get your gear together, Casey. You're comin' with us."

"What are you talking about? I . . . I have a job here—"

"The house is closed," Jessie said. "For good. I'm leaving. And I'm not going to leave you here for Shad—"

Casey gave a choked cry before Jessie could finish that sentence. "Give me a minute," she said. "I'll grab a few things, and then I'll be ready to go."

She ducked back into the room. While Casey was gathering her things, Preacher asked Jessie, "Do you have a carriage or a wagon, something we can use to get you and Casey away from here?"

"There's a buggy in the barn out back. I think all three of us can crowd into it."

Preacher nodded. He wanted to get the two women to Uncle Dan Sullivan, who could be counted on to do his best to keep them safe.

That would leave Preacher free to come back here to St. Louis and settle things once and for all with Shad Beaumont.

True to her word, Casey emerged from her room a minute later, carrying a small carpetbag. She had pulled on a gray dress instead of the robe she'd been wearing a few moments earlier. She looked pale and frightened but composed, a description that fit Jessie as well.

"I'm ready," Casey said. "Thank you for not leaving me here."

Jessie put a hand on her shoulder. "We'd never do that." She added, "Let's go down the rear stairs."

As they began to descend the stairs, Casey said, "What about Brutus? Is he coming with us?"

"I'm sorry, Cassandra. Brutus . . . is dead."

Casey gasped and stopped on the stairs to look at Jessie in shock. "Dead?"

"One of those shots you must have heard killed him."

"Who fired it?"

"Who do you think?" Jessie asked in a grim, angry voice.

"Beaumont," Casey breathed.

"That's right."

"Where is he now?"

"We don't know," Preacher said. "He busted through

a window and lit a shuck out of here. But I'm bettin' he didn't go far, and it won't be long until he's back."

They reached the house's rear entrance. Preacher gripped his pistol tightly and said, "Best let me go first and make sure nobody's lurkin' out there."

"Be careful, Preacher," Jessie said.

Casey turned her head to look at him. "Preacher?" she repeated. "I thought your name was Jim Donnelly? Or did Jessie mean that you're a minister?"

Preacher gave a short bark of laughter. "Not hardly. Preacher's just what they call me."

"Just like you evidently prefer to be called Casey," Jessie put in.

Casey's face flushed. "I'll explain that later," she said.

"You're right, there ain't no time now," Preacher said. "We've already spent too much time gabbin' and not enough takin' off for the tall and uncut."

He swung the door open and stepped outside. It was late afternoon, so there were no shadows for a bushwhacker to hide in. On the other hand, there was no darkness to conceal the movements of Preacher and the two women, either. He pivoted from side to side, the pistol leveled and ready, but there was no sign of danger. For the moment, this quiet neighborhood appeared to be safe.

Preacher knew how deceptive appearances could be, though, and how things could change in a hurry with little or no warning. He turned back and motioned for the women to hurry.

"Come on!"

They came out the back door. Preacher hustled them toward the barn.

"Can you hitch up the buggy horse?" he asked Jessie, expecting her to say that she didn't know how.

"Of course," Jessie answered without hesitation.

"I'll help," Casey added. "I used to live on a farm, so I know all about hitching up a team."

Despite the tension, Jessie let out a hollow laugh as they hurried into the barn. "I grew up on a farm, too. What is it about being farm girls that turns us into whores?"

"Being around the animals all the time while they're, well, you know?" Casey suggested.

Preacher stopped just inside the doorway and turned around to keep an eye on the house. "Just get that buggy ready to go," he said.

The women got to work while Preacher watched for trouble. The smooth, swift efficiency with which they got the horse hitched to the buggy told Preacher they'd been telling the truth about knowing what they were doing. Within just a few minutes, they had the buggy ready to roll. Casey's carpetbag was stuffed behind the seat.

"Aren't you taking anything with you, Jessie?" she asked as they started to climb onto the seat.

The look Jessie cast through the open doors of the barn at the house was positively venomous. "There's nothing in there that wasn't paid for by Shad Beaumont," she said. "I don't want any of it."

"I reckon I understand that feelin'," Preacher said as he sat down by Casey, who was in the middle. "Jessie, you'd better handle the reins, in case I have to do any shootin'."

"All right." She picked up the lines, slapped them against the horse's rump, and called, "Hyaaahhh!"

The horse surged forward against its harness, and the buggy rolled out of the barn. Jessie sent it rolling fast along the drive that circled around the house to the road.

When they reached the front of the house, Preacher saw that Beaumont's carriage was gone. He had expected as much. Beaumont had probably run straight back to the vehicle and ordered Lorenzo to get away from there as fast as he could. Because Beaumont believed that he had walked into a trap, he probably thought there were more men in the house who wanted to kill him.

It would have been nice to have some allies, Preacher thought, instead of just him and a couple of women and an old man declaring open war against the most powerful criminal in St. Louis, maybe the most powerful one west of the Mississippi. But at least things were out in the open now, and Preacher couldn't help but be a little relieved by that. He didn't know how Beaumont would react to what had happened, but it seemed likely that he would gather up a small army of hired killers and come after his sworn enemy.

That would be all right with him, Preacher mused as a bleak smile tugged at his mouth. "Head west out of town," he told Jessie. "I'll show you where to go."

If Beaumont came after him, that would save him the trouble of going after Beaumont. Preacher didn't care about the odds.

He just wanted to have Beaumont in his sights one more time.

Chapter 26

The sun sank toward the western horizon as the buggy rolled westward. After a few moments of silence, Casey said, "Do either of you want to tell me what's going on here?"

"I reckon you deserve an explanation," Preacher said. "Me and Beaumont are old enemies, even though we didn't ever actually meet until about a week and a half ago. He's been sendin' folks to the Rockies for the past year or so, tryin' to take over the fur trade out there, and I been stoppin' those plans."

"So you're a mountain man?"

"Yeah." Preacher smiled. "I just shaved off my beard and dressed in reg'lar clothes instead of buckskins to make Beaumont think I was somebody else. I told him my name was Jim Donnelly, and he believed me."

"Then there really isn't a Jim Donnelly?"

"Well, I reckon there must be at least one fella named that somewhere," Preacher said, "but I ain't him."

"If you hate Beaumont, why did you go to work for him?" Casey's eyes lit up as she thought about the question she had just asked. "Oh, I know! You were trying to get inside his organization so you could destroy it and get back at him for all the bad things he's done."

Preacher nodded. "That's about the size of it. Problem is, it never did work out quite like I figured it would. I reckon I just ain't cut out for playactin'."

Jessie said, "It would have worked if we'd had more time. We just didn't count on that bastard Garland Buckhalter showing up and recognizing you."

"That was his first name? Garland?" Preacher shook his head. "I don't reckon I ever heard it until now. Never expected to see the varmint again, either. I figured the Pawnee got him."

"He came into the house about an hour ago," Jessie explained as she snapped the reins and kept the horse moving briskly. "Brutus heard him talking to some of the girls. He said he'd been out on the plains for the past couple of weeks, on foot, dodging Indians. He was finally able to steal a horse yesterday, and that meant he was able to get the rest of the way to St. Louis a lot faster."

"Probably killed the fella he stole that horse from, too," Preacher said.

Jessie nodded. "More than likely. He also did a lot of talking about you, Preacher, mostly about how you had ruined all his plans and caused him to fail Beaumont . . . and how he was going to kill you if he ever saw you again. Brutus overheard that and warned me, and I told him that if you came in, he should keep you away from the parlor until Buckhalter was safely upstairs with one of the girls."

"He did his best," Preacher said. "He just didn't have any luck."

"Not this time," Jessie said, a catch in her voice. "Brutus's luck ran out . . . and so did ours."

Preacher grunted. "We're still alive, ain't we? I'd say we still got some luck on our side."

"We're alive, but Brutus isn't. He was a good man. He helped me a lot over the past couple of years, since Shad put me in charge of the house."

"Before that—"

"Before that, I was just one of the whores who worked there," Jessie said. "Is that what you wanted to know, Preacher?"

He grunted. "I didn't mean nothin' by it."

"I know. You don't strike me as the judgmental sort."

Preacher didn't say anything for a moment, then went on, "Anyway, I'm obliged to you for shootin' Buckhalter. Reckon you probably saved my life."

"For a second, I thought about letting him kill you," Jessie said bluntly. "If he had, that wouldn't have exposed what Cleve and I have been doing. We could have continued without your help."

"Why didn't you?"

For a long moment, Jessie didn't answer. Then she said, "I don't know. Instinct, maybe. I saw Beaumont and Buckhalter about to shoot you, and I didn't even really think about what I was doing. I just lifted my gun and . . . pulled the trigger."

"Well, I'm glad you did."

"So am I," Casey said. "I would have hated it if anything happened to Preacher. I'm glad you shot that man Buckhalter, Jessie."

A little laugh came from Jessie. "I was aiming at Shad. I'm afraid I'm not a very good shot with a pistol."

Preacher looked over at her, and then he laughed, too. Luck had been with him, all right, even more than he'd known.

By now dusk was settling down over the landscape west of St. Louis. Preacher directed Jessie toward the grove of trees where Uncle Dan was camped, while he kept an eye on their back trail for any signs of pursuit.

It was almost completely dark by the time they reached the place. When they had approached within earshot, Preacher motioned for Jessie to rein in, then lifted his voice and called, "Uncle Dan! It's me, Preacher! You in there?"

"Come ahead, boy!" the old-timer replied. "I heard the buggy comin', but didn't know who 'twas!"

Uncle Dan stepped out of the trees as Jessie drove up to the grove. Dog followed him, a ghostly gray shape in the shadows. Uncle Dan had his rifle in his hands, ready to use it if he needed to.

Preacher hopped down from the buggy as Jessie brought it to a halt. He slapped Uncle Dan on the back and gave him a rough hug.

"The plan's blowed all to hell," Preacher said.

"I figured as much when I seen you had somebody with you." Uncle Dan lifted his hat to Jessie and Casey. "Ladies. Your comp'ny is right welcome."

"We're hardly ladies," Jessie said as she looped the buggy's reins around the brake lever.

"The way I figure it, any woman is a lady until she proves otherwise," Uncle Dan said, "and that starts from when I meet her. Anything that happened afore that don't matter one little bit."

"Well, aren't you the gentleman." Jessie smiled at him.

"Somebody's gotta be, since this ornery young feller is rough as a cob most o' the time," Uncle Dan commented with a jerk of his thumb toward Preacher.

"I wouldn't say that," Casey chimed in. Both women climbed out of the buggy. "I think Jim is very nice. I mean, Preacher is very nice. It's going to take me some time to get used to the fact that you're not really Jim Donnelly, Preacher."

"That's fine," Preacher assured her. "I don't much care what folks call me—"

"As long as it ain't late for dinner," Uncle Dan interrupted and finished for him. "Speakin' of which, I'll rustle up some vittles. I got bacon to fry and a mess o' biscuits I cooked up earlier today. Reckon I must've had a feelin' somebody was comin'. These ol' bones o' mine are pretty good about that, you know."

"Don't you want to hear about what happened in town?" Preacher asked.

"Any hostiles directly on your trail?"

"Not that I know of."

"It can wait, then," Uncle Dan declared. "If there's trouble, folks tend to think straighter when they got a full belly and some coffee to drink."

As Uncle Dan led the women into the trees, Casey seemed to notice Dog for the first time. "Is that a wolf?" she asked worriedly as she shrank away from the big cur.

Preacher took the reins of the buggy horse to lead the animal into the woods. He laughed and said, "No, that's just Dog. Hold out your hand and let him sniff it."

"I'm not sure about that. He looks like he could bite it right off."

"But he won't," Preacher assured her. "Dog, these are friends. Jessie and Casey. Friends."

One by one, they let Dog sniff their hands. The big cur's bushy tail began to swish back and forth.

"You're safe from him now," Preacher said. "He'll never forget your scent. And he'll die to protect you, if I tell him to."

"I hope it won't ever come to that," Jessie said, "but with Shad bound to come after us . . ."

She didn't have to finish that sentence. Preacher and the two women knew that even though they had made it safely out of St. Louis, they weren't out of danger, by any means. In fact, you could say that even though they had reached the camp in the trees, they weren't out of the woods, Preacher thought.

He unhitched the buggy horse and picketed it near Uncle Dan's saddle mount and the pack horses. Meanwhile, the old-timer prepared supper over a small, almost invisible fire. When the food was ready, the four of them gathered around the embers to eat.

Jessie and Casey both said they weren't very hungry after everything that had happened, but Preacher noticed that they put away plenty of food anyway. Having an appetite, even if they didn't realize it, was a good sign. When they were finished with the meal, Preacher filled a cup with coffee and let the two women pass it back and forth, since he and Uncle Dan didn't have any extra cups.

"All right," the old man said. "Now you can tell me what happened."

Preacher proceeded to do so, telling Uncle Dan

about how he had fallen in with the campaign being waged against Beaumont by Jessie and Cleve. He drew a startled exclamation from the old-timer when he mentioned Buckhalter being alive and explained about running into the renegade wagon master at Jessie's Place.

"When he recognized me, that tore it," Preacher concluded. "There was some gunplay, and that fella Brutus who worked for Miss Jessie wound up dead, along with Buckhalter. Beaumont busted out through a window and got away."

Uncle Dan let out a low whistle. "So the polecat's still alive?"

"He is, as far as I know," Preacher confirmed.

Uncle Dan shook his head and said, "That ain't good. Beaumont's so full o' hate, he'll have to come after the three of you. He'll figure you double-crossed him, and he has to even the score."

"That's exactly the way he'll react," Jessie said.

Preacher clasped his hands together in front of him and leaned forward as he sat on a log. "Question is, will he send a bunch of hired killers after us . . . or will he come along, too?"

Jessie considered that for a moment, then said, "I think there's at least a chance he'll come after us himself. Along with as many men as he can gather up, of course. He'll want the odds overwhelmingly on his side."

"I was sort of hopin' you'd say that," Preacher replied as a grin stretched across his rugged face. "If Beaumont just sends men after us, Uncle Dan and I are right back where we started. But if he comes along, too, then we might be able to turn that to our advantage."

"I don't understand," Casey put in. "What makes you say that?"

"St. Louis is Beaumont's stompin' ground. But once he gets out of town, then he's in territory that's more to my likin'."

"He'll try to recruit some experienced frontiersmen to come along," Jessie warned.

Uncle Dan let out a cackle of laughter. "There ain't no frontiersmen better'n Preacher. Shoot, I'm a lot older'n he is, and I'll bet he's forgot more about survivin' out here than I ever knowed."

"I wouldn't go that far," Preacher said. "But if I've got to fight Beaumont and an army, I'd rather do it out away from town."

Jessie nodded. "That makes sense. You won't be fighting that army alone, though. You have the three of us."

"Not really." Preacher shook his head. "I want Uncle Dan to take you two gals and get you as far away from here as he can, as fast as he can."

Jessie and Casey both exclaimed in surprise at that statement.

Preacher held up a hand. "Hold on. I can do a better job of fightin' Beaumont if I know you two are safe."

"Forget it," Jessie snapped. "We have plenty of reason to hate Shad, too. You can't just send us away, Preacher."

"And what about me?" Uncle Dan put in. "I thought we was goin' after Beaumont together."

"That's the way it started out, but things have changed," Preacher said. "It's more important now for you to look after Jessie and Casey."

"We don't *need* looking after," Jessie argued.

Casey was a little less vehement, but she agreed. "I want to help you, Preacher. I want to see Beaumont get what's coming to him."

"Oh, he'll get what's comin' to him, all right," Preacher said. "You got my word on that. No matter what else happens, Beaumont's a dead man."

"But what if you wind up the same way?" Casey said.

"Well . . . some things are worth the price, I reckon." Preacher got to his feet. "I'm hopin' it'll be safe enough for the three of you to stay here tonight, so I can find you later."

Uncle Dan stared at him. "What? Where in blazes are you goin'?"

"Back to St. Louis," Preacher said.

Chapter 27

Even though it was too dark to see very well, Preacher sensed that all three of them were staring at him. Uncle Dan broke the surprised silence by saying, "Back to St. Looey? What in the blue blazes *for?*"

"Horse, for one thing," Preacher replied. "He's still in the stable behind Beaumont's house, I reckon. That big fella and me been trail partners for long enough that I can't just abandon him. For another thing, if I'm gonna be fightin' a whole army, I want my rifle and my other pistol, and they're in the servant's quarters at Beaumont's."

"How in the world do you intend to do that?" Jessie asked. "You can't expect Shad to let you just waltz in and take those things."

"I don't," Preacher said. "But I'm a pretty fair hand at sneakin' in and out of places."

"You'll need to be better'n a fair hand," Uncle Dan said. "You'll get yourself killed, that's what you'll do."

Preacher shook his head. "I got to try. Simple as that. I'll take one of the pack horses and ride back to town."

Casey stood up and came over to him. She laid a hand on his arm and said, "That sounds awfully risky to me. Can't you stay here with us? I don't want anything to happen to you. You can get another horse and some guns somewhere else, can't you?"

"You're wastin' your time, darlin'," Uncle Dan said. "I never seen anybody get Preacher to change his mind once he's got it made up. He's just about the stubbornest ol' cuss you'll ever see."

"That's because I'm right more often than not," Preacher said.

Jessie got to her feet and came over to Preacher, standing on his other side. She put a hand on his arm as well and said, "Are you sure that Cassandra and I can't change your mind, Preacher? We could give you plenty of good reasons to stay here tonight."

Uncle Dan let out a low whistle. Preacher had to laugh at the old-timer's reaction.

"You gals make it mighty temptin'," he said, "but like Uncle Dan said, my mind's made up. I'll be back by mornin', and then we'll figure out what to do next."

"Best sing out when you get close to camp," the old-timer advised. "My nerves is gonna be a mite on edge knowin' that Beaumont's out there with a powerful grudge against you three."

Preacher untied one of the pack horses. He didn't have a saddle and he wouldn't take Uncle Dan's, but he had grown up riding bareback and knew he wouldn't have any trouble doing so now. The horse wasn't used to having a rider and was a little skittish at first, but Preacher had fashioned a hackamore out of rope and soon had the animal under control.

He said so long to Uncle Dan and the two women

and rode out of the trees. He had a powder horn, shot pouch, one pistol, and his knife. It would have been nice to be better armed as he ventured back into the lion's den, but a man had to make do with what he had.

As he rode, he thought about what he planned to do. First he would go to Beaumont's house and size up the situation. He might have to create some sort of distraction in order to get into the barn where Horse was and then into the servant's quarters to get his rifle and his other gear. One way or another, though, he would get the things he was after and then head back to Uncle Dan's camp, hopefully without anybody on his trail.

There was a village of friendly Mandan Indians a ways up the Missouri. Preacher had been on good terms with them for a number of years. He thought he might send Uncle Dan and the two women to that village. Beaumont wouldn't think to look for them there, and the Indians would help protect Preacher's friends.

Once he didn't have to worry about them anymore, then he could turn his attention to finishing the chore that had brought him east from the mountains in the first place. He was confident that he could always ride into St. Louis and get close enough to Beaumont to put a bullet in the bastard before anyone could stop him, but that would probably get him a date with the hangman, as well. And while he didn't mind dying if that's what it took to square accounts with Beaumont, Preacher didn't particularly want to give up his life just yet. He'd prefer to survive the confrontation.

The best thing to do would be to lead Beaumont and his men on a chase that might extend all the way to the mountains. Preacher knew that if he could do that, he would have the advantage, no matter how many hired killers Beaumont brought with him. Preacher would stack his own skills up against any of them.

The lights of the settlement glittered in front of him. He circled to the south to come at it from that direction.

Preacher fully expected Beaumont to have guards posted at his house. Now that Beaumont knew the threat against him had originated within his own organization, he wouldn't trust anybody. He'd be on the alert for another attack. And knowing now that Preacher had been posing as Jim Donnelly, Beaumont might expect him to show up to get Horse. Of course, that was exactly what Preacher intended to do.

He left the pack horse tied loosely in some trees about half a mile south of town. If he got back later to reclaim the animal, that would be fine. If not, the horse wouldn't have much trouble getting free later on and undoubtedly would wander into town where someone would find it and give it a home. Preacher was willing to lose the pack horse in return for his gray stallion, if it came to that.

Sticking to the shadows, he approached Beaumont's house on foot. Dogs barked here and there, and wagons rattled past occasionally in the streets. This sedate residential neighborhood was too far from downtown and the riverfront for any of the raucous sounds originating in those areas to penetrate. To all appearances, it was a quiet, peaceful night in these parts.

Preacher's instincts told him that wasn't the case. Somewhere out there were armed men who wanted him dead.

He came at the barn from the rear, moving slowly

and carefully. When he was about fifty yards from the building, he stopped and let his senses reach out into the night. He listened for a cough or any other faint sound a guard might make. His eyes searched the shadows for any trace of movement. He sniffed the air like a wild animal trying to find the scent of an enemy, which in this case might be the lingering tobacco odor from a pipe.

After a few minutes, he was rewarded by a tiny scraping noise that came from the shadows near the rear door of the barn. That was a sentry changing position, he thought. As Preacher moved closer, he heard the man clear his throat. The guard was being quiet—for a city fella. To a man like Preacher, though, who had slipped in and out of Blackfoot camps on numerous occasions, the sentry might as well have been holding a lantern and a sign announcing his presence.

Preacher took his time about it. Five minutes later, he was within arm's reach of the man who stood near the barn door with a rifle cradled in his arms. The mountain man had approached in utter silence, and he was confident the guard had no idea he was there. Preacher struck in silence as well, looping his right arm around the man's neck and jerking him back while using his left hand to pluck the rifle out of the guard's grasp. The man tried to struggle, but Preacher's iron grip on his throat all but paralyzed him. Within a minute, the guard lost consciousness and slumped in Preacher's grasp. Preacher lowered him noiselessly to the ground.

He could have just killed the varmint with a thrust of his knife. Anybody who would work for Shad Beaumont had it coming, as far as Preacher was concerned.

But tonight he was more interested in getting what he'd come after.

Horses shifted around inside the barn, stomping their hooves and swishing their tails. That would make things a mite more difficult for Preacher, who figured there were guards inside the barn as well as outside. The noises the horses made would cover up any sounds that might help him locate the guards. But he couldn't stay out here all night. For one thing, the man he had just choked into unconsciousness would probably come to in ten or fifteen minutes.

Something made Preacher look up. The rear door into the hayloft was closed, but he knew it had only a simple latch on the inside. If he could get up there, he could slide his knife through the gap around the door and lift the latch.

A barrel sat against the rear wall. Preacher reached down, pulled the belt off the man he had knocked out, and climbed onto the barrel. He held onto one end of the belt and tossed it upward toward the beam that protruded from the wall just above the loft door. A block-and-tackle was fastened to the beam so that it could be used to lift bales of hay into the loft. Preacher had to try a couple of times, but using the belt he managed to hook the rope attached to the pulley and draw it down to him.

From there it was a simple matter to climb up to the door and work the latch open, just as he had thought.

A moment later he was inside the deep darkness of the loft, stretched out on the hay. Carefully, he crawled to the edge of the loft and peered over it. No lights burned inside the barn.

Again Preacher relied on his senses and his instincts

to tell him where the armed men were. He pinpointed three of them: one just inside the door, one beside the stall where Horse was, and a third man near the ladder that led down from the loft. Preacher's eyes had adjusted to the darkness so that he was barely able to make out the shape of that man only a few feet beneath him.

Preacher had draped the unconscious guard's belt over his shoulder when he climbed into the loft. He hadn't known if he would need it for anything, but he knew better than to discard something that might come in handy. Working in darkness now, he fashioned a loop from one end of the belt. Then he stretched out on his belly at the edge of the loft and studied the guard just below him. The fella wore a cap of some sort, rather than a wide-brimmed hat, which was a stroke of good fortune.

The guard must have been taken completely by surprise when the loop dropped over his head and jerked tight around his neck. He didn't have time to let out even a squawk. The muscles in Preacher's arms and shoulders bunched as he lifted the man's weight off the floor.

Unfortunately, the man dropped his rifle, which thudded to the hard-packed dirt floor. He managed to make a gagging sound, too, as he kicked frantically and clawed at the makeshift noose around his neck. The other two guards ran toward him, one of them calling, "Garrison! What's wrong?"

Preacher let go of the belt, dropping the man he'd been strangling. An instant later, Preacher leaped off the edge of the loft and plummeted down to crash into one of the guards who had just run up. The collision drove the man to the ground. Preacher's knees landed on the guard's midsection and dug deep, knocking all the breath out of his lungs and probably breaking some ribs, too. Using the momentum of his fall, Preacher rolled over and surged back to his feet just in time for the third man to tackle him.

Both of them went down, but Preacher twisted as he fell and managed to land on top. He hammered a fist at the spot where he thought the sentry's head would be and connected solidly. The man went limp as the blow stunned him. Preacher hit him again, just for good measure.

Then Preacher was back on his feet again. The ruckus hadn't made much noise, and all three of the guards inside the stable were out of action for the moment. Preacher hurried into Horse's stall and slapped blanket and saddle on the stallion with swift, efficient movements, even in the darkness.

He led Horse out of the stall and dropped the reins, knowing the animal would stand there patiently. Then Preacher felt around until he found the rifles the guards had dropped. He wouldn't need to get into the servant's quarters after all. He took their pistols, too, shoving the weapons behind his belt. He was armed for bear now.

Or for a war.

Preacher went to the double doors at the front of the stable and lifted the bar that held them closed. Then he swung up into the saddle and drew two of the four pistols. Guiding Horse with his knees, he urged the stallion forward. Horse hit the doors and knocked them open, bursting out into the open area between the stable and the back of Beaumont's house.

Throwing his head back as he rode, Preacher let out the wild howl of a wolf. From the corner of his eye, he spotted a man running toward him. Flame spurted from a rifle muzzle. The ball hummed past Preacher's head as he wheeled Horse around. He fired a pistol at the guard, the shot knocking the man over backward as it slammed into him.

"Beaumont!" Preacher yelled toward the house. "I'm comin' for you, Beaumont, you damned coward! I'll skin you alive!"

Another rifle boomed. Preacher saw the flash and returned the fire, but he didn't know if he hit the rifleman or not. He jammed the empty pistols behind his belt, grabbed the reins, and whirled Horse away from the house. The stallion leaped into a gallop as Preacher dug in his heels.

More shots rang out, but none of them came close to Preacher. Horse never broke stride as he raced away into the night. Preacher turned his head and let loose with one final crazy howl over his shoulder, then leaned forward in the saddle and let Horse run.

If that didn't get Beaumont to come after him, he thought, then nothing would.

Chapter 28

Preacher headed south again, then circled wide to the west before heading for Uncle Dan's camp. He didn't think Beaumont would have been able to mount a pursuit quickly enough to come after him tonight, but he wanted to be sure he didn't lead any pursuit back to the place where he had left Jessie and Casey. Once they were safely well away from St. Louis, then everything would be different. Then he would want Beaumont on his trail until he was ready to make his final move.

It was long after midnight by the time Preacher approached the grove of trees. He reined in and called softly, "Hello, the camp!"

Not surprisingly, Uncle Dan was awake and alert despite the hour. The old-timer responded from the thick shadows, "Come ahead, Preacher."

Just before Preacher heeled Horse into motion again, he heard a quiet clicking noise that he recognized as Uncle Dan lowering the hammer on his old flintlock rifle. If he had been anybody else, Preacher knew that Uncle Dan probably would have blasted him right out of the saddle.

When Preacher reached the camp deep in the trees and swung down from Horse's back, Jessie and Casey practically swarmed him.

"Are you all right?" Jessie asked.

"You're not hurt?" Casey said.

"No, I'm fine," Preacher told them. "And I got this stallion of mine back, too."

Uncle Dan grunted. "But not the pack horse you rode into town, I see."

"I didn't really want to take the time to go back where I left him," Preacher explained. "He'll be fine. I made sure he could get loose. Somebody will find him and get a good horse out of the deal."

"Yeah, I expect you're right."

"Any trouble out here?"

"Nary a bit," Uncle Dan said. "It's been mighty quiet ever since you left . . . 'cept for these here ladies frettin' their pretty heads off over you and wonderin' when you was gonna get back."

"We weren't worried," Jessie said, although the sound of her voice didn't convince Preacher of that claim.

"That's right," Casey added. "We know you can take care of yourself, Preacher."

"And the rest of us, too," Jessie said.

As Preacher unsaddled Horse, Uncle Dan asked, "What's the plan now?"

"I figure that first thing in the mornin', you and the gals will head on up the Missouri. There's a Mandan village about fifty miles upstream."

"I know the place," Uncle Dan said, and from the sound of his voice, Preacher knew the old-timer was nodding. "Chief name of Otter's Tail, or somethin' like that, is the boss of the village."

"Otter's Tail is right," Preacher said. "Him and me are old amigos. I don't reckon Beaumont would ever think to look for you there, and even if he did, he'd have a hard time gettin' you away from that bunch. The Mandan are plumb peaceful, but that's because they choose to be. I wouldn't want to tangle with 'em."

"Me, neither," Uncle Dan agreed. "Sounds like a good plan . . . 'cept for the fact that it means you'll be takin' on Beaumont all by your lonesome."

"That's the way I want it. I can go after him better if I'm not havin' to worry about the three of you."

"What about *us* worrying about *you?*" Jessie asked.

"No need for you to do that. I'll be fine. I don't plan on takin' any foolish chances. I'm gonna lead Beaumont out west where the odds will all be on my side."

"If he cooperates and chases you his own self," Uncle Dan said.

Preacher chuckled. "After the salt I rubbed in his wounds tonight, I got a hunch that's exactly what he'll do."

He told them about his raid at Beaumont's estate to reclaim Horse, then went on, "If that don't do the trick, I'll gig him again."

"You mean you'll go back to St. Louis?" Jessie asked.

"That's right."

"You'll be taking a terrible chance every time you do," Casey pointed out.

"That's a risk I'm willin' to take." Preacher had finished tending to Horse, so he continued, "You ladies better turn in and get some shut-eye. It ain't but a few hours until dawn. You need to be on the trail by the time the sun comes up, so you can get a good start."

"What about you?" Jessie said. "You need some sleep, too, don't you?"

"I figured I'd stand guard while Uncle Dan caught a few winks."

"Forget it, boy," the old-timer said. "The more decrepit I get, the less sleep it seems like I need. You get the shut-eye, Preacher, while I stand guard."

It was true that Preacher was mighty weary. The day had been a long, violent one. He thought about arguing with Uncle Dan but then shrugged and said, "All right. I reckon it wouldn't hurt for me to get a couple hours of sleep. But then you need to wake me up, so you can rest awhile, too. You'll be on the trail for a long time tomorrow, and you don't need to be tryin' that without any sleep at all."

Uncle Dan grunted. "Deal."

Preacher had left his bedroll here at the camp along with his buckskins. He crawled into his blankets now, fully expecting to fall asleep instantly as soon as he stretched out and closed his eyes, which was a knack that most mountain men had picked up.

He didn't doze off right away, though, because he realized that Jessie was spreading a blanket she had gotten from their supplies on the ground next to him. Not only that, but as Casey brought over another blanket, it appeared that she intended to bed down on his other side. The idea of having a beautiful woman lying within a foot or two of him on either side had a definite effect on Preacher. He was as human as the next fella, and Jessie and Casey were both mighty pretty.

Usually, though, when two gals set their cap for the

same man, it was a recipe for trouble. Preacher couldn't help but wonder if sparks were going to fly before he got the two of them packed off safely to that Mandan village.

But for tonight, at least, there didn't seem to be any signs of rivalry between them. Casey said, "Good night, Preacher," and then Jessie added, "Good night," and damned if both of them didn't reach over and pat him on the shoulder in a friendly manner.

After all that, it was no wonder that Preacher didn't doze off right away.

Despite the lack of sleep, when Uncle Dan whispered his name a couple of hours later, Preacher woke instantly and was fully alert. On the frontier, being able to wake up like that was sometimes the difference between life and death. He sat up and looked around the camp. A little silvery starlight penetrated the grove of trees, enough to show him the sleeping shapes of Jessie and Casey next to him. He had halfway expected to wake up with both of those gals cuddled against him. That would have been a pleasant—if somewhat nerve wracking—way to wake up.

Preacher got to his feet quietly and moved several yards away with Uncle Dan so the two of them could talk without disturbing the women.

"Anything been happenin' since I turned in?" Preacher asked.

"Nope. Ever'thing's mighty quiet. I reckon when you rode away from St. Looey last night, you give Beaumont the slip. You'll have to find some way to get him on your trail again if'n you want to lure him away from civilization."

"I can find a way to do that," Preacher said. He picked up one of the rifles he had brought with him from Beaumont's place. Earlier, before turning in, he had made sure they were all loaded, and he had reloaded the pistols he had fired as he burst out of the stable behind Beaumont's house. Now, as he tucked the rifle under his arm, he went on, "You go get some sleep, Uncle Dan. I'll wake all three of you in a couple of hours, and you and the gals can get ready to hit the trail."

"All right," the old-timer said, "but I don't know how well I'm gonna sleep without a couple o' nubile young women to keep me nice an' warm like *somebody else* around here."

Preacher just chuckled.

Uncle Dan rolled up in his blankets, and soon he was snoring loudly. The log-sawing didn't seem to bother Jessie and Casey. Preacher supposed they were so exhausted they could sleep through the last trump.

After a while, though, Casey stirred. She sat up and rubbed her eyes, then climbed slowly to her feet with the blanket still wrapped around her. She stumbled over to the log where Preacher was sitting and sank down beside him. The sky above the trees had begun to take on a tinge of gray because dawn was approaching, and that provided enough light for Casey to see her way around the camp, Preacher supposed.

"You're supposed to still be sleepin'," he told her.

"I know. And Lord knows, I'm still tired enough to sleep. But we're going our separate ways in the morning, and I wanted to talk to you, Preacher."

"What about?" he asked warily. In his experience, any time a gal wanted to talk about something, there was a significant chance it wasn't going to be anything good.

"I just wanted to say thank you."

Preacher frowned in surprise. "For what? Goin' after Beaumont?"

"Well, that, too. Whatever you do to him, he's got it coming . . . in spades." She paused. "I really wanted to thank you, though, for treating me the way you have."

Preacher still didn't understand. "I don't reckon I've done anything all that special."

"Yes, you did. When we were together . . . not once did you act like I was a . . . a whore. You just treated me like a woman you . . . liked."

"Well, hell, I *do* like you," he burst out. "I think you're a mighty fine gal."

"You're the first man who's treated me like that in a long time, though. Most of them . . ." Her voice trailed off and she shook her head. "You don't want to know how most of them treat me."

Gruffly, he said, "You're right about that."

She put a hand up, rested it on his beard-stubbled cheek. "Do you know why I asked you to call me Casey, when no one else in St. Louis does?"

"Nope. I know Jessie's mighty curious about that, too. I think maybe it hurt her feelin's a mite that she didn't know nothin' about it."

"I'm sorry about that," Casey said. "Jessie's been good to me, as much as she could under the circumstances, anyway. But you're different, Preacher. You reminded me of . . . a boy back home. A boy who used to . . . call me Casey. The only one who ever did."

"You were in love with him?" Preacher said softly.

She nodded without saying anything.

"And somethin' happened to him." It wasn't a question.

"He went off to fight in that stupid Black Hawk War a few years ago," Casey said with a note of bitterness in her voice. "He never came back."

"Got killed in the fightin'?"

"No. He took sick with the grippe and died. But if he had been home, it wouldn't have happened. I never told anybody what he called me when we were . . . together. And I never felt the same, until I met you."

Preacher wasn't sure what to say. He sat there in silence for a few moments, then finally said, "I'm mighty flattered I made you feel good, Casey, if that's what I did."

"Oh, don't worry," she said. "I'm not planning to marry you or anything. Although that might not be so bad. But I'm afraid things have gone beyond that by now. Too far beyond."

Preacher might have argued with her, but he wasn't looking to get married, either. He was too fiddle-footed for that, nowhere near ready to settle down. And he wouldn't try to drag a wife around in the sort of nomadic existence he led. That wouldn't be fair to any woman.

"I wouldn't mind sitting here with you for a little while, though, if that would be all right," Casey went on.

"That'd be just fine," Preacher said, and a smile touched his lips as Casey leaned against him and rested her head on his shoulder.

By the time Preacher roused Jessie and Uncle Dan from their slumber, Casey had built up the fire and gotten the coffee on to boil. Jessie looked at her in surprise and said, "I didn't know you were so . . . domestic."

"Just a farm girl at heart, remember?" Casey said lightly.

They had breakfast and then packed up all their gear. Preacher went into the bushes, peeled out of the town clothes, and put on his buckskins. He felt almost like himself for the first time in weeks as he emerged from the brush and settled his hat with its wide, floppy brim on his head. If his beard was longer, everything would be back to normal again.

Or as normal as it could be . . . while Shad Beaumont was still alive.

"I've been thinking," Jessie said as they got ready to leave the camp. "What happened to Cleve?"

"My guess is that he heard what happened at your place yesterday and is lyin' low," Preacher said. "Beaumont don't know that Cleve had any part in the plans against him, and as long as Cleve keeps his mouth shut, it can stay that way. Cleve struck me as a pretty smart fella."

"He is," Jessie agreed.

"Then he'll know to keep quiet. He can plunk himself down at a table in Dupree's and play poker until this whole business is over."

"I hope you're right. I'd hate for something to happen to him because he tried to help me."

A short time later, they were ready to go. Uncle Dan and the women would take the pack horse with them. Preacher planned to travel as light as possible once he started leading Beaumont on a merry chase across the prairie.

Jessie and Casey both hugged him tightly. "When it's over, you'll come find us?" Casey asked.

"I sure will," Preacher promised her.

"And maybe you'll spend some time with us in town before you go back to the mountains?" Jessie suggested.

That could prove interesting in more ways than one, Preacher thought, but he just nodded and said, "Sure."

He shook hands with Uncle Dan, who groused, "I still think I oughta be goin' with you, Preacher."

"You've got a more important job—keepin' these ladies safe."

"I know it, I know it. I just hate to see you havin' all the fun, that's all."

"You sure you know how to find that Mandan village?"

"Yep. Don't worry."

Preacher embraced the old-timer roughly and slapped him on the back. "So long, Uncle Dan."

"So long, Preacher."

He rode with them until they were within sight of the Missouri River. Then he reined Horse to a halt and sat there watching with Dog alongside him as Uncle Dan and the two women in the buggy headed northwest. Any direction that was away from St. Louis represented safety, Preacher thought. He lifted a hand and waved farewell, even though none of them were looking back.

Then he turned Horse and headed toward civilization.

Bloody, damned civilization.

Chapter 29

He had only gone about half a mile when he heard popping sounds in the distance. Preacher's keen ears instantly recognized the sounds as gunshots.

And they were coming from the direction Uncle Dan and the two women had gone a short time earlier.

Preacher hauled back on the reins and turned around in the saddle to gaze off toward the Missouri River. Beside him, Dog stared in that direction as well, ears pricked forward. A low, throaty growl came from the dog.

Fear made Preacher's heart slug heavily in his chest. Not fear for himself. The life of peril and adventure he led had long since pushed him past the point that he worried much about his own fate. He knew that in all likelihood, one of these days he would die with a gun or a knife in his hand, battling against some son of a bitch who needed killing—and he could live with that knowledge.

He had never learned how not to worry about the

people he cared for, though, and right now, Uncle Dan, Jessie, and Casey were at the top of that list.

The shooting continued for almost a minute, then an ominous silence took its place. Preacher wheeled Horse around and dug his heels into the stallion's flanks.

"Trail, Horse!" he called. "Come on, Dog!"

Horse leaped ahead into a gallop. Dog bounded along, keeping up as best he could.

Preacher rode hard toward the river, and as he did so, worry gnawed at his guts. He hadn't expected his friends to run into any trouble. Of course, they were far enough from town that the possibility of encountering a Pawnee or Cheyenne war party existed, and bands of white renegades sometimes roamed through these parts, too.

The threat that loomed the largest, though, was Shad Beaumont. He had more reason to hate Preacher and want to strike at him through his friends than anyone else. Preacher wasn't sure how Beaumont could have found them, though.

The time it took him to reach the river and then turn northwestward stretched out interminably, although Preacher knew logically it was only a few minutes. He scanned the morning sky, looking for dust that would betray the presence of riders. He had heard quite a few shots, which meant several people had been involved in the battle.

Maybe the shots hadn't had anything to do with Uncle Dan and the two women, he told himself. He couldn't quite bring himself to believe that, though. The tight, cold ball in his guts wouldn't let him.

He topped one of the rolling hills and spotted something up ahead. A second later as he galloped toward it, he recognized it as Jessie's buggy, which now lay overturned on its side. The horse that was hitched to the vehicle was still in its traces, lying on its side, motionless. A saddle horse was a couple of hundred yards away, moving around skittishly. Preacher recognized it as Uncle Dan's mount.

His heart plummeted as he recognized those things. Now there was no hope that the trouble hadn't involved his friends. The evidence that it had was right before his eyes.

But he didn't see Uncle Dan or either of the two women anywhere. It was possible they had been taken prisoner and carried off somewhere. Preacher didn't slow Horse as he raced toward the wrecked buggy. Wherever the men who had done this had gone, he would track them down. He made that vow to himself.

A rifle suddenly boomed from some brush to the left of the overturned vehicle. Preacher saw the puff of powder smoke from the bushes. The ball didn't come anywhere near him, though, whining off harmlessly instead. Whoever was holed up in there wasn't a very good shot. Using his knees to guide the stallion, Preacher veered Horse so that the buggy provided some cover for them. Rifle in hand, he leaped from the saddle while Horse was still moving and landed behind the buggy. He crouched and aimed over the top of the vehicle at the brush.

"Whoever you are, best throw out your guns and come out after 'em with your hands up!" he shouted.

He wasn't sure what response he was expecting, but the one he got sure wasn't it. A weak voice called, "Preacher? Is that you?"

"Uncle Dan!" Preacher exclaimed. He straightened

and ran out from behind the buggy. A few fast, long-legged strides brought him to the bushes. He parted them, paying no attention to the way the branches clawed at his buckskins, and plunged into the thicket. He spotted Uncle Dan lying on the ground and went to his knees beside the old-timer.

Several dark splotches of blood on Uncle Dan's buckskins told Preacher that he'd been shot through and through. It was a wonder the old man was still alive. Carefully, Preacher lifted him so that he was sitting up halfway. Uncle Dan's hat was gone, and his long white hair was tangled around his head. Blood had trickled from his mouth, leaving a crimson trail in the snowy beard.

"Well, I'm . . . shot all to hell, Preacher," he managed to say.

"It ain't that bad—" Preacher began.

"The hell . . . it ain't. I'm a goner, and we . . . both know it."

Preacher didn't waste time arguing. He got right to the point of what he needed to know.

"What happened?"

"Some fellas . . . jumped us. They come up . . . behind us. We tried to outrun 'em, but their horses was too fast. Couldn't . . . get away." The old man's weathered face twisted in a grimace. "I'm plumb sorry, Preacher! I put up . . . as good a fight as I could . . . and so'd them gals . . . but they was too many . . ."

"Beaumont," Preacher grated.

Uncle Dan licked dry lips. "Yeah. He was the boss of 'em. And there was a fella with him . . . Miss Jessie called him . . . Cleve. Said he was . . . a double-crossin' . . . son of a bitch."

A fire of hatred and fury sprang up within Preacher. Jessie had been worried about Cleve that very morning, and then the gambler had gone and betrayed her. Cleve knew where their camp was. He must have heard about Jessie's plot against Beaumont being revealed and had gone straight to Beaumont to sell him that information. That would not only enrich Cleve, it would help keep Beaumont from suspecting his connection with Jessie, too.

Cleve had made it clear from the first that he had joined forces with Jessie for money and power, so it didn't come as any surprise that he had switched sides as soon as it was better for him to do so. Preacher understood that, but it didn't make him hate Cleve any less.

Those thoughts flashed through Preacher's head while Uncle Dan paused to take a deep, ragged breath that made the old-timer wince in pain.

"Things're all busted up . . . inside me," Uncle Dan went on. "I took a bad tumble from my hoss . . . just about the time the buggy . . . turned over. I managed to . . . crawl into this here thicket . . . and throw some lead at the sons o' bitches . . . but I was already hurt and they winged me a few times . . . to boot. Reckon they figured . . . I was done for . . . and they was right." A grim chuckle came from him. "I must've . . . passed out for a little spell. Came to and heard a horse . . . I wasn't thinkin' too straight . . . I shoved my rifle out and squeezed off a shot. That was you comin', weren't it, Preacher? I didn't . . . hit you?"

"Nope, don't worry about that," Preacher assured him. "I'm fine. Now, I need to get you out of these bushes—"

"Don't . . . waste the time on me. You best get after . . .

Beaumont. After they . . . stopped shootin' . . . he yelled at me . . . said if I was still alive to tell you . . . that he'll be waitin' for you . . . at his place . . . if'n you want to see . . . Jessie and Casey alive again."

The old-timer's voice was getting weaker. It was barely above a whisper now. Preacher had to lean close to make out all the words.

"You . . . find Beaumont . . . and save them gals. And when you . . . settle the score . . . with Beaumont . . . you'll be settlin' up . . . for me and Pete, too . . ."

Uncle Dan's breath went out of him in a long sigh. The light in his eyes faded at the same time. Preacher knew that his friend was crossing the divide. Hoping that Uncle Dan could still hear him, he rasped, "I'll see you on the other side one of these days, old-timer."

Then he gently closed the lifeless, staring eyes.

Preacher sat there for a minute with his own eyes closed, then drew in a deep breath. He lowered Uncle Dan carefully to the ground and left the thicket. One of the wheels on the buggy had shattered when it overturned. He looked at the broken spokes and picked out one that he thought could be used as a shovel. Then he got a blanket from his pack and went back into the brush to wrap the old-timer's body in it.

A part of Preacher cried out for him to hurry back to St. Louis and head straight for Beaumont's house, as Uncle Dan had urged him to do. But that was what Beaumont would expect, so Preacher decided to wait. He didn't think Beaumont would hurt Jessie or Casey right away. They were the bait in the trap Beaumont had set for Preacher, so he couldn't just kill them outright.

Besides, Uncle Dan deserved to be laid to rest properly.

Preacher lifted the body onto Horse's back and tied it in place. Then he led the stallion along the river until he found a suitable spot, a high, tree-shaded hill with a good view of the valley and the broad stream flowing through it. Uncle Dan should have been buried in the Rockies, but they were too far away. This would have to do.

Using the broken spoke, Preacher began digging. It was hard work, and as the day grew warmer, sweat sprang out on his face. He kept at it until he had a nice, deep grave.

Then he lowered Uncle Dan's body into the hole and covered it. When he was finished, he stood beside the grave with his hat in his hand and said, "Lord, you know I ain't much for speechifyin', and even though they call me Preacher, You and me never been all that close. But I'll say this . . . I don't reckon there's anybody in this world who appreciates the mountains and the streams and the prairie You made more than I do, and if that counts for anything with You, I'd ask You to look kindly on this old fella who showed up on Your doorstep a while ago. He's one of the finest men I ever knew, and if You can find a fiddle up there in heaven for him to play, he'll have the angels dancin' a jig 'fore You know it. I reckon that's all I've got to say, so I'll wrap this up the way the real preachers do by sayin' amen."

With that, he put his hat on and turned away from the mound of dirt that marked the final resting place of Uncle Dan Sullivan. He took hold of Horse's reins, swung up into the saddle, and motioned for Dog to follow him as he hitched the stallion into motion. Preacher started at an easy lope toward St. Louis.

There was no need to hurry now. It was all over

except for the rest of the killing . . . and that would come later, once night had fallen.

It looked like every lamp in Shad Beaumont's house was lit. Yellow light glowed from all the windows. From the roof of a building a couple of blocks away, Preacher used the spyglass he had taken from his pack to study the place. He didn't see anybody moving, but he was confident that Beaumont was in there, and so were Jessie and Casey. Also, he had no doubt that a dozen or more well-armed men were hidden around the house, just waiting for him to show up.

Not that they would kill him if he waltzed up there, he knew. Their orders would be to take him prisoner, not to slay him. Beaumont would want the pleasure of killing him.

Of course, if Preacher attacked openly and forced the men to gun him down, Beaumont probably wouldn't lose too much sleep over that. He had wanted Preacher dead for a long time, and if that was the way things played out, Beaumont would be able to live with it.

And then, once Preacher was gone, he could take his time with the two women . . .

Preacher had a hunch that Beaumont had watchers posted all around the settlement, waiting for him to show up. When he did, Beaumont's plan probably called for the sentries to send word to the house that he was on his way.

That was why Preacher hadn't ridden in openly. He had spent the day building a small raft, barely big enough for him to lie on with his rifle beside him, along with a few other things he had worked on during the day. He'd had to leave Horse and Dog behind, because this was a chore he could only handle by himself. In the dark buckskins he wore, and with his face smeared with mud, he knew that the raft would look like a floating log in the darkness. Before the moon came up, with only starlight washing over the Mississippi, he made his slow way downstream, letting the current carry him.

When he reached the riverfront area, he had steered the tiny raft in among the wharves that jutted out into the water. Being careful to keep his rifle and pistols out of the muck, he had slid off into the mud under one of the wharves and listened intently for several minutes before crawling out into the open. He stayed in the shadows, moving like a shadow himself, a phantom who carried death with him. He was confident that none of Beaumont's men had seen him.

With the same level of stealth Preacher would have employed sneaking into an Indian village, he made his way through the streets of St. Louis, staying in the deepest, darkest shadows, until he reached a position that commanded a view of Beaumont's house. That was where he lay now, on the roof of a general store that was closed for the night. He had climbed up here from the alley that ran behind the store.

Slowly, Preacher moved the spyglass, checking each window in turn, trying to see if he could make out what was going on inside. All the curtains on the ground floor were pulled tightly shut, and the windows themselves were closed.

That wasn't the case on the second floor. Some of those windows were open for ventilation, and the night breeze stirred the curtains inside the rooms, creating occasional gaps through which Preacher caught glimpses of what was inside.

After almost an hour, he stiffened as he saw what appeared to be a flash of fair hair. Casey? He fixed all his attention on that particular window and waited for another gust of wind to move the curtains. He would wait all night if he had to. He wasn't going to strike until he was good and ready.

Time went by, and then the curtains parted briefly, and this time he saw a large shape move past the window. Beaumont, he thought. Beaumont was in there with Casey. Preacher didn't know that for a fact, but his instincts told him it was true.

Jessie was probably in the same room. Beaumont would want to keep them together, so that it would be easier for him to keep an eye on them.

Suddenly, the curtains were thrust open, taking Preacher by surprise. As he squinted through the spyglass, he saw the reason why. Beaumont had moved a couple of straight-back chairs up close to the big window. Jessie and Casey sat in those chairs. From the way their arms were pulled back, Preacher knew their hands were tied behind them. Beaumont was using them as bait, all right, and he was making sure they were right out there where Preacher couldn't help but see them. Beaumont's nerves were probably getting tired of the waiting. He wanted to goad Preacher into action.

Preacher's jaw tightened as he studied the faces of the two women through the glass. His breath rasped between his teeth. He wouldn't have thought it was possible for him to hate Shad Beaumont any more than he already did, but he discovered now that it was.

Jessie and Casey had been beaten. Preacher saw the

blood and the bruises on their faces, and if Beaumont
had stepped into view at that moment, Preacher
might have put a rifle ball through the bastard's head
and been done with it. He wished he had done that a
couple of weeks earlier. Uncle Dan would probably
still be alive if he had.

Preacher wasn't the sort to brood about what might
have been, though. Instead, he took action to deal with
what was. Now that he knew where Jessie and Casey
were being held in the house, he could put his plan
into effect. It was risky, no doubt about that, but with
the odds stacked against him the way they were, there
was no way he could rescue the women without putting
them in danger first. As long as they were in Beaumont's hands, they were doomed to die eventually,
anyway.

Preacher climbed down into the alley again. He went
to the back door of the emporium and used his knife to
bust the lock, which wasn't very strong. He went inside,
and his eyes were accustomed enough to the darkness
by now that he was able to find his way around the store
and locate the things he needed. He made a bundle out
of some burlap, slung it over his shoulder, and climbed
up on the roof again, leaving some money on the
counter to pay for what he had taken.

He was two blocks away from Beaumont's house.
That was a pretty far distance for what he had in
mind, but he was confident the bow he had fashioned
during the day would send the arrows that far. He had
made half a dozen arrows, not bothering with trying
to carve flint heads for them. Now he dumped them
out of the makeshift quiver he had used to carry them
and tore strips off the bolt of cloth he had taken from

the store. He wrapped the strips around the ends of the arrows. Once he had done that, he dipped each cloth-wrapped arrowhead in the keg of pitch he had found in the store as well.

Preacher tore up some brown paper he had brought from below, making a pile of it in a metal bowl that would contain the fire. Then he took out his flint and steel and struck sparks with them, leaning over to blow on the tiny flames and make them leap higher.

Once the fire was burning well enough, he stood up and nocked one of the arrows to the bow. He held the pitch-soaked head of the shaft in the flames until it caught and began to blaze. Then he straightened, drew back the bow, aimed, and let fly.

The burning shaft arced through the darkness. Preacher watched it soar through the air and then curve downward . . . to land on the opposite end of the roof from the room where Jessie and Casey were being held prisoner.

Chapter 30

Even though Preacher watched the flight of the flaming arrow, by the time it landed he had set another one ablaze. With a grunt of effort, he drew the bow-string taut and sent the second arrow flying through the air after the first one. He knew he had the range, so he didn't even watch this one. He just nocked the next arrow and let fly, then again and again and again.

By the time the sixth and final arrow landed on the roof of the big house, the flames had caught hold. Preacher heard yelling and knew that Beaumont's men had seen the blazing streaks in the sky and figured out what was going on. They leaped out of their hiding places and hurried toward the house. Most people feared fire worse than anything else, and with good reason.

Preacher dropped the bow and snatched up his rifle. He lifted the weapon to his shoulder and drew a bead. He aimed at one of the lighted windows, and when one of Beaumont's men was unlucky enough to pause between him and the window, Preacher pulled the trigger.

The rifle boomed, and the man dropped like a rock as the heavy lead ball tore through him.

Preacher reloaded swiftly and downed another man the same way. With all the yelling and confusion going on around the house now, he wasn't sure anybody even noticed. He glanced at the fire, saw it spreading across the roof, and figured he could risk taking the time for another shot or two. He reloaded, waited a few seconds for another target to present itself, and killed a third man.

That was all he could stand. He had to get down there. He couldn't wait any longer.

He left the empty rifle where it was, ran to the front of the building, clambered out onto the awning over the boardwalk, hung from it, and dropped to the street. Some of the citizens of St. Louis who were still out and about at this hour had noticed the flames leaping from the roof of Beaumont's house, and a number of them ran toward it, shouting questions. Preacher joined them, blending into the crowd. He drew two of the four pistols he carried behind his belt as he hurried along the street.

When he reached the lawn in front of Beaumont's house, he looked around to see if Jessie and Casey had been brought outside already. Failing to spot them anywhere, he looked up instead. Smoke billowed from the burning roof and coiled around the house, but it didn't obscure the window where he had seen the women earlier. He grimaced as he saw that they were still there, tied to the chairs. That meant he had to get inside the house to free them.

Beaumont had to realize that Preacher was the reason his house was on fire. That meant he would know that Preacher was coming for Jessie and Casey.

He would wait in there as long as he could, still hoping to have the final showdown on his terms.

Preacher was willing to oblige him on that score. The mountain man headed for the front door as people started trying to form a bucket brigade stretching back to the nearest well. They would fail in that effort, Preacher knew. The fire was too well entrenched on the roof. The best the citizens could do was to keep the blaze from spreading. Preacher wished them luck with that, but he couldn't stop to help them. He bounded toward the porch.

A knot of Beaumont's men emerged from the house just as Preacher reached the steps. They had been warned to look out for him and probably had a good description of him, thanks to Cleve. They wouldn't be looking for a seven-foot-tall giant anymore.

Sure enough, one of the men recognized him and yelled, "Hey, it's him! Preacher!"

They grabbed for their guns, but Preacher's pistols were already coming up. Smoke and flame geysered from the muzzles of both weapons. At this distance, the double-shotted loads wreaked havoc, blowing holes in three of the men and driving them off their feet. A fourth man fell to his knees and howled from the pain of a shattered elbow.

That left just two men blocking the door, and Preacher struck before they could bring their guns to bear. He leaped onto the porch and lashed out right and left with the empty pistols. Their barrels thudded against the skulls of the guards. The men dropped.

Preacher hurtled over them and into the house. He had spent a lot of time here over the past couple of weeks, so he knew where he was going. The curving staircase was right in front of him. He stuck the empty pistols behind his belt and drew the remaining pair as he started up the stairs, taking them two and three at a time.

Cleve appeared at the top of the stairs, clutching a shotgun. Preacher's keen reflexes enabled him to fire before the treacherous gambler could pull the scatter-gun's triggers. Traveling at an upward angle, one ball ripped into Cleve's throat and bored on up into his brain, while the other smashed into his chest. He went over backward, his finger contracting involuntarily as he died. Both barrels of the shotgun discharged, blowing a huge hole in the ceiling above the second-floor landing.

Cleve had paid the ultimate price for his betrayal. Preacher ran past the dead man and headed for the room where Jessie and Casey were being held prisoner. He knew Beaumont would be there, and maybe some of Beaumont's hired killers. But no matter what the odds, Preacher intended to prevail. It was time for Beaumont to die.

He heard footsteps thudding behind him and knew that some of Beaumont's men must have pursued him into the house. Before he could swing around, another figure stepped into the hallway in front of him, blocking his path. This man held a shotgun, too, and Preacher barely had time to recognize him as Lorenzo before the twin barrels were leveled at him.

"Get down, boy!" Lorenzo shouted.

Preacher threw himself forward, diving to the floor as Lorenzo triggered both barrels in a deafening roar. At this range, the double load of buckshot hadn't had a chance to spread much by the time it passed over the sprawled-out mountain man. Preacher looked back over his shoulder and saw that the lead pellets had scythed into the three men who'd been pursuing him, splattering them in a bloody mess all over the second-floor hallway.

He scrambled to his feet as Lorenzo lowered the smoking scattergun. "You come to rescue them gals?" the old black man asked.

"That's right."

"And to kill Beaumont?"

"You're not gonna try to stop me, are you, Lorenzo?"

"Stop you?" Lorenzo let out a disgusted snort as he started to reload the shotgun. "Hell, boy, I'm gonna cover your back. Probably nobody ever told you . . ." His voice caught for a second. "But Brutus was my son."

That was a shock, all right. "I'm sorry about what happened to him," Preacher said.

Lorenzo finished ramming fresh charges down the bores and gave Preacher a curt nod. "You just go finish it with Beaumont. That son of a bitch been lordin' it over folks for too damn long. I won't let nobody sneak up behind you."

Preacher gave the man's shoulder a quick squeeze and then started along the hall toward the door of the room in which Jessie and Casey were being held prisoner. He was confident that Shad Beaumont was on the other side of that door, waiting for him.

To go charging in blindly would be the act of a damned fool. So Preacher came up to the door, lifted his foot, and kicked it open, then spun to the side, away from the opening, as a gun discharged inside the room.

He didn't say anything. If he did, Beaumont could aim at the sound of his voice and shoot through the wall. Instead, Preacher stood to the side with the pistol leveled at the door. Coils of smoke curled through the hallway, and he heard the fierce crackling as the fire made its inexorable way through the house.

"Preacher!"

The angry shout made a smile tug at Preacher's mouth. He had figured that Beaumont's nerves wouldn't be able to stand the strain of waiting.

"Preacher, I know you're out there!"

Preacher still didn't say anything.

"You'd better get in here," Beaumont warned, "or I'm going to kill one of these sluts!"

A scream of pain ripped out from the room. Preacher couldn't tell if it came from Jessie or Casey. The cry trailed away into a sob.

"I just slashed the blonde's face," Beaumont said. "The next one goes right across her throat."

Preacher didn't doubt for a second that Beaumont was crazy and mean enough to kill Casey. He would still have Jessie to use as a hostage.

"All right, Beaumont," Preacher called. "I'm comin' in."

"Empty-handed!"

Preacher lowered the hammer on his pistol and stuck it behind his belt. With his hands open and empty at shoulder level, he stepped into the doorway. As he did, flames began to lick at the ceiling in the corridor.

Beaumont stood between the chairs where the women were tied. His clothes were disheveled, and his eyes were wide with rage and insane hatred. He didn't look much like the suave, wealthy, powerful man he had been before Preacher came back to St. Louis.

Beaumont had a knife in his left hand, a pistol in his right. He grinned at Preacher as he raised the gun.

"You're an uneducated fool," he said. "I'm going to kill you, then kill these two bitches of yours. I may even leave them here to burn to death. Knowing that they're doomed will pay you back for all the trouble you've caused me, Preacher."

"You sure you ain't gonna talk us all to death instead?" Preacher drawled. He glanced at Jessie and Casey. Both women had been beaten, and blood ran from an ugly cut on Casey's cheek. But Preacher saw anger and defiance and determination still blazing in their eyes, so he wasn't too surprised by what happened next.

Both women threw themselves at Beaumont, chairs and all.

They crashed into his thighs and sent him toppling forward just as he pulled the trigger. The shot missed, the ball humming past Preacher's ear to smack into the wall on the other side of the corridor. Preacher leaped forward and swung his leg, kicking the knife out of Beaumont's other hand. Then he backed off and drew the pistol that was still loaded.

"Get up, Beaumont," he ordered. "Get up and get away from those gals."

Beaumont pushed himself onto hands and knees, then climbed to his feet. He backed away from where Jessie and Casey lay on the floor, still tied to the overturned chairs. The smoke in the room was getting thicker now. Lorenzo spoke from the doorway behind Preacher.

"We'd best be gettin' outta here, boy. This place is gonna be comin' down 'fore you know it."

Preacher slid his knife from its sheath and handed it back to Lorenzo. "Cut the women loose and see that they get out of the house," he said. "Just don't get between me and Beaumont while you're doin' it."

Lorenzo hurried to do as Preacher said. He cut Jessie's bonds first, then Casey's.

"Why are you helping him, you stupid nigger?" Beaumont demanded. "You work for me!"

Lorenzo straightened and handed the knife back to Preacher. "So did my son," he said. "His name was Brutus. You *knew* that, and you ain't even said you're sorry for what happened to him."

"Sorry? Why should I be sorry? None of you matter!" Beaumont laughed. "You're just a bunch of niggers and whores and bumpkins! You're nothing compared to me, you hear? Nothing!"

"Well, then, it's nothin' that brought you down, boss," Lorenzo said.

Preacher sheathed the knife and said, "Get 'em out of here, Lorenzo."

Casey caught at his arm. "What about you, Preacher? You have to come, too!"

"She's right," Jessie added. "You have to come with us, Preacher."

"I'll be along directly," Preacher promised. "As soon as I'm finished here."

The women didn't want to go, but Lorenzo succeeded in hustling them out of the room. The crackling of the flames was loud now, and smoke hung in the air so thickly that Preacher's eyes and nose and mouth stung.

A fit of coughing wracked Beaumont, but when he recovered, he laughed. "What are you going to do now?" he asked. "Give me a gun so we can fight a duel? Let me have my knife back so we can settle this with cold steel?"

Preacher peered over the barrel of his pistol at Beaumont, locking eyes with the man. Thinking of

Uncle Dan and Brutus and everyone else who had died, he said, "I'm gonna do what I should have done a couple of weeks ago."

Beaumont's eyes barely had time to widen in shocked realization before Preacher pulled the trigger.

Preacher left the body where it fell. The burning mansion could serve as a suitable funeral pyre for Shad Beaumont. It was more than the man actually deserved. His corpse should have been tossed into the mud for the pigs, but Preacher was too damned tired to do anything but turn and walk out as the place burned down behind him.

Casey, Jessie, and Lorenzo were waiting for him outside. The two women ran to him and threw their arms around him. As good as that felt, Preacher knew they couldn't afford to waste any time.

"Let's get out of here while everybody still ain't quite sure what's goin' on," he said. They slipped away into the shadows, leaving the shouting, agitated citizenry of St. Louis behind them, along with Beaumont's men who weren't aware yet that their employer was never coming out of that inferno.

A couple of blocks away, they found Beaumont's carriage, with the team hitched to it. Some of Beaumont's men must have driven it out of the carriage house to save it in case the fire spread that far. Nobody was around at the moment, so Lorenzo opened the door and grinned as he motioned for Preacher, Jessie, and Casey to climb inside.

"Ladies. Gentleman."

"It ain't fittin'," Preacher started to protest.

"It damn sure is!" Lorenzo responded forcefully.

"Now get in there, boy, and let's light a shuck outta here."

Preacher chuckled and shook his head, but he didn't argue anymore. He just climbed into the carriage after Jessie and Casey. Lorenzo closed the door, scrambled up to the driver's seat, and took up the reins. A moment later, the carriage was rolling away.

That was how it came to be parked on a hillside several miles north of town the next morning, overlooking the Mississippi River. Preacher had directed Lorenzo to the spot where he had left Horse and Dog when he started downriver on the little raft, so he could pick up his two old trail partners. Then they had found this spot and camped. Jessie was preparing some breakfast from the supplies Preacher had been planning on taking with him as he headed west with Beaumont in pursuit. Things hadn't worked out that way, of course, but Beaumont was still dead and the two women were safe. Preacher knew he was going to miss Uncle Dan, though, and he was sure Lorenzo would miss Brutus.

Preacher cleaned the wound on Casey's cheek as best he could. "That'll need a sawbones to sew it up, or it'll leave a scar," he told her.

She shook her head. "I'm not going back to St. Louis, and I don't care if there's a scar. Do you, Preacher?"

"Why would it matter to me?" he asked with a frown.

"Because I'm coming with you."

Before Preacher could give her a "hell, no," Lorenzo spoke up, saying, "I'm comin', too. I always had me a hankerin' to see some real mountains."

"Now wait just a doggoned minute," Preacher said. "What makes you think the Rockies are any place for a—"

"A whore?" Casey challenged him.

"And a nigger?" Lorenzo added.

Preacher scrubbed a hand over his face and heaved a weary sigh. "I was gonna say, a gal and a carriage driver. I don't give a damn about them other things, and you two know it."

"Yeah, I reckon," Lorenzo said gruffly. "But I been around horses all my life. I'll be all right on the frontier."

"And I was raised on a farm, remember?" Casey put in. "I'm used to being outdoors. At least, there was a time I was, and I'd like to experience that again."

"Well, if that don't beat all." Preacher turned to Jessie. "I suppose you want to come along and see the mountains, too."

She smiled up at him from where she was frying some bacon over the fire and said, "Actually, no. It's been too long since I lived on a farm. I'm afraid I'm a city girl now."

Preacher frowned. "You can't mean to go back to St. Louis. Too many folks there know you were plottin' against Beaumont. Somebody's gonna take over where he left off, you know, and whoever it is might consider you a threat."

"That's why I'm going to take one of those horses, ride *around* St. Louis, and catch a ride on a riverboat somewhere downstream." Jessie got a gleam in her eyes. "I've always wanted to see New Orleans. I think I'll do just fine there."

Preacher couldn't help but laugh. "You know, I got a hunch you're right about that."

"And that way, Casey and Lorenzo can have two of the other horses, and you can use the fourth one as a pack animal. See how neatly that works out?"

Casey said, "Yes, but what will we do with the carriage? Just leave it here?"

Preacher's eyes narrowed as he studied the slope leading down to the river. It was pretty steep, and the bank dropped off sharply to the water.

"I got me an idea . . ." he said.

The others agreed, and after breakfast, they un-hitched the four horses that would now carry them their separate ways, Jessie to the south, Preacher, Casey, and Lorenzo to the west. The carriage was empty. Preacher took the brake off and got behind the vehicle. The others joined him.

"Put your shoulders in it," he said.

They pushed, and after a moment the heavy carriage began to move, slowly at first and then faster as its weight began to work against it. Gravity took over, and the carriage started rolling down the hill. Preacher and his companions trotted after it for a second, keeping it going, then stopped and stepped back to watch as the vehicle's momentum made it pick up speed as it headed for the river.

A moment later, the carriage went sailing off the bank to land with a huge splash in the Mississippi. Preacher let out a whoop, and Jessie and Casey clapped their hands. The carriage wound up on its side, floating slowly out of sight around a bend in the river.

"There goes the last of Shad Beaumont," Jessie said.

Preacher grunted. "Good riddance."

Casey said, "People in St. Louis are going to be mighty puzzled when they see it floating past, though."

"It'll make a good story," Lorenzo said. "And folks do like a good story."

Turn the page for an exciting preview of the next
book in the *USA Today* bestselling new series

MATT JENSEN, THE LAST MOUNTAIN MAN:

SNAKE RIVER SLAUGHTER

by William W. Johnstone
with J. A. Johnstone

On sale February 2010
Wherever Pinnacle books are sold

Chapter 1

Sweetwater County, Wyoming

The Baker brothers, Harry and Arnold, were outside by the barn when they saw Jules Pratt and his wife come out of the house. Scott and Lucy McDonald walked out onto the porch to tell the Pratts good-bye.

"You have been most generous," Jules said as he climbed up into the surrey. "Speaking on behalf of the laity of the church, I can tell you that every time we hear the beautiful music of the new organ, we will be thinking of, and thanking you."

"It was our pleasure," Scott said. "The church means a great deal to us, more than we can say. And we are more than happy to do anything we can to help out."

"We'll see you Sunday," Jules said, slapping the reins against the back of the team.

Lucy McDonald went back into the house but before Scott went back inside, he looked over toward the barn at the two brothers.

"How are you two boys comin' on the wagon?" Scott called toward them.

"We're workin' on it," Harry called back.

"I'm goin' to be needin' it pretty soon now, so you let me know if you run into any trouble with it," McDonald replied, just as he went back inside.

Harry and Arnold Baker were not permanent employees of the MacDonalds. They had been hired the day before for the specific purpose of making repairs to the freight wagon.

"Did you see that money box?" Harry asked.

"You mean when he give that other fella a donation for the organ? Yeah, I seen it," Arnold replied.

"There has to be two, maybe three hunnert dollars in that box," Harry said.

"How long would it take us to make that kind of money?" Arnold asked.

"Hell, it would take the better part of a year for us to make that much money, even if we was to put our earnings together," Harry said.

"Yeah, that's what I thought," Arnold said. "Harry, you want to know what I'm thinkin'?"

"If you're thinkin' the same thing I'm thinkin', I know what it is," Harry replied.

"Let's go in there and get that money."

"He ain't goin' to give up and just give it to us," Harry said.

"He will if we threaten to kill 'im."

Harry shook his head. "Just threatenin' him ain't goin' be enough," he said. "We're goin' to have to do it. Otherwise, he'll set the sheriff on us."

"What about the others? His wife and kids?"

"You want the two boys to grow up and come after us?"

"No, I guess not."

"If we are goin' to do this thing, Arnold, there's only one way to do it," Harry insisted.

"All right. Let's do it."

Pulling their guns and checking their loads, the two brothers put their pistols back in their holsters, then crossed the distance between the barn and the house. They pushed the door open and went inside without so much as a warning knock.

"Oh!" Lucy said startled by the sudden appearance of the two men in the kitchen.

"Get your husband," Arnold said, his voice little more than a growl.

Lucy left the kitchen, then returned a moment later with Scott. Scott wasn't wearing his gun, which was going to make this even easier than they had planned.

"Lucy said you two boys just walked into the house without so much as a fare thee well," Scott said, his voice reflecting his irritation. "You know better than to do that. What do you want?"

"The money," Harry said.

"The money? You mean you have finished the wagon? Well, good, good. Let me take a look at it, and if I'm satisfied, I'll give you your ten dollars," Scott said.

Harry shook his head. "No, not ten dollars," he said. "All of it."

"I beg your pardon?"

Harry drew his pistol, and when he did, Arnold drew his as well.

"The money box," Harry said. "Get it down. We want all the money."

"Scott!" Lucy said in a choked voice.

"It's all right, Lucy, we are goin' to give them what they ask for. Then they'll go away and leave us alone. Get the box down and hand it to them."

"You're a smart man, McDonald," Arnold said.

"You'll never get away with stealing our money," Lucy said as she retrieved the box from the top of the cupboard, then handed it over to Harry.

"Oh, yeah, we're goin' to get away with it," Harry said as he took the money from the box. Folding the money over, he stuck it in his pocket. Then, without another word, he pulled the trigger. Lucy got a surprised look on her face as the bullet buried into her chest, but she went down, dead before she hit the floor.

"You son of a bitch!" Scott shouted as he leaped toward Harry.

Harry was surprised by the quickness and the furiousness of the attack. He was knocked down by Scott, but he managed to hold onto his gun and even as he was under Scott on the floor, he stuck the barrel of gun into Scott's stomach and pulled the trigger.

"Get him off of me!" Harry shouted. "Get him off of me."

"Mama, Papa, what is it?" a young voice called and the two children came running into the kitchen. Arnold shot both of them, then he rolled Scott off Harry and helped his brother back on his feet.

"Are you all right?" Arnold asked.

"Yeah," Scott answered. "I've got the money. Come on, let's get out of here."

The next day

Matt Jensen dismounted in front of the Gold Strike Saloon. Brushing some of the trail dust away, he tied his horse off at the hitching rail, then began looking at the other horses that were there, lifting the left hind foot of each animal in turn.

His action seemed a little peculiar and some of

pedestrians stopped to look over at him. What they saw was a man who was just a bit over six feet tall with broad shoulders and a narrow waist. He was young in years, but his pale blue eyes bespoke of experiences that most would not see in three lifetimes. He was a lone wolf who had worn a deputy's badge in Abilene, ridden shotgun for a stagecoach out of Lordsburg, scouted for the army in the McDowell Mountains of Arizona, and panned for gold in Idaho. A banker's daughter in Cheyenne once thought she could make him settle down—a soiled dove in The Territories knew that she couldn't, but took what he offered.

Matt was a wanderer, always wondering what was beyond the next line of hills, just over the horizon. He traveled light, with a Bowie knife, a .44 double-action Colt, a Winchester .44-40 rifle, a rain slicker, an overcoat, two blankets, and a spare shirt, socks, trousers, and underwear.

He called Colorado his home, though he had actually started life in Kansas. Colorado was home only because it was where he had reached his maturity, and Smoke Jensen, the closest thing he had to a family, lived there. In truth though, he spent no more time in Colorado than he did in Wyoming, Utah, New Mexico, or Arizona.

At the moment, Matt was on the trail of Harry and Arnold Baker for the murder of Scott McDonald, his wife, Lucy, and their two young sons, Toby and Tyler. Before he died, Scott McDonald managed to live long enough to scrawl the letters BAK on the floor, using his finger as a pen, and his own blood as the ink. McDonald had hired the Baker brothers, not because he needed the help, but because he thought they were down on their luck and needed the job.

Matt had known the McDonalds well. He had been a guest in their house many times, and had even attended the baptism of one of their children. When the McDonalds were killed, Matt took it very personally and had himself temporarily deputized so he could hunt down the Baker brothers and bring them to justice.

One of the Baker brothers was riding a horse that left a distinctive hoof print and that enabled Matt to track them to Burnt Fork. That brought him to the front of the Gold Strike Saloon where he was checking the shoes of the horses there were tied off at the hitching rail. On the fourth horse that he examined, he found what he was looking for. The shoe on the horse's left rear foot had a "V" shaped niche on the inside of the right arm of the shoe.

Loosening his pistol in the holster, Matt went into the saloon.

A loud burst of laughter greeted him as he stepped inside, and sitting at a table in the middle of the saloon were two men. Each of the men had a girl sitting on his lap and the table had a nearly empty whisky bottle, indicating they had been drinking heavily.

Matt had never seen the Baker brothers, so he could not identify them by sight, but the two men resembled each other enough to be brothers, and they did match the description he had been given of them.

"Hey, Harry, let's see which one of these girls has the best titties," one of the men said. He grabbed the top of the dress of the girl who was sitting on his lap and jerked it down, exposing her breasts.

"Stop that!" the girl called out in anger and fright. She jumped up from his lap and began pulling the top of her dress back up.

"Ha! Arnold, you done got that girl all mad at you."

They had called each other Harry and Arnold. That was all the verification Matt needed. Turning back toward the bar, he signaled the bartender.

"Yes, sir, what can I do for you?" he asked.

"I need you to get the women away from those two men," Matt said, quietly.

"Mister, as long as those men are paying, the girls can stay."

"I'm about to arrest those two men for murder," Matt said. "If they resist arrest, then I intend to kill them. I wouldn't want the women to be in the way."

"Oh!" the bartender said. "Oh, uh, yes, I see what you mean. But, I don't know how to get them away without tellin' what's about to happen."

"Go down to the other end of the bar and take out a new bottle of whiskey. Tell the men it's on the house, you're giving it to them for being good customers. Then call the women over to get it."

"Yeah," the bartender said. "Yeah, that's a good idea."

Matt remained there with his back to the men while the bartender walked down to the other end of the bar. He put a bottle of whiskey up on the bar.

"Jane, Ellie Mae," he called. "Come up here for a moment."

"Hey, bartender, you leave these girls with us. They're enjoyin' our company," one of the men said. This was Arnold.

"We are enjoying your company too, sir," the bartender said. "You've spent a lot of money with us and you been such good customers and all, we're pleased to offer you a bottle of whiskey, on the house. That is, if you'll let the girls come up to get it."

"Well, hell, you two girls go on up there and get the

bottle," Harry said. "And if you are good to us, why, we'll let you have a few drinks. Right, Arnold?"

"Right, Harry," Arnold answered.

From his position in the saloon, Matt watched in the mirror as the two girls left the table and started toward the bartender. Not until he was sure they were absolutely clear, did he turn around.

"Hello, Harry. Hello, Arnold," he said.

"What?" Harry replied, surprised at being addressed by name. "Do you know us?"

"No, but I know who you are. I was a good friend of the McDonalds," Matt said.

"We don't know anyone named McDonald," Harry said.

"Sure you do," Matt said. "You murdered them."

The two men leaped up then, jumping up so quickly that the chairs fell over behind them. Both of them started toward their guns, but when they saw how quickly Matt had his own pistol out, they stopped, then raised their hands."

"We ain't drawin', Mister. We ain't drawin'!" Arnold said.

When Matt returned to Green River, Harry and Arnold were riding in front of him. Each man had his hands in iron shackles, and there was a rope stretching from Harry's neck to Arnold's neck, then from Arnold's neck to the saddle horn of Matt's saddle. This was to discourage either, or both, from trying to bolt away during the return journey.

Chapter 2

Within a week of their capture, the two brothers were put on trial in the Sweetwater County Courthouse. Although seats were dear to come by, Sheriff Foley had held a place for Matt so he was able to move through the crowd of people who were searching for their own place to sit. Rather than being resentful of him, however, those in the crowd applauded when Matt came in. They were aware of the role Matt had played in bringing the Baker brothers to trial.

Matt had been in his seat for little more than a minute, when the bailiff came through a little door at the front of the courtroom. Clearing his voice, the bailiff addressed the gallery.

"Oyez, oyez, oyez, this court of Sweetwater county, Green River City, Wyoming, will now come to order, the Honorable Judge Daniel Norton presiding. All rise."

As Judge Norton came into the courtroom and stepped up to the bench, Matt Jensen stood with the others.

"Be seated," Judge Norton said. "Bailiff, call the first case."

"There's only one case, Your Honor. There comes now before this court Harry G. Baker and Arnold S. Baker, both men having been indicted for the crime of murder in the first degree."

"Thank you, Bailiff. Are the defendants represented by council?"

The defense attorney stood. "I am Robert Dempster, Your Honor, duly certified before the bar and appointed by the court to defend the misters Baker."

"Is prosecution present?"

The prosecutor stood. "I am Edmund Gleason, Your Honor, duly certified before the bar and appointed by the court to prosecute."

"Let the record show that the people are represented by a duly certified prosecutor and the defendants are represented by a duly certified counsel," Judge Norton said.

"Your Honor, if it please the court," Dempster said, standing quickly.

"Yes, Mr. Dempster, what is it?"

"Your Honor, I object to the fact that we are trying both defendants at the same time, and I request separate trials."

"Mr. Dempster, both men are being accused of the same crime, which was committed at the same time. It seems only practical to try them both at the same time. Request denied."

Dempster sat down without further protest.

"Mr. Prosecutor, are you ready to proceed?"

"I am ready, Your Honor."

"Very good. Then, please make your case," Judge Norton said.

"Thank you, Your Honor," Gleason said as he stood to make his opening remarks.

Gleason pointed out that the letters BAK, written in the murder victim's own blood were damning enough testimony alone to convict. But he also promised to call witnesses, which he did after the opening remarks. He called Mr. Jules Pratt.

"Mr. Pratt, were you present at the McDonald Ranch on the day of the murder?" Gleason asked.

"Yes," Jules replied. "My wife and I were both there."

"Why were you there?"

"We went to see the McDonalds to solicit a donation for the church organ."

"Did they donate?"

"Yes, they did. Very generously."

"By bank draft, or by cash?"

"By cash."

"Where did they get the cash?"

"From a cash box they kept in the house."

"Was there any money remaining in the cash box after the donation?"

"Yes, a considerable amount."

"How much would you guess?"

"Two, maybe three hundred dollars."

"Was anyone else present at the time?"

"Yes."

"Who?"

Jules pointed. "Those two men were present. They were doing some work for Scott."

"Let the record show that the witness pointed to Harry and Arnold Baker. Was it your observation, Mr. Pratt, that the two defendants saw the cash box and the amount of money remaining?"

"Yes, sir, I know they did."

"How do you know?"

"Because that one," he pointed.

"The witness has pointed to Arnold Baker," Gleason said.

"That one said to Scott, 'That's a lot of money to keep in the house.'"

"Thank you, Mr. Pratt, no further questions."

Gleason also called Pastor Martin who, with four of his parishioners, testified as to how they had discovered the bodies when they visited the ranch later the same day. Then, less than one half hour after court was called to order, the prosecution rested its case.

The defense had a witness as well, a man named Jerome Kelly, who claimed that he had come by the McDonald ranch just before noon, and that when he left, the Bakers left with him.

"And, when you left, what was the condition of the McDonald family?" the defense attorney asked.

"They was all still alive. Fac' is, Miz McDonald was bakin' a pie," Kelly said.

"Thank you," Dempster said. "Your witness, Counselor."

"Mrs. McDonald was baking a pie, you say?" Gleason asked in his cross-examination.

"Yeah. An apple pie."

"Had Mrs. McDonald actually started baking it?"

"Yeah, 'cause we could all smell it."

"What time was that, Mr. Kelly?"

"Oh, I'd say it was about eleven o'clock. Maybe even a little closer on toward noon."

"Thank you. I have no further questions of this witness." The prosecutor turned toward the bench. "Your Honor, prosecution would like to recall Pastor Martin to the stand."

Pastor Martin, the resident pastor of the First Methodist Church of Green River City, Wyoming, who had, earlier, testified for the prosecution, retook the stand. He was a tall, thin man, dressed in black, with a black string tie.

"The court reminds the witness that he is still under oath," the judge said. Then to Gleason he said, "You may begin the redirect."

"Pastor Martin, you discovered the bodies, did you not?" Gleason asked.

"I did."

"What time did you arrive?

"It was just after noon. We didn't want to arrive right at noon, because Mrs. McDonald, kind hearted soul she was, would have thought she had to feed us."

"You testified earlier that you and four other parishioners had gone to thank the McDonalds for their generous donation to the organ fund?"

"Yes."

"And that all five of you saw the bodies?"

Pastor Martin pinched the bridge of his nose and was quiet for a moment before he responded. "May their souls rest with God," he said. "Yes, all five of us saw the bodies."

"You have already testified as to the condition of the bodies when you found them, so I won't have you go through all that again. But I am going to ask you a simple question. You just heard the witness testify that Mrs. McDonald was baking a pie when they left, just before noon. Did you see any evidence of that pie?"

Pastor Martin shook his head. "There was no pie," he said. "In fact, the oven had not been used that day. It was cold, and there were no coals."

"Thank you. No further questions."

"Witness may step down," the judge said.

In his closing argument to the jury, the defense

attorney suggested that the letters BAK were not, in themselves, conclusive.

"They could have referred to Mrs. McDonald's intention to bake an apple pie. After all, the letters BAK, are the first three letters of the word bake. Perhaps it was a warning that the oven needed to be checked, lest there be a fire," he said. "Don't forget, we have a witness who testified that the Bakers left the McDonald Ranch with him on the very day the McDonalds were killed. And, according to Mr. Kelly, the McDonalds were still alive at that time they left. The burden of proof is on the prosecution. That means that, according to the law, in order to find Harry and Arnold Baker guilty you are going to have to be convinced, beyond a shadow of a doubt, that they did it. Prosecution has offered no evidence or testimony that would take this case beyond the shadow of a doubt."

During Gleason's closing, he pointed out that Kelly was not a very reliable witness, whereas the two witnesses who had seen the Baker brothers at the ranch on the morning of the murder, were known citizens of good character. He also reminded the jury that the witness said that the donation had come directly from a cash box and that Arnold Baker had commented on the money.

"Mr. Pratt said he believed there was at least three hundred dollars left in the box, and maybe a little more. An affidavit from the bartender in Burnt Fork says that the two men spent lavishly while they were in the saloon, and Matt Jensen, acting as a duly sworn deputy, found two hundred sixty-eight dollars on them when he made the arrest."

In addition, the prosecuting attorney pointed out that, according to Pastor Martin, whose testimony was also unimpeachable, that there was no evidence of any apple pie having been baked, which cast further doubt on Kelly's story.

"With his own blood, as he lay dying, Scott McDonald scrawled the letters, BAK. BAK for Baker. He hardly had time to actually leave us a note, so he did what he could to see to it that those who murdered him, and his family, would pay for their act. We owe it to this good man to make certain that his heroic action is rewarded by returning a verdict of guilty of murder in the first degree for Harry and Arnold Baker."

Less than one hour after the court had been called to order, the jury returned from their five-minute deliberation.

"Gentleman of the jury, have you selected a foreman and have you reached a verdict?" Judge Norton asked.

"We have, Your Honor. I am the foreman," a tall, gray-haired man said.

"Would you publish the verdict, please?"

"We find the defendants, Harry and Arnold Baker, guilty of murder in the first degree."

There was an outbreak of applause from those in the gallery, but Judge Norton used his gavel to restore order. "I will not have any demonstrations in my court," he said sternly. The judge looked around the courtroom. "Bailiff, where is the witness, Jerome Kelly?"

"He's not present, Your Honor."

"Sheriff Foley?"

"Yes, Your Honor?" the sheriff said, standing.

"I'm putting out a bench warrant on Jerome Kelly for giving false testimony. Please find him, and take him into custody."

"Yes, Your Honor."

"Now, Bailiff, if you would, bring the convicted before the bench."

The two men were brought to stand before the judge.

"Harry Baker and Arnold Baker, I have presided over thousands of cases in my twenty six years on the bench. But never in my career, have I encountered anyone with less redemptive tissue than the two of you. Your crime in murdering an entire family, a family that had taken you into their bosom, is particularly heinous.

"You have been tried, and found guilty by a jury of your peers. Therefore, it is my sentence that, one week hence, the sheriff of Sweetwater County will lead the two of you to the gallows at ten of the clock in the morning. Once upon the gallows, ropes will be placed around your necks, all support will be withdrawn from under your feet, and you shall be dropped a distance sufficient to break your necks. And there, Harry Baker and Arnold Baker, you shall continue to hang until it is obvious that all life has left your miserable bodies. May God have mercy on your souls, for I have none."

Chapter 3

One week later

The gallows stood in the middle of Center Street, well constructed but terrible in the gruesomeness of its function. A professionally painted sign was placed on an easel in front of the gallows.

On this gallows
At *ten o'clock* on Thursday morning
Will be hung
The murderers Harry and Arnold Baker.

☞**All are invited.**

Attendance is Free.

The idea of a double hanging had drawn visitors from miles around, not only because of the morbid curiosity such a spectacle generated, but also because the McDonald family had been very well liked, and the murders the two condemned had committed, including even the murder of Scott McDonald's wife and children, were particularly shocking

The street was full of spectators, and the crowd was growing even larger as they all jostled for position. Matt glanced over toward the tower clock in front of the courthouse to check the time. It was five minutes after ten.

The judge had said they would be hanged at ten o'clock, which meant that the prisoners should have been brought out by now. Some in the crowd were growing impatient, and more than one person wondered aloud what was holding up the proceedings.

Matt began to have the strange feeling that something was wrong, so he slipped away from the crowd and walked around into the alley behind the jail. He was going to look in through the back window but he didn't have to. The moment he stepped into the alley he saw the Baker brothers and the man who had given false testimony on their behalf, Jerome Kelly, coming through the back door.

"Hold it!" Matt called out.

"It's Jensen!" Harry Baker shouted, firing his pistol at the same time.

The bullet hit the wall beside Matt, sending little brick chips into his face. Matt returned fire and Harry went down. By now both Arnold Baker and Kelly were shooting as well, and Matt dived to the ground, then rolled over and shot again. Arnold clutched his chest and went down.

Kelly, now seeing that both Bakers were down, dropped his gun and threw up his hands. At that moment Sheriff Foley came out of the jail, holding his pistol and one hand, while holding his other hand to a bleeding wound on his head.

"Jensen, are you all right?" the sheriff called.

"Yes, I'm not hit. How about you?"

"They killed my deputy, and I've got a knot on my head where this son of a bitch hit me," Foley said. The sheriff looked at Harry and Arnold Baker, then chuckled. "I wonder if you saved the county the cost of the execution, or if we will have to pay the hangman anyway? Or, maybe we can just go ahead and have the hanging, only it'll be Kelly instead of the Baker brothers."

From the Boise, Idaho, *Statesman:*

Deadly Shootout in Wyoming !

MURDERERS KILLED WHILE TRYING TO ESCAPE.

Last month the brothers Harry and Arnold Baker committed one of the most heinous crimes in recent memory when they murdered Scott McDonald, his wife, Lucy, and their two young sons, Toby and Tyler. The crime, which happened in Sweetwater County, Wyoming, raised the ire of all decent citizens who knew Scott McDonald as a man of enterprise, magnanimity, and Christian faith.

The murderers were tracked down and arrested by Matt Jensen, who had himself deputized just for that purpose. Jensen brought the brothers back to Green River City for a quick and fair trial, resulting in a guilty verdict for both parties. They were sentenced to be hanged, but moments before they were to be hanged, Deputy Sheriff Goodwin was killed, and Sheriff Fred Foley knocked unconscious, resulting in the prisoners being broken out of jail. All this was accomplished by Jerome Kelly, a cousin of the Baker brothers. Jerome Kelly was himself wanted for having provided false testimony at the trial of Harold and Arnold Baker.

Had Matt Jensen not discovered the escape in progress the two brothers would have made good their getaway. In the ensuing shootout Matt Jensen dispatched both murderers with his deadly accurate shooting. The accomplice, seeing that further resistance was futile, threw down his gun and surrendered. A quick trial found him guilty and he is to be hanged for murdering Deputy Goodwin.

Some readers may recognize the name Matt Jensen, as he has become a genuine hero of the West, a man about whom books and ballads have been written. Those who know him personally have naught but good things to say of him. Despite his many accomplishments, he is modest, a friend of all who are right, and a foe to those who would visit their evil deeds upon innocent people.

The Boise Statesman, being published in the territorial capitol, was the largest newspaper in Idaho. And though only five thousand copies were printed, it was circulated by railroad and stage coach throughout the territory so that a significant number of the thirty two thousand people who lived in Idaho, were aware of, and often read, the newspaper.

Sawtooth Mountains, Idaho Territory

Colonel Clay Sherman was a tall man with broad shoulders and narrow hips. He had steel gray eyes, and he wore a neatly trimmed moustache which now, like his hair, was dusted with gray. He was the commanding officer of the Idaho Auxiliary Peace Officers' Posse. The posse consisted of two officers and thirty-two men, all duly sworn as functioning, though unpaid, deputies to the Idaho Territorial Task Force. Clay Sherman had received his commission from the assistant deputy attorney general of the territory of Idaho, and as such, was duly authorized to deputize those who joined the posse. Sherman and his Auxiliary Peace Officers wore deputies' badges, but because they were not paid by the territorial government, the posse supported itself, and supported itself very well, by acting as a private police force. Most of the posse's income was generated when it was hired by the disgruntled to get justice where they felt justice had been denied.

So far the posse had managed to avoid any trouble with territorial or federal law agencies, because they managed to find loopholes to allow them to operate. But their operations always walked a very narrow line between legality and illegality, and had either the territorial or federal government taken the trouble to conduct a thorough investigation, it would have discovered that, in fact, the posse often did cross over that line.

There were many citizens, and a few quite a few lawmakers, who felt that the posse was little more than a band of outlaws, hired assassins who hid behind the dubious authority of deputies' badges. It was also pointed out by these detractors that very few of the wanted men they went after were ever brought back alive, including even some who were being pursued for the simple purpose of being served a subpoena to appear in civil court. *The Boise Statesman* and other newspapers had written editorials critical of the Idaho Auxiliary Peace

Officers' Posse, pointing out that, despite its name, it had nothing to do with "peace." Some of those newspapers had paid for their critical observations by having their offices vandalized by "irate citizens who supported the posse," or so it was claimed.

At this moment, Sherman and few members of the posse were engaged in one of the many private police force operations by which it managed to earn its keep. They were operating in the Sawtooth Mountains, and Colonel Sherman stepped up on a rock and looked down toward a little cabin that was nestled against the base of the sheer side of Snowy Peak. The posse had trailed Louis Blackburn to this cabin, and now their quarry was trapped. The beauty of it was that Blackburn had no idea he was trapped. He thought he was quite secure in the cabin.

Part of the reason for Louis Blackburn's complacency was due to the fact that he didn't even know he was being trailed. Two weeks earlier, Louis Blackburn had been tried for the murder of James Dixon. At least three witnesses testified that Dixon not only started the fight, he had also drawn first. The jury believed the witnesses, and found Blackburn not guilty, and not guilty by reason of self-defense. The judge released him from custody and Blackburn went on his way, a free man.

The problem with the court finding was that not everyone agreed with the verdict, and principal among those who disagreed was Augustus Dixon, James Dixon's father. And because the senior Dixon had made a fortune in gold and was now one of wealthiest and most powerful men in Idaho, he was able to use both his money and influence to find an alternate path to justice, or at least the justice he sought.

Dixon managed to convince a cooperative judge to

hold a civil trial. It was Augustus Dixon's intention to sue Louis Blackburn for depriving him of his son. No official law agency of the territory of Idaho would serve a subpoena for the civil trial, but then, Dixon didn't want any official law officer involved in the process. Dixon hired Clay Sherman and his Idaho Auxiliary Peace Officers' Posse to run Blackburn down and bring him back for civil trial.

Sherman had eight men with him, and as he looked back at them he saw that everyone had found a place with a good view and a clear line of fire toward the cabin.

"Lieutenant," Sherman said to Poke Terrell, his second in command.

"Yes, Colonel?"

"It is my belief, based upon our conversation with Mr. Dixon, that he doesn't particularly want us to bring Blackburn back alive."

"Yes, sir, that is my belief as well," Poke replied.

"You know what that means then, don't you?"

"Yes, sir," Poke said. "We have to get him to take a shot at us."

"You know what to do," Sherman said.

Poke nodded, then cupped his hand around his mouth. "Blackburn!" he called. "Louis Blackburn! Come out!"

"What?" Blackburn called back, his voice thin and muffled from inside the cabin. "Who's calling me?"

"This is Lieutenant Poke Terrell of the Idaho Auxiliary Peace Officers' Posse. I am ordering you to come out of that cabin with your hands up!"

"What do you mean, come out with my hands up? Why should I do that? What do you want?"

"I have a summons to take you back for the murder of James Dixon!" Terrell shouted, loudly.

"You're crazy! I've already been tried and found innocent."

"You're being tried again."

"My lawyer said I can't be tried again."

"Your lawyer lied. And if you don't come out of your cabin now, I'm going to open fire," Poke called.

"Go away! You ain't got no right to take me back."

"You are going back, whether it's dead or alive," Poke said.

As Sherman and Poke expected, a pistol shot rang out from inside the cabin. The pistol shot wasn't aimed, and was fired more as a warning than any act of hostile intent.

"All right, boys, he shot at us!" Sherman called.

"Beg your pardon, Colonel, but I don't think he was actual aimin' at us. I think he was just tryin' to scare us off," one of the men said.

"That's where you are wrong, Scraggs," Sherman said. "He clearly shot at us. I could feel the breeze of the bullet as it passed my ear." Smiling, Sherman turned to the rest of his men. "That's all we needed, boys. He shot at us, so now if we kill him, it is self-defense. Open fire," he ordered.

For the next several minutes the sound of gunfire echoed back from the sheer wall of Snowy Peak as Sherman, Poke, and the other men with them fired shot after shot into the cabin. All the windows were shot out and splinters began flying from the walls of the little clapboard structure. Finally Sherman ordered a cease-fire.

"Lieutenant Terrell, you and Scraggs go down there to have a look," Sherman ordered.

With a nod of acceptance, Poke and Scraggs left the relative safety of the rocks, then climbed down the hill to approach the cabin. Not one shot was fired from the cabin. Finally the two men disappeared around behind the cabin and, a moment later, the front door of the cabin opened and Poke stepped outside then waved his hand.

"He's dead!" Poke called up.

"Dead—dead—dead!" the words echoed back from the cliff wall.

"Gentlemen, we've done a good day's work here, today," Sherman said with a satisfied smile on his face.